The Good Luck Stone

8/20

The Good Luck Stone

a novel

HEATHER BELL ADAMS

Haywire Books
Richmond
Virginia

HAYWIRE BOOKS

ISBN: 978-1-950182-04-6
Library of Congress Control Number: 2020931450

Cover Design: Baxton Baylor
Copy Editor: Nicole van Esselstyn
Author Photo: Megan Cash

First Edition

This book is dedicated to my husband, Geoff Adams

Part One

CHAPTER 1

Wearing the brooch was a risk, but surely no one would recognize it. Audrey Thorpe lingered by the wall in the lobby of Savannah's Jepson Center for the Arts. Waiters circulated with trays of champagne and bite-sized crab cakes while the museum's donors mingled and congratulated themselves on another fine exhibition.

Audrey leaned against a linen-skirted table for support and returned a friend's wave across the crowd. At her age, the room's pale stone floor was almost as treacherous as an ice rink. She'd gone her entire life—ninety years—without a broken bone. Now her sense of balance worsened with each passing day. At home, she resorted to using a cane when she felt unsteady, but she didn't like to be seen with it on social occasions.

The last of the evening sun filtered in through the glass façade overlooking Telfair Square. Trying to quell her impatience, she touched the brooch pinned to her dress. The cloudy green stone—flawless jade still as smooth as when she'd first held it long ago—had been carved to resemble a hibiscus bloom. A tiny seed pearl glimmered from its center.

As soon as her granddaughter approached, Audrey dropped her hand, which had begun to tremble. She didn't want Deanna to notice the brooch. This particular jewel hadn't seen the light of day since the war.

Deanna, a thirty-eight-year-old woman who monogrammed practically everything she touched, straightened the name tag pinned to her navy sheath. It had been printed with *Deanna Gayton*, but she'd added *Thorpe* with a hyphen in blue ink. Obsessed with social standing, she used the family's name every chance she got.

"Are you looking forward to the new exhibit?" Deanna tilted her head to appraise Audrey's dress, made of pale green silk printed with purple irises. She didn't appear to notice the brooch. Then again, when it came to the family jewelry, Deanna had always been most interested in her grandmother's diamond-encrusted watch, an anniversary gift from Audrey's late husband.

Deanna repeated her question about the exhibit, louder, even though Audrey had heard her perfectly well the first time. Her granddaughter often spoke to her the same way she spoke to her ten-year-old son.

Audrey nodded. As a member of the museum's board, she'd studied the oversized color photographs of ancient Filipino artifacts. A stem cup and footed jarlet discovered in Leta-Leta cave. A copper plate inscribed in Kavi. Blue and white porcelain from Palawan. A death mask made of gold. Burial jars from the Late Neolithic period, some with traces of their original red paint. It was astonishing, really, what survived, hidden deep within the earth while battles raged.

"You drove yourself, I'm guessing. Didn't you get my message? I offered to swing by and pick you up," Deanna said.

"I got it, thank you. But I can manage on my own."

"It might be getting dark by the time we head out."

Audrey ignored her granddaughter's warning and turned her attention toward the front of the lobby where the museum director had stepped behind the podium. The chattering died down and the catering staff withdrew behind the service doors.

After a brief introduction, the director stepped aside for the curator, a no-nonsense woman in her sixties whom Audrey admired for her intelligence. Reporters jotted notes and photographers from *Low County Lifestyle* and *Art South* discreetly snapped pictures.

Between the echoing height of the room and the rustling of programs, Audrey couldn't make out what the curator said, but as soon as the speeches concluded, she shuffled forward. Of all the lovely exhibits she'd toured over the years, this one would be the most personal for her, the most meaningful. With each step she tried to work out the kink in her hip. She felt more anxious than she'd let on to her granddaughter, who had no idea about the time she'd spent in the Philippines.

No matter how difficult it might prove, she wanted—needed—to stay calm. Although tonight might offer closure, it was a private matter. After she'd seen the exhibit, she would return to her life unchanged, without so much as a hint of any personal connection.

But when Audrey glimpsed the map on the wall, her breath quickened, and the sepia tones swam before her eyes. Back when she saw the archipelago for the first time from the ship, so many years ago and from such a distance, the islands looked like nothing more than specks of coral. Here, the music drifting from the museum's speakers sounded misplaced, the traditional gongs and lizard skin drums a stark contrast to her memories of Jimmy Dorsey and Glenn Miller on the Armed Forces Radio. Slightly dizzy, she grabbed the velvet rope separating her from the display of clay and hematite pottery. Perhaps coming here had been a mistake.

Just as Audrey took a deep breath to steady herself, a heavily made up woman whose pink pantsuit matched her fuchsia lipstick bumped into her and crushed her foot in its sensible low heel.

She stammered an apology. "You're Mrs. Thorpe, right? I've seen you at events, of course, but we've never officially met."

Audrey, so accustomed to strangers wanting something from her, barely registered the woman's words. She forced herself, spine popping, to stand up straighter even as her foot throbbed. "No apology needed. Please don't give it another thought."

Deanna thrust her hand forward to shake the stranger's. "I'm her granddaughter. My husband is around here somewhere."

Audrey's attention drifted as the two women discussed whether they'd met at another charity event. In time, this new acquaintance would drop hints about a donation request. When your name appeared all over town—Savannah Episcopal Day School,

Christ Church, various historical preservation fundraisers—it was expected. Neither woman mentioned Audrey's most cherished event, the garden club gala she hosted at her house on palm tree-lined Victory Drive, where she lived blissfully alone.

When Audrey caught the word *legacy* in the woman's prattle, she winced. Did everyone think she had so little time left? Grateful for the carpeted floor, she concentrated on putting one foot in front of the other, inching closer to the artifacts on display.

Beyond the map, at last they entered the exhibit proper. The crowd thinned as donors fanned out to examine items of interest. Audrey should've been able to breathe more easily, but the word *legacy* thrummed in her mind. Somehow, she felt hot and cold at once, shivering in the air-conditioning while sweat trickled down her neck. Behind the glass, a death mask winked in the light like an ominous forecast. Spots danced in front of her eyes and the mask appeared to tilt sideways.

"What's the verdict, Miss Audrey?" Another stranger, this one a tall, slender middle-aged man in khakis, stooped down, his voice low in her ear.

Confused by the word *verdict*, Audrey shook her head and struggled to stay upright. The room was starting to spin.

"I'm afraid I don't know what you mean." Shocked at how tremulous her voice sounded, she took a step back. "You have no business passing judgment on me."

Eyebrows raised, the stranger turned to the attractive woman at his side. Her toned arms were crossed over her chest and her navy dress, with its lace overlay and grosgrain trim, looked expensive.

"Deanna," Audrey said, reminding herself that she was her granddaughter.

Deanna stepped closer, the slender man not far behind. Desperate to find the exit, Audrey turned away. In the press of the crowd, the sharp pin of the brooch pricked her chest and she gasped, surprised at the sting. A spot of blood bloomed on her dress.

"Where are you going?" Deanna's voice sounded shrill, almost excited. "What's the matter?"

At the thought of her granddaughter peering closer at the brooch, of having to explain herself, Audrey twisted the flower around and fumbled for the clasp. It broke off with a pop and she lost track of where it landed on the beige carpet.

"You're coming with me," Deanna said, much louder than necessary. "Excuse me, we have a problem here." The crowd, murmuring in concern, parted to let them through.

The tall man came too, but in the brighter light of the hallway, Audrey realized he wasn't a stranger after all. He was Neal, of course. Deanna's husband.

He handed Audrey the clasp, which she slipped in her satin clutch along with the brooch. Once her heart slowed, she ventured excuses for her confusion. The exhibit hall was dark. Her glasses had fogged up. Deanna prodded her toward a chair while Neal, muttering about a glass of water, hurried away.

"What happened in there?" Deanna crouched in front of her. She pressed one hand against her abdomen, as though suffering from cramps or a stomachache. With her other hand she gripped Audrey's wrist.

"I got a bit overheated, that's all."

"It seemed more serious. Was it like the grocery store last week?"

"That was a simple accident. They make the aisles so narrow these days, the carts so unwieldy. I'm not the first person to knock over a produce display."

"But just now you didn't even recognize Neal. He asked a simple question and you weren't making any sense at all." Deanna's grip on her wrist tightened. "How many more incidents like this does it take? I'm worried about you in that big old house by yourself."

Audrey twisted away, appalled at what she was suggesting. For some time, she'd suspected her granddaughter doubted her ability to care for herself. Tonight's scene would only provide her with ammunition. Even so, Audrey wouldn't back down. She came from good stock, her own mother hosting bridge club and judging horse shows into her nineties.

Surely Audrey had a few good years left. Preparing for the day took longer than it used to. Getting in and out of the bath was a laborious process and the shaking in her hands made putting on makeup painstakingly slow. She didn't cook much anymore, the Le Creuset pots and pans too heavy for her to handle, food labels impossible to decipher. And yet, whether the day was spent in the garden or committee meetings, she managed perfectly well.

"We should take her home." Deanna looked up at Neal who'd returned to her side. "She's in no shape to drive. How she still has her license—"

Neal handed Audrey a glass of water. "You're looking better," he said.

"I'm fine," Audrey said, a sentiment she had to repeat quite often these days.

Deanna stood with a sigh. "We can talk about it tomorrow, but I'm thinking it's time to hire some help. An in-home aide of some kind, maybe a nurse."

"We'll do no such thing." Rattled by the suggestion, Audrey tried to sound polite and in control. After a quick sip of water, she handed the glass to a passing waiter and pushed herself up from the chair. "I'd like some fresh air. All the perfume around here has gone to my head." She directed this last part to Neal, who suffered from allergies and would be understanding. He hadn't responded to Deanna's comment about hiring help. Whether this meant he would be Audrey's ally in the matter remained to be seen.

Outside, she took a deep breath of the muggy August air. Although it was past eight o'clock, the evening still pulsed with heat.

She let go of Neal's arm. "I'm much better, thank you. I'd like a minute to myself if you don't mind."

"In this humidity?" He pointed over his shoulder. "You might be better off inside where it's cooler."

Audrey eased onto a bench in the tree-lined square and waved him away.

"Go see the rest of the exhibit with Deanna. If you don't mind, I'd like a commemorative brochure, one of the color ones. They have them in the gift shop. I'm not going anywhere," she said, even as she fingered her car keys tucked in her clutch. The Mercedes was around somewhere, parked under an oak tree even older than her, its branches strung with Spanish moss as silver as her hair.

At the moment, Audrey couldn't recall precisely how to get home. But once she made it to the car, it would come to her—a way around the squares of trickling fountains and bronze statues, past rows of antebellum townhouses and churches studded with stained glass, to the white Greek Revival where she'd lived since the war. Already she anticipated the familiar crush of the oyster shell driveway beneath the car's wheels, the comfort she would find in a cup of chamomile tea and her stack of feather pillows.

Once Neal disappeared, she picked her way along the cobblestones, the path lit by ornate lamp posts, so old-fashioned they might have belonged to another time altogether.

Chapter 2

From the ship, the islands of the Philippines looked like stepping stones of impenetrable jungle and jagged cliffs. Barely past her twenty-first birthday and fresh out of nursing school, Audrey stared out at the Pacific. With no way to know what was in store, she could only worry that she'd made a mistake, the biggest of her life. Maybe she would've been better off staying home in Kentucky.

They'd had layovers in Hawaii and Guam, the destination of Manila Bay ever present in everyone's mind. Between her nerves and seasickness, she'd spent most of the trip curled on the bottom bunk, leaving her with little sense of how many days had passed.

Now that land was in sight, the humidity clung like an unwanted blanket. She tried to steady herself with both feet planted on the deck. As the wind picked up, she picked at a hangnail until she drew blood. Her mother would have been appalled at her lack of decorum. But here on the other side of the world, Audrey was finally free of her mother's unwavering scrutiny, her father's cigar-scented sighs of disapproval. Her younger sister had married—the wedding ceremony at St. John's, a cocktail reception at the country club—and settled down. Although Audrey didn't want to disappoint her family, she'd envisioned something different for herself. The expansive horizon stretched out in front of her seemed a good start.

She was surrounded by other nurses, some as young as her but most with a year or more of experience, names Audrey had only heard in passing and couldn't remember, women from St. Louis, Omaha, Jackson, Richmond, all over the country. Their chatter grew louder once they drew closer to the coast where gently sloped volcanoes, cloaked in green and ringed with clouds, appeared in the mist. The wind gathered strength until it whipped Audrey's hair from its pins.

At Manila Bay, chauffeured cars whisked them away to cocktails at the Army Navy Club, which stretched wide across the Calle San Luis extension, its oversized arched windows flanked on both sides by three-story wings. In the reception room, Audrey stood to the side by herself. Her legs felt oddly stiff even when she pressed the heels of her lace-up walking shoes against the black and white tile floor. A wobbly looseness, like gelatin, she might've expected. Not this strange woodenness that made her wonder how she'd managed to climb the entrance steps.

"That was some welcome we got out there, the band playing and everything. I felt like Joan Crawford on the red carpet," a petite Army nurse said. Despite her youth, she appeared self-assured and held her head high. She looked so fashionable, she could've graced the cover of *Glamour*. Even after their long journey, her makeup was flawless and her wavy brown hair was swept into crisp rolls.

Audrey tried to smooth her own strands back into some semblance of order and, pretending not to notice, the other nurse took a delicate sip of what Audrey assumed to be gin. Her red lipstick left a mark on the glass. "I'm Kathleen. But I've decided to go by Kat. Here, come sit with me if you're free."

Impressed with the other woman's frankness, the certain way she carried herself, Audrey smiled and said hello. She didn't think they'd met earlier on the ship, at least not that she could remember. Before that had been a long trip in a crowded Pullman car to the West Coast, a coffee-scented blur of close quarters, the country hurtling by through the windows in streaks of muddy brown. She sat and leaned back against the chair cushion. All around them the other nurses chattered with the airiness of once captive birds now set free. "Where are you from?" Audrey asked.

"Tennessee." Kat settled next to her, her slender legs in pristine nylons crossed at the ankle. "But that's a lifetime away now, isn't it?"

Audrey agreed. She looked around at the wicker lounge chairs, the gently turning ceiling fans, the trays of food and drinks. In the corner of the room, a brass stand held a large American flag. No matter what was coming, she wanted to be of some use.

"Why the new nickname?" she asked.

Kat checked her lipstick in a shell-shaped mirror she withdrew from her purse. Everything about her appeared polished to a fine sheen, from her alabaster skin to her red lacquered nails and the small pearl studs in her earlobes. "It's a new start. Being here, I mean."

Audrey was considering her point when a broad-shouldered woman wandered over. So tall she towered over the other women, her plump round face held an expectant, hopeful expression.

"Come sit with us." Kat patted the empty chair on her other side. "We've got plenty of room."

The newly arrived woman grinned, showing her dimples, and introduced herself as Penelope Carson. She sat down and smoothed her rumpled skirt over her plump knees. In stark contrast to Kat's glossy elegance, Penelope's complexion was ruddy, as though she spent most of her time outdoors. Her fingernails were bare of polish and she didn't seem to be wearing a speck of makeup.

"Penelope." Kat said. "It's pretty. I was saying how I'm going to be Kat from now on, short for Kathleen."

Penelope straightened in her seat. "I'd like a nickname too. I've always worried Penelope is kind of old-fashioned."

"What about Penny?" Kat looked to Audrey who nodded in approval.

"That's simple enough. I'm Penny from now on." She popped a tart in her mouth and rested her plate on her lap.

Kat asked Audrey if she wanted a nickname too, but Audrey laughed and explained she already went by her middle name.

For the rest of the afternoon, the women huddled in the corner and exchanged stories about their time in nursing school. Kat had won a scholarship for reciting William Wordsworth's "I Wandered Lonely As a Cloud." At the last minute she chose nursing over secretarial school, although she already knew shorthand. "Money was tight. Always has been," she said. "Nursing suits as well as anything else, don't you think?"

Audrey couldn't tell whether her new friend's shrug was genuine or exaggerated for effect. Either way, it made her want to stay by Kat's side.

Penny had been set on nursing from the start. "It was nursing or serving up fried crab legs in my father's diner at the beach," she said. "I guess the other nurses, the ones from places like New Jersey, call it the shore."

"We've got that in common," Audrey said. "I call it the beach too."

"Same here," Kat said, "although I never envisioned being on a Pacific beach. I still remember the day my orders arrived. The neat, white envelope was like a ticket and a penalty slip all at once."

"After I got sworn in, as soon as I got home, my father already had my Service Star in the front window," Penny said. "He was telling all the neighbors."

"How about you? Was your family the same way?" Audrey asked Kat. She didn't want to reveal that her parents thought she belonged at home. They had directed a housemaid to put her star wherever she saw fit.

Kat's crisp, brunette curls bounced as she shook her head. "I was born in a home for unwed mothers in Knoxville and raised in an orphanage."

For a few seconds, the only sounds were the clink of cocktail glasses and spirited conversations from the nurses in the center of the room. Overhead the ceiling fans whirred.

"I'm sorry," Audrey whispered. "I shouldn't have pried."

"Don't be silly," Kat said. "You only asked a sensible question. And I've had my whole life to get used to the idea." With her thin fingers, she slid an ambrosia square from her plate to Penny's.

Audrey leaned forward, emboldened by the intimacy that already linked them together. "The truth is, as glad as I am to be here, my family didn't want me to join up."

"Let me guess. They wanted you to get married and pop out a baby or three." Penny winked.

Audrey was relieved at how easily she'd been understood. "Marry the boy from down the road and raise a family with him."

"You said Kentucky, right? Does this beau of yours have horses?" Penny asked, stuffing the ambrosia square in her mouth.

"He's not my beau," Audrey said. "But most everyone in Lexington has horses. That's part of why I'm here, to see something different. My mother wants me sitting at home wearing pearls, not doing unseemly work, God forbid emptying bed pans."

She'd been studying art history at Peabody, a thick volume about the great masters on her nightstand, when her grandmother fell ill with liver disease. Audrey noticed the nurses taking such care with her and the way her grandmother's eyes brightened when they entered the room. Before long, she set aside the colored plates depicting Renaissance paintings in favor of biology and anatomy textbooks.

She was taking a sip of her water, a delicate sprig of mint dangling in the glass, when a sudden crash sounded nearby. Kat screamed and jumped out of her seat. Penny darted to her side and held Kat's tiny figure, the way a mother might comfort a child. Audrey gripped her glass, the water ice cold as it made its way down her throat, and scanned the room. If they were under attack—she tried to remember what they should do, how best to take cover—but a waiter waved and called out an apology. He bent to pick up shards of broken porcelain.

"It's nothing," she told Kat. "Look, someone dropped some dishes. That's all."

Kat's cheeks flushed bright red. "Now don't I look foolish."

"You're not the only one," Penny patted Kat's shoulder. "I worry too. A whole heck of a lot. We have no idea what's coming. Imagine all this under attack. Destroyed even." She gestured at the high ceiling supported by mahogany beams, the windows looking out onto swaying palms and the expanse of Manila Bay. Arched doors along the back of the reception room led to manicured tennis courts bordered with purple bougainvillea.

Audrey had thought as much on the ride in. Everything they saw was beautiful and vibrant, yet could disappear in an instant.

Sprawling under the moody peaks of the Mariveles Mountains to the north, Manila bustled with activity. Young soldiers in pressed uniforms strode between the white stone buildings. Expansive tree-lined boulevards crossed the modern, sophisticated city like ribbons. The scent of salt water on the air, weathered churches dating from the seventeenth century stood next to bright new government buildings and horse-drawn calesa carts jostled for room between cars and trucks. Everywhere Audrey looked, tangled vines of flame-colored flowers looped across grand archways.

But they had all heard the same rumors. As they ate pastries and sipped drinks from crystal tumblers, the Imperial Japanese military could be stockpiling weapons and preparing troops to attack American bases in the Pacific. The islands of the Philippines were dotted with potential targets—the U.S. naval base at Canaco, Fort Stotsenburg, where the cavalry was based, Clark Air Field, Fort McKinley—any of which the Japanese could approach from the South China Sea. No wonder President Roosevelt had called General MacArthur out of retirement to help. Audrey stared at the tennis courts out back and gradually realized why they were empty. The military dependents stationed in Manila, all the wives and children, had already evacuated.

Penny twisted her watch around until the gold buckle was where the face should be. "Maybe I shouldn't admit to being scared," she said. "Forget I said anything, will you?"

Audrey reached over to pat Penny's knee. "I feel the same way. I'm glad you said it first."

After they'd talked for a while longer, Penny glanced again at her bulky watch. Its leather band was as thick as a man's. She pushed the buckle back into place and checked the time.

"Girls, I think we've missed supper."

"Gabbing with you two has been worth it." Kat held up her glass and finished her drink.

Unlike Penny's, her slender wrist was bare. Audrey wore a petite Rolex with a fawn-colored, braided leather band and a delicate gold rim surrounding the watch face.

"The mess hall will still be there tomorrow," Kat continued. "We'll get breakfast before our shifts."

"Bright and early." They were assigned to Sternberg General Hospital, a Spanish-style, multi-acre complex in a busy part of the capital, which they'd passed on the drive in. Audrey vaguely remembered the typed schedule ordering her to report to the surgical ward for her first assignment.

In the nurses' quarters behind the medical buildings, they found their trunks and duffel bags. By the light of a lamp in the corner, they could make out gleaming tile floors, ceiling fans, and rows of beds with Army blankets—unneeded in the tropical heat—folded at the foot. They managed to find three beds in the back corner and got to work making them up. Yawning, they left their trunks to unpack later. Despite the lateness of the hour, they talked into the night even as another nurse down the row hissed at them to be quiet.

Close to dawn, they were drifting off when Kat sat up in bed, her arms wrapped around her knees. Her pale cheeks glistened with cold cream.

"What is it?" Penny asked, her voice groggy with sleep.

"Anything could happen," Kat whispered. Perhaps she was remembering the sudden crash at the club earlier in the evening. Peace could so easily splinter into chaos. "But I'm awfully glad we've got each other."

Penny had propped herself on her elbows. "Me too," she said before lying back down. "More than you know."

Audrey nodded in the dark. "Let's meet up after our shifts. Breakfast too, but I'm thinking about after we've finished."

It seemed too much to hope for that they would share an assignment, but at least after a long day she'd have Kat and Penny to look forward to.

When she was a young girl, she'd gotten up at night to look out her bedroom window at the paddocks, velvety smooth under the moon. Gravel paths led down to the barns and the little stone cottage that served as an office for the property manager, a potted geranium by the door. The paths ended at the edge of the property and Audrey would invent different possibilities for what lay beyond. A lone white horse, like something she'd read about in a story. A shimmering pond visible only by her. A carpet of golden leaves that never turned brown or brittle.

Being here on the other side of the world seemed just as fanciful a destination, a far-fetched and surreal sort of dream. Back home she would climb back into her four-poster bed, the sheets smelling of the lavender spray the housemaid, Eugenia, used when she pressed them.

Now Audrey looked first at Penny, snoring lightly, her arm flung across her forehead, and at Kat who'd pulled her knees into a fetal position. No matter what happened, the three of them were in it together. She tried to memorize their faces before she let her eyes close.

She didn't know it then, but their trio would be tested in ways they never imagined. In less than a year's time, one of them would be gone, one left behind, and one dead.

CHAPTER 3

Sunday morning, Audrey drove herself to church just as she'd done for the last twelve years, ever since her husband, Whit, died. The route took her from Victory Drive to the downtown historic district where Georgian and Italianate townhouses with granite steps and flickering gas lanterns lined the cobblestone streets. Park-like squares offered shade and respite and the branches of live oaks stretched overhead, twisting and linking so that one became indistinguishable from another.

After she'd left the museum the night before, she'd made it all the way to Bull Street before Neal and Deanna caught up with her wandering around Wright Square. She'd gotten turned around in the dark and headed east instead of south—an easy enough mistake. Deanna tried to convince her to ride home with them, especially when Audrey stumbled on the herringbone brick path made uneven by the roots of live oaks. But she wouldn't hear of it. She was perfectly capable of driving. They found her car on York Street and waited by a lamp post until she drove away. She'd been so relieved to arrive home safely that she'd sat in the car for a moment. She breathed in the scent of leather upholstery and tried to banish the night's embarrassment from her mind.

A short drive from the bustling historic district and up-and-coming Victorian district, Victory Drive stretched from Ogeechee

Road to Tybee Island. Palms lined its center grassy median as a World War I memorial. The houses were spread apart on wide lots with semi-circular drives bordered by pink azaleas and bougainvillea. To the casual observer, Audrey's two-story Greek Revival might appear imposing. But the white paint softened the brick façade and the deep veranda anchored by fluted columns welcomed visitors with the gift of shade. She'd climbed the steps, fumbled her way inside, and eventually collapsed onto her four-poster bed.

Come Sunday, the night's rest had left her in good spirits. When her great-grandson, Ford, found her in her regular spot at Christ Church, he waved and squeezed into the pew beside her, leaving Deanna and Neal to greet their friends. Ford wore a seersucker suit and Sperry loafers, his rosy cheeks scrubbed clean. This—seeing Ford, having this time with him to herself—was easily the best part of Audrey's week. She hugged him and took a deep breath of his cherry bubblegum scent.

"Hey Nana," he said, grinning. "Ready to play our game?"

Since Deanna's insinuation that she couldn't take care of herself, tension had been gathering in Audrey's neck and shoulders. As if by magic, Ford's exuberance made her feel looser and lighter, almost like she was young again. She found the pad of paper she kept in her purse for this purpose, what her great-grandson called their special game. While they waited for the service to begin, she drew elaborate mazes and Ford, his brow furrowed in concentration, tried to trace a way to the middle. As was their custom, she drew a star in the corner for each successful finish.

Ford was the reason she put up with Deanna and her meddling ways. It didn't matter that Audrey held the family purse strings. If Deanna wished, she could keep her from seeing her great-grandson except for perfunctory visits on formal holidays. In the blink of an eye, he'd be a teenager and perhaps he'd want little to do with her. For now she had moments like these. He tapped the paper and looked up at her, his eyelashes enviably full, his knees bouncing with impatience.

After church, Deanna stopped by the house unannounced. Her granddaughter rummaged through her kitchen cabinets and poked around the cubbyholes in the antique secretary where she kept bills and correspondence, insistent on seeing for herself whether Audrey could manage her affairs.

In the kitchen, Audrey showed her the homemade potato salad she planned to eat for dinner and handed Deanna a waxed paper bag of fresh pralines to take home to Ford. She was surprised when Deanna stuffed one in her mouth, groaning as the brown sugar dissolved on her tongue.

"I don't know why I'm so hungry lately." Her granddaughter wiped her mouth with her forefinger. "It's possible, in all of history, no one has ever been this ravenous."

Noting Deanna's tired eyes and the unusual slump in her posture, Audrey handed her another sweet. "Not to worry, they're worth every calorie."

Audrey was starting to think the visit was going well when Deanna, still crunching the bits of pecan, demanded to see whether her checkbook was balanced.

"I'm perfectly capable of keeping track of my money," Audrey said. The truth was, she had trouble entering numbers onto the impossibly tiny blank lines, but she wouldn't ask Deanna for help—especially not now. She had to distract her granddaughter.

"Wouldn't you like to wash your hands after that sticky candy?" Audrey touched Deanna's wrist and maneuvered her toward the powder room, which she'd recently freshened up with new pear-scented soaps.

Late Monday morning, Deanna called to say she was bringing someone over. Audrey watched out the front window, its glass slightly rippled with age, as her granddaughter strode up the front walk with an unfamiliar woman. Although she looked to be around Deanna's age, this woman appeared less polished than Deanna's friends, wobbly in her sandals, the full skirt of her sundress a bit rumpled.

Angelic countenance aside, if Deanna thought she would hire this woman to take care of her, she was sorely mistaken. Audrey planned to send them politely on their way with nothing more than a glass of tea and a cheese straw. She straightened the area rug in the foyer and her back creaked as she stood again.

Deanna didn't bother ringing the bell. Instead she used her key, which was meant for emergencies, and burst inside bringing with her the scent of the expensive bergamot and grapefruit perfume she bought on her annual girls' shopping weekend in Atlanta.

Minutes later, the three women sat in the rear parlor, a book-lined room with a marble fireplace.

"Nana, this is Laurel Eaton. We met at school drop-off."

"It's always lovely to meet my granddaughter's friends."

Mrs. Eaton shook Audrey's outstretched hand. Audrey had assumed the visitor was the same age as Deanna, but upon closer inspection, she appeared a year or two older. Her heart-shaped face looked pretty in an innocent, fair maiden way that brought to mind a Pre-Raphaelite angel. In addition to her wrinkled cotton sundress, she wore modest silver earrings and a plain gold wedding band. Her brown sandals were scuffed around the edges, but it was apparent she'd made an effort to look nice.

"We barely know each other, but Laurel's looking for a job," Deanna explained. She pushed a stack of enamel bracelets up her wrist. "She asked if there was something at the shop and I thought why not bring her by here instead?"

Audrey raised her eyebrows. Never mind that Deanna always seemed stressed about the gift shop she'd opened in the historic district. She ought to have called before bringing someone over.

Although Audrey wanted to confront Deanna about her audacity, politeness dictated that she offer her guest refreshment. By the time she stood, her hip still bothering her, Deanna was halfway to the kitchen.

"I'll get some tea," her granddaughter called out. "Y'all relax for a minute."

Audrey looked at Mrs. Eaton, whose hands rested in her lap. Her hair had turned frizzy from the humidity. "This is such a nice surprise," Audrey said as she retook her seat. "I don't get many visitors. Deanna brings my great-grandson after school occasionally. Not as often as I'd like."

"Ford and my son, Oliver, are in the same class," Mrs. Eaton said. She kept glancing around the room, her gaze darting from the ebony inlay on the mahogany coffee table to the ceiling medallion and crown molding carved from plaster.

Deanna reappeared with an overloaded tray from the kitchen. "Speaking of Oliver, how's he keeping up? I heard he—well, what I mean is I'm sure he'll do great." She passed around glasses of iced tea, wedges of banana bread on Haviland saucers, and linen cocktail napkins.

"He's still getting settled in." Mrs. Eaton fidgeted as she sipped her tea, but when their eyes met Audrey sensed kindness in hers, a softness her granddaughter hadn't displayed since she was a little girl.

"Episcopal has a lot of top-notch programs," Deanna said as she settled into the club chair in the corner. "Anyway, like I was telling you earlier, my grandmother has been showing her age lately." When she laughed, Mrs. Eaton's kind eyes widened slightly.

"Has she told you I need assistance of some sort?" Audrey asked. "A sitter or caregiver?"

Mrs. Eaton rested her glass on her lap. "She said you might need some help. I'm not trained as a nurse or anything, but I could be useful around the house, which is beautiful, by the way." She gestured toward the windows along the back of the room, which overlooked the garden. Audrey followed her gaze to the manicured shrubbery and the stone water feature, its gurgling sound faint by the time it reached her ears.

"I'm very sorry, but my granddaughter has wasted your time. The truth is, I'm not in need of any in-home care at the moment." Audrey drew herself up straighter.

"The family begs to differ," Deanna said. "There have been some incidents recently."

Mrs. Eaton looked back and forth from Audrey to Deanna. Audrey wished there was a polite way to bring the meeting to a swift close.

"She's ninety," Deanna said as if this explained everything.

"Age is merely a number, Deanna."

"What if you forgot to take your medicine? There's your blood pressure. Your vertigo too. What if you left the gas range on? The whole house could burn down."

"I've never once left the range on or forgotten to take my medicine."

"It's only a matter of time. The other night at the museum you were very confused."

Mrs. Eaton squirmed in her seat and Audrey regretted subjecting the poor woman, a stranger, to what should be a private discussion. She offered her more tea, but Mrs. Eaton declined, tugging the hem of her dress past her knees.

"Mrs. Eaton, do you really need the job all that much?"

"I'm afraid so." She let her chin rest in her hand for a moment. Then she reached for her left wrist and, in what seemed like a nervous gesture, flipped her stainless steel Timex around until the clasp landed where the face should be. Audrey was shocked to be reminded of Penny. Her old friend had a habit of doing the same thing with her watch.

"You might find another position. I could put in a good word around town."

Although Mrs. Eaton attempted a smile, it faltered. "I like the idea of taking care of someone. It's nice to feel needed. Helpful."

"We could keep you in mind for the future, if my health declines."

"That's awfully generous of you. But I'm afraid I need the income now."

"And you need someone now, Nana." Deanna brushed invisible crumbs off her slacks.

Audrey started to pick up the argument again, but Mrs. Eaton's neck had grown splotchy. The poor woman must have been anxious to extricate herself from the uncomfortable situation.

Deanna's cell phone rang and, as she answered it, Audrey leaned over to Mrs. Eaton. "Would you like to step outside for a minute? Sometimes fresh air helps."

She remembered the relief she felt leaving the art museum, that rush in her lungs, the sense of a tightness loosening.

Deanna, her phone pressed to her cheek, waved like she was granting them permission, and Audrey took Mrs. Eaton's elbow and led her out to the back porch where the ceiling fans created a welcome breeze. Although she offered one of the rocking chairs or a wicker chaise lounge, Mrs. Eaton sat on the top step and looked out over the garden like she was trying to calm herself.

Audrey's knees popped in protest as she sat down beside her. From this angle, the entire garden spread out before them. The paths meandering around the neatly trimmed bushes and bright flower beds. The water feature fashioned from a vintage Parisian gate. The ornamental fruit trees lining the perimeter. She'd spent many pleasant hours coaxing ivy along the trellis, clipping the bushes, planting bulbs and seedlings, fertilizing and weeding. Every season she designed a new color scheme for the annuals. Now she couldn't help admiring how the pinks transitioned gradually from the palest blush to vermillion scarlet, an effect she found quite striking.

"When I need comforting, this is where I go," Audrey said. "I come out if I'm not feeling well or I'm worried about my family or stewing over an unpleasant conversation. The flowers help—or at least they offer a distraction."

The younger woman said, "I can hardly believe how peaceful it is back here. Like another world." With a sigh, she dug in her bag and held out a folded piece of paper. "We keep getting bills from the school, one after another. The latest is a five-hundred-dollar technology fee." She stuffed the paper back where she found it. "Sorry, I'm not being very professional."

Audrey waved off her apology. "Deanna intimated that your son—Oliver was it?—might need some extra help."

"He has dyslexia. It's pretty severe unfortunately. Some other issues too. The people at his old school meant well, but the kind of help he needs isn't in their budget, not for public schools."

"Episcopal is an excellent choice. I hope he's adjusting and settling in."

"Oliver needs this school. It's the only place around with a one-on-one program. It's so expensive though. And his scholarship doesn't cover everything."

"You're doing what you can, I'm sure. Mothers will always worry though."

"My husband is infuriating sometimes. We can barely talk about it," Mrs. Eaton said with a slight frown. "I don't know why I'm telling you all this."

"Please don't apologize. Tell me what you mean about your husband."

"He acts blasé about the whole thing, no matter how many reading levels Oliver falls behind."

"You should trust yourself, my dear. You know what your son needs. Are he and Ford the same age? Ten?"

"Right. That's another thing. He used to depend on me, you know? He needed my help. Now he slinks away and begs me to leave him alone."

Mrs. Eaton's voice cracked and Audrey imagined her self-worth draining away a bit more every day.

"It's been a long time, but I remember this age with my son, Tripp," she said. "He was a third—William Trevor Thorpe, the third. A mouthful to be sure." If the young woman noticed her use of the past tense, she didn't visibly react. "And Ford is a nickname for the fourth."

The name had skipped Deanna's generation, but when she and Neal had a son, they picked it up again. Given how her granddaughter relied on her heritage every chance she got, it wasn't surprising. At times, Audrey wondered if Deanna put too much stock in the Thorpe name. Then again, look at how she'd been brought up. In some ways, she might feel it was her most valuable asset. Even when loved ones died—and Deanna was appallingly aware of that reality—their legacy endured.

They sat in silence while Audrey considered what to do. If she sent this young woman away, she would have to look for another job. She seemed desperate, on some sort of precipice—and Audrey liked her. The last time she'd experienced such immediate intimacy might have been when she first met Kat and Penny. Like her old friends, Mrs. Eaton came across as forthright and genuine, a refreshing combination when so many people hid their true selves behind a polished veneer.

Of course, if she agreed to a caregiver, Deanna would win the battle. What might come next? Deanna could try to take over her bank accounts, perhaps move her out of this house.

The French door clicked closed behind them and Deanna called out. "What are y'all doing sitting on the steps like that? Nana, I swear it'll take a forklift to get you up again. Your knees will be stiff for days."

Mrs. Eaton stood and offered her hand. Without so much as a word passing between them, she helped Audrey up and held her elbow until she was steady. Then, as if by tacit agreement, she let go. They'd only just met, but they already understood each other.

Chapter 4

They soon settled on the details. Mrs. Eaton, whom Audrey agreed to call Laurel, would arrive at her house each weekday after she dropped Oliver off at school. During their time together, she would help with laundry, meals, lifting anything heavy, errands around town. Since the idea had been Deanna's, she would pay Laurel's modest salary. In a way, the arrangement played into Deanna's hands, but Audrey could help Laurel and her son—and perhaps agreeing to a companion would satisfy Deanna, at least for now.

For their first day together, Audrey dressed in cream-colored dress slacks and a pale blue blouse. She wore sapphire studs in her earlobes, never mind how long it took her trembling fingers to fasten them, and her diamond watch, which left her arm only for bathing and sleep.

As soon as Laurel parked under the porte-cochère and climbed the veranda's front steps, Audrey opened the front door.

"Lovely to see you, Laurel. I have coffee if you'd like some."

"I'm supposed to be taking care of you," Laurel said. "Not the other way around."

"Oh, Deanna hasn't deemed me unfit to run the Keurig, at least not yet."

With a timid laugh, Laurel turned to follow her into the house. Audrey described how her husband, Whit, used to put so much cream in his coffee it turned light as sand. She liked to tease him about it.

"Would you like some coffee with your cream?" she would ask him.

"It's perfect this way," Whit would say. He'd hand Audrey her cup—no cream, no sugar—and shudder at how bitter it must taste. "My father used to say black coffee would put hair on your chest. I don't think you want that."

"Guess I'll take my chances," she would say after the first sip.

From the doorway to the kitchen, their housemaid would shake her head at their easy banter.

Since he'd passed, the house had been so quiet. Audrey hadn't realized how nice it would be to have companionship during the day. Deanna and Ford were the only family she had left, and, although they stopped by when they could, it wasn't as often as she would've liked. At Audrey's urging, Laurel settled into a chair at the breakfast table in the corner of the kitchen.

"How long has Whit been gone?"

"Twelve years. Some days it seems much more recent," Audrey said. "I come into the kitchen expecting to find him standing at the sink washing his hands or looking out at the garden. We had help, of course, but he used to gather up the fallen blooms every morning. Sometimes he'd put them in a dish of water and set them here." She tapped the soapstone counter.

"I wish I'd been able to meet him."

Audrey took a deep breath as if she could conjure the scent of gardenia from some lost memory. "He was an admirable person," she said eventually.

Laurel glanced at the black and white checkerboard floor and the glass-fronted cabinets displaying glassware and scallop-edged china. "I'm sure this house carries a lot of memories."

"The garden, of course, is my retreat." Audrey pointed toward the back yard. "It was nothing but overgrown bushes when I set out. These days, a landscaping company does the heavy lifting—putting out mulch, clipping the hedges, that sort of thing. I'm not as strong as I once was. But I still putter around out there every chance I get."

"I saw some pictures online from the gala. The newspaper archives—at least the free ones—only go back a couple years, but I love how Ford is always right by your side."

"Yes, I suppose pictures are out there." Audrey paused. "I forget how much shows up online these days. There's something very exposed about the way we live now." Too late she realized she sounded like she was hiding something. "Let me give you a tour of the house," she said quickly.

All the walls were painted a creamy custard color, the trim and millwork bright white. In addition to the rear parlor, where they'd sat yesterday, she walked Laurel through the front parlor with its matching marble fireplace and grand piano. In the dining room, Laurel pointed at the chandelier dripping with crystals and joked it would take up half her living room.

On the second floor they passed one bedroom after another. The four-poster beds were piled high with crisp white linens and sisal rugs ran along the wide-plank oak floors.

Over the years Audrey had collected the artwork adorning the walls. A coastal landscape collage crafted from strips of burlap and shards of oyster shells. The last Irena Wheeling before she stopped painting— swirls of yellow and black against a stark white background called "The Eye of the Storm." A Danish still life depicting firm cheeses and plump grapes arranged on everyday earthenware.

The master bedroom overlooked the garden. In the *en suite* bathroom, she'd scattered discreet rubberized mats across the tile floor, a necessary concession to her age. Along one wall Whit had long ago designed an antique sideboard fitted with two sinks.

On their way back downstairs, Laurel paused at the top of the sweeping staircase. Audrey followed her gaze to the gallery wall of framed pictures.

Laurel skipped over Deanna's bridal portrait, her billowing train spread across the steps of Christ Church, instead pointing to a couple in old-fashioned wedding clothes.

"My parents, Lillian and John Merrick," Audrey explained. She leaned on the handrail, its wood rubbed ebony black from years of use.

"Were they married here? In Savannah?"

"Lexington, Kentucky." The conversation was swerving, and Audrey felt caught between a surprising recklessness and a twinge of uneasiness deep within her chest, the sense that something was about to unravel.

"Is that where you grew up?"

"I haven't been back in a while." So many people assumed she'd always lived here simply because her name appeared on donor lists around town. "The Thorpes have been in Savannah for a long time," she explained. "Whit's ancestors started out here and soon fanned across the country. Some eventually went up to Pittsburgh—steel mills. His grandfather became interested in breeding horses, which brought them to Lexington."

"So, your families knew each other in Lexington?"

"We lived down the road from Whit's family. How long have you lived in Savannah, my dear?" It was a blatant change of subject, but one Audrey assumed the younger woman would graciously ignore.

"About a year. Clay and I are both from western North Carolina, but we didn't meet until college. The company he works for—they do home security systems—assigned him this new district this past spring." Laurel paused and started to bite her nail, then stopped herself. Her nails were bare of polish, most of them bitten to the quick. "He helps schedule installs and service calls. Hoping to work his way up, but he's got to learn more about how the systems work first. Meanwhile, I'd applied to jobs all over town before I lucked out and got this one." When she smiled, her face, which looked as freshly scrubbed as a child's, seemed suffused with light.

Audrey gripped the handrail to steady herself as they went down a couple steps. Her flats were rubbing against her bunions and she longed to take them off.

"What do you think of Savannah so far? Besides the heat, of course."

Laurel reached back to offer her hand, but she brushed it off.

"That first time we crossed over the Talmadge Bridge, it was like plunging into an enchanted fairytale kingdom. You know what I mean? Looking down over the river, you see a tangle of ancient trees, the white church steeples, that gold dome."

"City Hall." Audrey nodded. "Savannah is very European in some ways. The wrought iron everywhere. The carriage blocks and weathered stucco. Beautiful to be sure. But it can be a difficult, exacting place."

They stood in silence, the traffic from Victory Drive muffled by the thick plaster walls.

"When we came here," Audrey continued, "the family name eased our way, opened doors."

"Surely it's the same now."

Coming from someone else, her words might have sounded bitter, but Audrey didn't detect any rancor, even as Laurel mentioned Deanna and how she seemed to think the name helped.

"My granddaughter has gotten worse as she's grown older." She pointed to a picture of Deanna as a toddler nervously clutching a stuffed rabbit. Her smocked dress had been embroidered with her initials.

Then she wiped a speck of dust off an image of her son, Tripp, at his college graduation, back when he was a young man in horn-rimmed glasses. They'd tried to give him everything he might ever want. Maybe that was a mistake. "I don't believe my son and his wife raised her to care so much about money or about what other people think."

"Sometimes money goes a long way toward solving problems."

"And some days I feel dispensing money is all I'm good for."

The mood had shifted, and Laurel frowned when their eyes met. Audrey wondered what the younger woman thought of her. As they continued down the stairs, she let Laurel hold her elbow. By the time they reached the foyer, she inhaled the scent of lemon furniture oil and smoothed her forehead like she might slip a mask back into place.

"What about Ford?" Laurel asked as though she didn't want the moment to pass without saying something helpful. "Look how he snuggles up next to you. The two of you look close. I saw it in the newspaper pictures. The garden gala, year after year, he's by your side."

"I want so much more for him, more than I ever had."

Laurel gestured toward the dining room where a silver urn holding silk magnolia blooms was centered on the table. "Hard to imagine having more than this."

"I don't mean the house. I want my great-grandson to have friends, to find love." She tried to take a step forward, but her leg wobbled like it couldn't support her frame. "Whit and I were married for fifty-six years. To look at us, you would see a perfectly happy couple."

"Where's your cane?" Laurel scanned the foyer.

"Plenty of money," Audrey continued. "A lovely son who carried on the family name. Relatively good health. Friends. Vacations. A charmed life." She stared into the distance, vaguely aware she might tip over at any moment, that Laurel was asking again about her cane. "But it hasn't been the fairytale people think."

Laurel helped her into a chair she'd pulled over from the dining room.

"Nobody's life is perfect, I know," Laurel said. She waited with her hand at Audrey's back, perhaps hoping for some sort of explanation.

Perched in the center of the foyer, Audrey felt disoriented and out of place. "It's a long story. Too long for today." Already she regretted her outburst. Since the exhibit opening, she'd felt as though she might choke on her own memories. Now she'd said too much.

Determined to change the subject, she rose—perfectly steady— from the chair and ushered Laurel into the kitchen where they prepared lunch, croissants piled high with butter lettuce and chicken salad. She considered reminding Laurel not to divulge what she'd said. Although she was still a relative stranger, she seemed trustworthy enough. So she left the admonition unsaid.

When the time came for Laurel to leave, she was surprised at how sorry she felt to see her go. All day she'd let Audrey tackle whatever task she felt up to doing, attending close by in case she stumbled or needed help. Being around her was remarkably easy.

Laurel had parked her Toyota, which was missing a hubcap, under the porte-cochere. When she climbed in, she waved back at Audrey with a wide smile.

After she left, Audrey returned phone calls. With the other museum board members, she chatted about the exhibit's success. Never once did she mention being haunted by the memories it dredged up. Pushing aside the embarrassment of Saturday evening, she drew up plans for the animal rescue organization's fundraising gala. Once she was finished, in some sort of penance for her earlier comment about Whit, Audrey picked up a framed picture and polished the glass with the hem of her blouse.

On the occasion of their son Tripp's marriage to Joyce Price, father and son had stood shoulder to shoulder at the front of the church, dressed in tuxedos and bowties the same mustard yellow favored by Vermeer. The tall, handsome men appeared evenly matched with their dark hair and smiles so wide, so open, their white teeth blurred ever so slightly in the camera's flash. Even in the picture, the warmth between them appeared obvious. The photographer had captured Tripp turning toward his father before his bride came down the aisle. Whit's head was tilted as though nodding to reassure his son.

Audrey traced her finger over their faces before replacing the picture on the table. She told herself she did the best she could, especially under the circumstances, but it was tempting to revisit history.

CHAPTER 5

The following day, Audrey gave her new caregiver a key to the house and pulled out a leather address book to jot down her phone numbers. She clenched the pen with her arthritic fingers, guessing Laurel wanted to take the pen and finish the job herself. Their time together proceeded like this. As much as they enjoyed each other's company, Laurel wanted to prove her worth and Audrey was fiercely determined to stay independent.

Still, it only took days for her to make space for Laurel. They moved around each other easily, co-existing in the cool quiet space of the house and on their drives together around town. Before long, their friendship provided an essential contribution to her days.

One afternoon, Laurel helped her order some books for Ford—a boy in sixth grade saves the world or something along those lines. He talked about them constantly.

"You ought to see him in his favorite spot"—Audrey pointed to the wingchair in the corner—"with his knees drawn up and his book balanced just so." She wanted Ford to visit as much as he was willing, for their routine to remain the same as long as possible.

For now, maybe Deanna was satisfied. It was difficult to know how far her granddaughter would push things. With Laurel helping out, perhaps she'd bought herself a little time. She wouldn't be able to live alone indefinitely, nor stay in the house once she could no longer manage the stairs. One day she would have the grace to surrender her independence on her own terms. For now, she had no intention of being strong-armed into giving up.

The end of the following week, the pharmacy called to report that Audrey's prescriptions were ready.

"I'd give anything to be young again." Audrey plucked the pharmacy card from the corkboard by the phone. "Every day there's a new struggle."

Laurel flipped the dishwasher closed and wiped her hands on the dish towel. "Do the medicines help at least?"

"As long as I keep my blood pressure under control, the dizziness stays at bay. The older I get, the more I have to watch what I eat too. Bananas are good for my potassium." She pointed toward the bowl of fruit on the kitchen counter. "If I go for too long without vegetables or fruit, my blood pressure skyrockets. I can feel my heart in my throat, and I become so light-headed that I can't see straight."

Laurel touched her arm. "I'm sorry. That sounds hard. What do you say we pick up your medicines while we're thinking of it?" She slung her purse over her shoulder and rummaged around for her keys.

"I can still drive you know. You don't need to keep chauffeuring me around." Audrey nodded toward the garage out back where the Mercedes was parked.

"Just this once. I've got my keys right here."

Audrey let out a sigh but followed Laurel to her car.

They were on Abercorn when Laurel's cell rang and she asked Audrey if she would mind answering.

After some difficulty, she managed to press the correct buttons on Laurel's phone and through the speaker the headmaster's assistant explained she was calling about Oliver.

"Your son isn't hurt, but he's been out of sorts and it's reached the point—well, it's distracting for the other children to have him so distraught," she said.

"Have you asked him what's wrong? What happened?" Laurel's voice cracked and she glanced at Audrey with something close to panic in her eyes.

"We don't know. He won't say much. His science teacher called in the guidance counselor. She had no luck with him either, I'm afraid."

"I'll come get him as soon as I can," Laurel said.

Audrey jabbed at the screen to hang up. "Let's go right now. We aren't far." She hoped Laurel's son was all right.

"I've never gotten a call like this." Laurel fiddled with her silver earrings, first one ear, then the other. "I mean, he has trouble following the lessons in school, but did she really say distraught?"

From the passenger seat, Audrey pointed at the road as if she could make the car turn around. "Never mind about the pharmacy. We'll go another time."

"Are you sure? I'm on the clock you know."

"Goodness, I wish you wouldn't think of it like that. Let's go get your son."

"I can't let anything happen to him," Laurel said as she turned the car around to head toward Episcopal.

"I understand. He's your only child. I know what that's like." Audrey closed her eyes for a moment. When her own son was ten, his ears had stuck out and he'd worn white knee socks. He would stuff butterscotch candies in his mouth until he looked like a chipmunk. She opened her eyes again in time to see Laurel pressing her hand against her chest.

"At this point, we've given up on having any more. There's this hole right here." She tapped her chest again. "An emptiness. Silly, I know."

"Not at all, my dear. What you feel is entirely understandable."

"And once Oliver is a teenager, he won't need me anymore."

"He'll need you in different ways. Besides, it's only natural for him to grow up. You'll have prepared him well."

Audrey wished she could smooth away the furrow from the younger woman's brow, but it seemed etched there permanently.

*

Laurel came out of the school's whitewashed brick administration building with a young boy whose gangly limbs suggested he'd yet to grow into his height. As he climbed in the backseat, Laurel reminded him to say hello, and Oliver mumbled some sort of greeting punctuated by hiccups.

Laurel settled into the driver's seat and checked Oliver in the rearview mirror. She nudged the face of her watch around her wrist. "He won't say what's wrong."

"Is that Deanna and Ford?" Audrey squinted in the afternoon sun to be sure. Across the parking lot, her great-grandson spotted her and jogged over, his mother close behind.

With a slight sigh, Laurel rolled down the window.

"I'm wondering what y'all are doing here," Deanna said, the sweetness in her tone belying her true intent. "I assumed it went without saying that my grandmother isn't to tag along on your personal errands."

"This is the first time," Laurel said. "Won't happen again, I promise."

"Whatever y'all want to do, I guess. It's not what you're being paid for but—"

"Who's paying for what?" Ford asked. "You're paying her to be Nana's friend? Hey, maybe I'm going to charge Kirkman to be my friend." Both boys laughed, unfettered and innocent.

"Laurel and I are having a lovely time together." Audrey smiled when Ford came to her window and gave her a high five. "And look how nicely this has worked out."

"Guess what, Nana?" He grinned, waiting for her to answer. She ventured a silly guess, that his homeroom was getting a pet porcupine, and Ford chuckled and gave her another high five. "Microscopes. So we can look at bugs' wings and stuff."

Audrey was trying to convey how impressed she was when Deanna tapped on the car to interrupt. "End of the week I'll expect a full report," she said to Laurel.

From the corner of her eye, Audrey spotted a familiar heavyset figure heading across the parking lot. "Deanna, aren't you going to say hello to Judge Parker? You know he and your father were very close."

Deanna gave a perfunctory wave in the judge's direction, which hardly seemed sufficient given Tripp's friendship with him. Then she turned back around toward Audrey and sucked in her breath.

"What is it?" She didn't understand why her granddaughter's forehead had such an odd sheen to it or why she was blinking so rapidly.

"I would've said hello, you know. You didn't need to prod me."

Audrey held up her hands in a gesture of innocence. "I only thought—"

"Keeping up is exhausting," Deanna said. "Don't you realize that?"

Audrey glanced at Laurel, who was unnaturally focused on a sand gnat batting against the front windshield. She turned back to her granddaughter. "I don't know what you're talking about."

"The constant name dropping—who knows who and where they're from. Code for how much money or influence or power people have, what they're worth."

"Maybe you need a vacation or a break of some sort." Deanna usually held her head high, her pedigree like an invisible crown. She'd never heard her granddaughter talk this way, never imagined she might grow tired of the circles in which she moved.

"Come on Ford," Deanna said. Already moving away, she looped her arm protectively around her son's shoulder. If nothing else, she'd always been refreshingly maternal.

She'd also married for love. Young men from the most well-known families in town had courted her, and she'd chosen Neal, a kind, mild-mannered sort from a small town near Athens. A good choice as it had turned out.

Ford leaned closer to his mother, seemingly oblivious to her earlier outburst, and waved goodbye. "Love you, Nana."

Audrey blew him a kiss, then another. As they pulled out of the parking lot, it struck her as odd that Ford was leaving school early too. She ought to have probed why.

On the drive, Laurel peppered Oliver with questions, trying to learn what upset him at school. It had been a long time, but Audrey recalled boys sometimes felt hesitant to open up to their mothers, as well-intended as they were. Often, she had the best luck with Tripp when they used to toss a ball in the garden, his sneakers squeaking on the cobblestones. He would grunt when he reached high to make a catch, his t-shirt riding up to show his flat stomach. She didn't ask outright how school was going. As he launched the ball toward her, he would let slip a complaint about the science teacher or confess that he hoped a certain girl would ask him to the Sadie Hawkins dance, that sort of thing.

When they arrived back at Audrey's house, Oliver couldn't stop looking around, his eyes wide, his mouth ajar.

"Whoa, this is like a mansion. Are there hiding places and secret tunnels and stuff?" His glasses were crooked, and he wrinkled his nose in a half-hearted attempt to straighten them.

Audrey couldn't remember at what age Tripp had started wearing his glasses. It horrified her sometimes, the things she tried to recall and failed.

"I've never found any secret passage ways, but you never know." She winked, resisting the urge to dab at a smudge on his chin. "You can explore if you'd like."

"Does it have a name? Is it super old?"

"Let's see, the house was built in 1912 so it's fairly old."

"Oliver, can you do the math? If it's 2010," Laurel prompted. Oliver frowned instead of answering.

"It's even older than I am," Audrey said.

"How about a name? You could put a sign in the yard," he said. Audrey guessed he'd noticed the historic landmarks around town.

"What do you think might be a good name?"

He studied the high ceilings. "How about Raven Hall?"

Laurel raised her eyebrows.

"We're the ravens at school, Mom. It's the mascot."

"Raven Hall is a splendid name. I'm so glad you thought of it," Audrey said.

"Can I go upstairs?"

"Certainly."

At the top of the staircase, he slung his backpack to the floor and took out a crinkled piece of paper. He folded it carefully into a paper airplane, which he launched off the landing.

"Yes!" Oliver cheered and hurried down. "Did you see that? Your stairs are awesome."

"I'm glad you like them," Audrey said. "You make very nice paper airplanes."

"Do you know why Ford was picked up early too?" Laurel asked.

"I've been wondering the same thing. Even if I ask, my granddaughter won't tell me unless she feels like it."

Laurel looked toward Oliver, who shrugged and switched the subject back to planes. "I've never flown on a real plane before. Have you, Miss Audrey?"

Although it was a simple question, she didn't want to dampen the mood. Oliver watched her and swooped his paper airplane up and down.

"I've flown before," Audrey said eventually. "But I haven't flown since—well, in a few years."

"You could fly all the way to Alaska. Or Spain."

"There are lots of interesting places to go." She tried to keep her voice steady. She could almost hear her son's hearty laugh, could almost smell the subtle scent of his aftershave wafting through the foyer. For a moment she let herself imagine that he'd traveled through time and space to be with them. "But I'd rather not get on a plane again."

Even though Oliver appeared to expect an explanation, it was much too sad to share with a child. Audrey suggested a snack and, chattering away about ravens, he followed her to the kitchen.

Chapter 6

On their first afternoon off duty, Audrey, Kat, and Penny wandered over to the marketplace in Manila, a lively spot where local merchants sold everything from orchids to wooden prayer beads to freshly harvested shellfish. A local woman displaying handwoven baskets drew their attention to a bouquet of white blooms, their slim petals narrowing to a dainty point.

Sampaguita, she said. "The Filipino national flower, the symbol of divine hope."

Audrey touched the flower with her fingertips, careful not to bruise it.

"I've seen those white blooms everywhere," Penny said. "Maybe they're a good sign."

The following week, a group of handsome soldiers escorted them to Fort McKinley, some seven or eight miles from Manila's city center. The air thick with the heady scent of jasmine, they ate *pastilles de leche* and buttery cassava cakes until their fingers were greasy and their stomachs pleasantly full. Before heading back to their quarters, one of the soldiers tugged Kat over to the streetcar station.

"There's a bowling alley a few blocks away," he said. "A swimming pool, a movie theater. Whatever you want."

"Come on, girls, we've got loads of time." Kat hopped on board after him. As she stumbled, Penny jumped up to steady her. Audrey, smiling at how her friends were game for most anything, followed.

Despite Penny's preference for swimming, they ended up at the bowling alley, where Kat whooped and cheered, even when her ball went into the gutter. The sounds of lighthearted revelry, the streetcar's jangling, and big band music from a nearby radio carried across the air well into the evening.

Once night fell, the island of Corregidor across the bay dissolved into darkness, its rocky outcrops barely distinguishable from the ink-blue water. Anyone stationed there must have been jealous seeing Manila so far from reach. Unlike the gaiety of the capital, Corregidor seemed cloaked with seriousness. Searchlights panned across the water. Along the armed batteries, guns stood at the ready. Audrey had heard rumors of an underground network of tunnels. One day they might be used as a last retreat from the Japanese. A desperate hunkering down, hiding beneath the volcanic rock, like being buried alive.

As they settled into life in Manila, most evenings they attended dances at the Army Navy Club, the patio strung with white lights and a record player set up to play Glenn Miller and Billie Holiday. Audrey jitterbugged and foxtrotted with rosy-cheeked men from Ohio and Pennsylvania and Texas, their names a hazy series of Henry, Charlie, Peter. They slid tropical flowers behind her ear and told her—in whispers so close they made her shiver—how lovely she looked. They took breaks from dancing to smoke cigarettes and laugh at bawdy jokes with their friends.

"Any one of them could end up being a hero," Penny said one evening.

Audrey followed Penny's gaze. A man with a dark buzzcut danced with Kat, his hand pressed low on her back. She wore a full-skirted chiffon dress of pale mint green. Her eyes fluttered closed, like she'd traveled to some faraway place. She didn't talk much about her past—growing up in the orphanage, whether she'd ever had a beau.

"They don't look afraid," Audrey said. "Anxious maybe, but not afraid." The cigarette smoke lingering on the air made her want to sneeze.

Penny nodded. "Kat isn't too worried anyway. She's too busy flirting."

They both laughed. Audrey, so naïve and inexperienced she sometimes felt she was back in grade school, ached to be held again by some young man whose name she would soon forget, in whose arms she might believe the horizon held, instead of war, some immeasurable, romantic glow.

By day, everyone prepared for the possibility of war. Active duty meant travel and adventure, but the possibility of sacrifice loomed around the corner.

Worried about imminent attack, most civilians had fled for home. Rumors swirled about how General MacArthur would defend the alabaster city. He had his work cut out for him. Most of the hangars held only observation planes and obsolete bombers. There were few—if any—tanks in Manila, and the Asiatic Fleet anchored at Cavite was a skeleton force.

Meanwhile, Audrey's unit worked at Sternberg General Hospital, a series of white wooden buildings with arched walkways and open-air verandas situated at the corner of Calle Arroceros and Calle Conception. There they took care of the American troops' everyday medical issues—lacerations and sprains sustained during training exercises, abscessed teeth, ear aches, heart palpitations. In the tropical climate, patients often presented with stomach ailments.

As the chief nurse's first deputy, Lieutenant Johnson set work schedules and made assignments. Stern but kind, every day she organized the stack of file folders on her desk, each labeled with handwriting so neat it bordered on calligraphy. When their shifts weren't busy, she handed out what she called *readiness tasks*. They had to be prepared, which meant organizing supply closets and double-checking requisition forms. War might arrive any minute.

One afternoon, Audrey thought she'd finished for the day when Lieutenant Johnson ordered her to re-wrap an entire cart of bandages.

"The bundles must be tight," she said, demonstrating. Barely five feet tall, freckles darkened her pale cheeks as if she'd been slapped. "Now start again."

Audrey checked the Rolex her childhood friends had given to her at her going-away party. Disheartened that she'd likely miss dinner, she spread out a bolt of linen. One day the bandages would protect injured soldiers from infection. If Japan attacked, they would be needed soon.

"Oh honey, do all of these have to be re-done?" Kat appeared at Audrey's side, her red lipstick still impeccably applied after her shift in the pharmacy. "Every last one?"

"Apparently so, but it's my job, not yours. You should get dinner."

"Not a chance. We're in this together." Kat reached up to adjust the ceiling fan so the breeze would cut through the afternoon humidity.

Had the situation been reversed, Audrey wasn't sure she would've offered to help. Back home, she and her friends had shared hairstyle tips and the latest *McCall's*. She couldn't recall taking on someone else's job.

Kat picked up a bundle of the cloth bandages. As they worked, car horns and sirens clanged from the busy streets outside. At the surprising sound of an animal braying Kat blinked and shook her head like she must have imagined it. Audrey tugged her to the window where they discovered a donkey pulling a cart along Calle Conception.

By the time they finished, their fingers ached and their stomachs growled. Audrey was resigned to going to bed hungry when they got back to the barracks, but Penny had managed to save some dinner rolls, wrapped in a napkin to keep warm.

"I snuck them out." She passed one to Kat and gave the other to Audrey. "And I have some canned peaches in my footlocker for your dessert."

"You're a peach yourself." As she brought the bread to her mouth, Kat fluttered her eye lashes as though practicing how to flirt.

During their afternoon breaks, they often went to the beach club where colorful umbrellas dotted the sand and a beverage counter sold sodas and lime rickeys. A rack at the entrance held piles of navy and white striped towels.

"Lucky ducks, all of us, getting this plumb assignment. If we were in Europe, we'd be mucking around in the cold rain," Kat said one day. She set down the canvas bag they'd packed with fresh pineapple and canteens of water. Audrey shivered despite the afternoon heat and then lifted her face to the sun and burrowed her toes into the sand. From the shore she watched Penny race toward the water and dive into the waves.

"Do I look like a porpoise?" Penny called out. She arched her back and dove again. "See what I mean?"

Audrey looked at Kat and they both laughed. Audrey's legs, so much thinner and paler than Penny's, were dotted with flecks of powder fine white sand, drying in the sun. "You most certainly do," she yelled back at Penny.

"The sleekest, most elegant porpoise I've ever seen," Kat added.

Kat usually wanted to leave first. "Come on girls, I want to lie down for a bit. I can't sleep out here, it's too hot," she would say, wiping sweat from her forehead. Along the sweetheart neckline of her swimsuit the sun had tinged her porcelain skin with pink, like a slightly faded hibiscus bloom.

"We only just got here," Penny said. She chugged water from a canteen—Audrey's mother would've deemed her coarse and unladylike—and turned back for more swimming. "Can't we can stay a little longer?" she called out over her shoulder.

"If we don't scorch ourselves first." Kat would groan and adjust her sun hat but make no move to get up from the sand. Penny's outlook was always sunny and guardedly optimistic. But this, being out on the water, was the happiest they'd seen her.

Even now, so many years later, the image came easily to Audrey's mind—how when it was time to go, they stood with their arms slung over each other's shoulders and watched Penny wring the salt water from her hair.

CHAPTER 7

Monday morning, Audrey called Laurel and asked her to bring Oliver with her.

"School is out for Labor Day, isn't it? You won't want to leave Oliver home alone." According to Deanna, Ford was too busy with his friends to come over, a disappointment that threatened to cast a damper on the day.

"Clay was planning to take him to an install. Shouldn't take more than an hour or so."

"I'm sure there's nothing to interest him at an old lady's house. All the same, I'd love to visit with him. He left his paper airplane here the other day." Her voice trailed off as she realized how silly she sounded.

"I'll ask. He'll probably go with Clay though."

But when Laurel showed up, Oliver accompanied her, carrying the same backpack as before.

Laurel shrugged. "He picked to come here."

Audrey patted his shoulder. "It's nice to see you again, Oliver. What do you want to do today?"

He swung his full backpack around and patted it. "I have all sorts of things in here. Some stuff for school. Paper for drawing."

"He forgot to charge his laptop so it's at home," Laurel explained. She reached to pat her son's head, but he ducked and she let her hand drop. Her heart-shaped face seemed to sag ever so slightly when she sighed. Her hair was falling out of its ponytail but she made no move to tighten it.

"You forgot to charge it, Mom. You left it on the counter."

"Either way, it'll be ready for you this afternoon," Laurel said.

They worked in the garden for a bit. Oliver collected ladybugs in a jar Laurel found for him. He asked over and over again if Audrey had ever seen a snake in the yard, each time acting mildly disappointed when she said no.

Back inside, he had a snack of shortbread cookies, the kind slathered with icing—which Audrey kept on hand because they were Ford's favorite—and a glass of lemonade.

"Did you want to get some school work done?" Laurel asked. "I'm going to help Miss Audrey for a few minutes." At the kitchen counter she dispensed Audrey's remaining pills into an easy-open plastic container with seven slots, one for each day of the week.

Oliver found his backpack and dumped it out on the floor of the rear parlor. As papers and loose change and pencils landed in a heap, his mother groaned from the doorway.

"It's fine," Audrey assured her. "Will you help me sort through Saturday's mail? I can't find my letter opener and my hands feel a bit stiff."

She sat at the secretary and smiled at Oliver who was shuffling papers. One by one, Laurel handed over bills and Audrey filed them away to pay later. When Laurel opened an envelope with an unfamiliar return address in Wilmington topped by a crown-shaped logo, she paused.

"It's a handwritten letter—how nice—and a newspaper article." Laurel flipped back and forth between the pages. "Look, it's a picture of you at the exhibit opening." She held out the newspaper article.

Audrey's vision blurred and she held the paper further away and willed the image to come into focus. Clearly taken in the lobby of the art museum as the event began, the picture conveyed the size of the gathering. Standing beside her grandmother, Deanna appeared to be scanning the crowd for a familiar face. Her complicated up-do and navy lace sheath looked well-tailored and elegant.

Despite Deanna's youth and beauty, the photographer had focused on Audrey. She came across as both elderly—bordering on frail—and thoroughly engaged in the evening's proceedings. Perhaps due to a trick of the light in that white, high-ceilinged room, what came through most clearly was the jade brooch. It would have been instantly recognizable to anyone who'd seen it before.

Laurel passed the already-opened envelopes and the junk mail to Oliver.

"Will you please take these to the recycling? Remember the green bin in Miss Audrey's pantry?"

Oliver took the stack of papers from his mother, but didn't leave the room. Instead, he dropped the pile beside his backpack. Audrey realized she was crumpling the newspaper page and forced herself to lay it on the secretary.

"Here's the letter." Laurel glanced at a sheet of ivory paper bearing the same crown logo as the envelope. "Actually, two letters." She unfolded a pale blue sheet of paper that looked more like personal stationary and handed both to Audrey.

Audrey studied the thick paper embossed with the crown logo and the longer letter written on personal stationary. Both appeared to be hand-written, one in print, the other cursive. She couldn't make out what they said. She took the letters, folded them in half, and slipped them in her pocket as though for safekeeping. "I'll read them later," she explained.

Laurel handed over the next item. "Looks like the Jacksonville Museum of Contemporary Art is inviting you to preview a new exhibit."

Audrey took the brochure and feigned interest in its photographs depicting extreme close-ups of nature—bumps on tree bark, ridges in blades of grass, a bruised petal. As compelling as the images were, her mind remained on the letters, wondering who sent them and if they had anything to do with the brooch.

"How's your homework going, Oliver?" Laurel crouched beside her son on the rug. "Looks like you've only written your name and the date. Surely we can make more progress than that."

He sighed. "It's a paper for history and I don't know what to write about. Plus, you know how I have trouble with spelling. If I had my laptop, there's spellcheck on it."

"What are you studying in class?" Audrey fingered the folded papers in her pocket. *Was it possible she was still alive?* She considered excusing herself to the powder room for a moment of privacy, but the lighting was poor and she wouldn't be able to read what the letters said.

"We're only getting started. This one's free choice," he answered, reminding her of the question she'd asked only seconds earlier. "We can write about whatever we want."

"Why don't you write about World War II?" The words were out before Audrey could quite evaluate whether they were wise.

"As long as there are guns and fighting," Oliver said.

"I bet some boys in your class might write about Europe, but you could write about the Pacific."

"What kinds of planes did they have?"

"The Japanese had lots of planes with great big red circles on them."

"Did they shoot stuff? Like bombs?"

"Yes, exactly." She leaned forward with her elbows on her knees. "Imagine one day you're—let's say you're a nurse or a doctor working in Manila at a big hospital so bright and clean it sparkles in the sun. The war hasn't arrived—not there anyway—so you dance at parties and go swimming with your friends." She showed Oliver the article from the newspaper and pointed at the brooch. "One day your friend Penny buys you and your other friend, Kat, matching brooches made of jade."

At his dubious look, Audrey realized her mistake. "Perhaps your friend buys something else. A belt or a wallet."

"Okay, I guess. But I don't have any friends named Penny or Kat."

She laughed. "You're right. Let's call your friends John and Charlie. Does that work?"

Laurel took a seat beside Oliver on the floor with her legs crossed in front of her. Audrey envied how fluidly she moved, the easy way she sat like a child.

CHAPTER 8

"The old woman at the market said she only made three." Penny held out the brooches on her palm. "It was meant to be." Although much plainer than Kat—easily the prettiest of any woman in the unit—Penny's demeanor was always warm and inviting. In that moment, her heart had never shown more clearly in her countenance.

Kat grabbed one, grinning, and held it up to her uniform. "Nobody has ever bought me jewelry before—ever, I tell you."

Penny handed Audrey a brooch. Their fingers brushed in the exchange. "The jade means good luck," she said. "It promotes healing and surrounds the wearer with a shield of protection."

Audrey rubbed the cool green stone. "And we'll need all the good luck we can get. Thank you."

"The way this Whit boy keeps writing you, I'd wager a guess he wants to give you jewelry one day." Kat nudged Audrey.

Audrey shook her head. "I told you, he was my neighbor growing up. A close friend, but more like a brother than a beau."

"That's what you say, but—"

Penny interrupted Kat. "She'll find another beau, you'll see. Somebody she doesn't think of like a brother."

"Watch, Penny, you'll be the first to get married," Kat said, still fingering the brooch in her hand.

"Not me. My head's not turned so easily. Besides, you're the one who's been out late every night this week."

Kat didn't respond, only raised her neatly plucked eyebrows and pressed her lips together in a way Audrey didn't recognize.

From then on, they wore the brooches whenever they were off duty. When they were on their shifts, they wrapped the jewels in scarves and tucked them in their footlockers.

By the start of December, she began to hear more rumblings about what the Japanese might do. The American and Filipino troops readied themselves for an attack. Even as Audrey went through the motions of treating the routine needs of the American soldiers stationed there—rotating among the surgical, orthopedic, and emergency wards—she hoped they might, against the odds, emerge unscathed. Thus far, the worst emergency she'd seen was an appendectomy and the private who'd been wheeled in clutching his stomach was already in recovery begging for ice cream. Despite the prescribed preparations, most everyone in Manila assumed they might be left untouched, at least for a few months, that for all the talk, one day would flow into the next as gently as the waves in the harbor overlapped again and again.

So when a last-minute meeting was called, Audrey didn't know what to expect. Perhaps the chief nurse had changed the shift schedule. At most, she expected a stern lecture about some damage done to the Army Navy Club by late night revelers.

Lieutenant Johnson ushered everyone who could be spared toward the mess hall.

"Let's push these back to make room." She pointed at the benches and tables where they took their meals in shifts. Nurses and corpsmen hurried to follow her orders. Once the center of the room cleared, the rest of the unit shuffled in.

Given her lack of height and her wideset eyes, in other circumstances Lieutenant Johnson might have appeared meek. But, like armor, her crisp white uniform must have bestowed confidence. She stood as tall as she could muster, her shoulders squared, her gaze unflinching.

"Captain Deegan is on her way," she said, an announcement which lent increased importance to the meeting. If the unit's leader was speaking, then it was probably serious.

When the captain appeared, the two women conferred in whispers at the front of the room. Captain Deegan towered above the lieutenant.

Kat nudged Audrey and tilted her head toward Captain Deegan, who looked surprisingly disheveled. The back of her skirt was creased with wrinkles, her loose bun lopsided beneath her cap.

"Let's find Penny." If something significant had happened, Audrey wanted to hear it alongside her friends. She noticed Penny in the crowd and waved to get her attention. Squeezing their way through the crowd and apologizing for any feet they trampled, they reached Penny as Captain Deegan called for everyone to quiet down.

"What do you think is happening?" Penny whispered.

Kat rubbed her hands together like she was cold, but Audrey guessed it was a sign of nerves. "No more dances probably."

Captain Deegan paced back and forth in front of the crowd. Her sensible brogues squeaked on the sticky tile floor. Audrey had never before noticed the crease between her brows. She held a single sheet of paper. The chatter died down once she cleared her throat and began to explain.

"Yesterday the Imperial Japanese Navy launched a surprise attack on the U.S. Naval Base at Pearl Harbor," she said. A murmur stuttered through the room. "Nineteen American ships scuttled. More than a hundred planes destroyed."

When Audrey tried to swallow, her throat felt blocked. They'd known of course, or at least they should have known. Now, like something heavy descending, it was actually happening.

"What about casualties?" someone called out.

Captain Deegan looked sternly over her glasses. "Thousands," she said and the murmur grew louder. Kat shook her head. Penny reached for Audrey's arm and squeezed it. "Thousands killed or badly wounded." Their chief nurse crumpled the paper she held in her hand until it was the size of a penny. Lieutenant Johnson took it from her and stuffed it in the pocket of her uniform.

All around the room, nurses burst into tears. Others began listing people they knew who were stationed at Honolulu—boyfriends and brothers, sisters and friends from school—as though by saying their names out loud they might shield them from harm.

On their way out of the meeting, they collected steel Army helmets and gas masks. Audrey carried hers around in a daze and found herself wishing this slight armor would keep away any further bad news. The sounds around the base intensified, the sharp beeping of trucks in the street, the deep voices of officers barking orders.

Normally she would have slept after the night shift, but as soon as she lay down she twitched nervously. Kat must have felt the same way. Audrey found her outside, a trail of spent cigarettes at her feet. Kat's face looked less vibrant than usual and Audrey realized it was because her lipstick and rouge had worn off.

"Hi there, pretty gal," she said, nonetheless, and Kat smiled in return and fell in step beside her.

They linked arms and headed for the clinic where Penny was assigned.

From the doorway, Audrey watched Penny give a patient an injection. After she sterilized the needle and placed it on the metal tray with the others, she leaned over him to adjust the sheet across his chest. From where they stood Audrey heard the faint clink of the metal tray, the rustling of the starched sheet. They'd been dealing with ordinary, relatively easy cases like broken bones and lacerations, toothaches, and the occasional tonsillectomy, but soon their work would become more frenzied and bloody.

When Penny stood up, she flipped her watch around and arched her back in a stretch. She made a quick note in the patient's chart and hung it back on the end of his bed.

Kat waved. "Aren't you due for a break?"

Penny jumped at the sound of Kat's voice and turned to wave back. Once the nurse in charge of the ward nodded her approval, Penny peeled off her gloves and signed out.

"This is for you." Audrey gave Penny a hibiscus flower she'd picked along the way. The bright blooms, some as large as bread plates, were almost brazen in their showiness. Women in Manila wore them behind their left ear if they had a beau, behind their right if they didn't.

"You two know exactly how to cheer me up," Penny said. She stuck the bloom behind her right ear, its delicate petals incongruous against her sturdy frame. Penny reminded Audrey of a sunny-faced peasant woman, the type painted by the Dutch masters. "I'm sure everything will be fine." Penny sounded so certain, it was tempting to believe her.

But the news only worsened as the day dragged on. Audrey listened, stunned, to reports on KZRH, the Voice of the Orient, about bombs falling on Baguio, only a few hundred miles north. By lunchtime, the Japanese attacked Clark Air Field and Fort Stotsenburg, the news announcer said, reminding listeners of its location eighty kilometers north of Manila in the foothills of the Zambales Mountains where cavalry and artillery regiments were based. The maintenance crews were working on the newly arrived P-40s and B-17s, frantically trying to get them ready, when the first bombs dropped.

During the afternoon, the chief nurse called another meeting. The commanding officer at Fort Stotsenburg's hospital had put in a request for additional nurses. Audrey chewed on her lip and did the math in her head. Eighty kilometers meant about fifty miles. It wasn't about the distance though, was it? It was about barreling straight into the mouth of the beast.

The chief nurse asked for volunteers to make the trip. The mess hall fell silent save for a fly buzzing around the overhead light. Despite the fresh air coming in through the screen doors, the room smelled like greasy leftover fried fish. Audrey's stomach rolled.

Straight into it, whatever might come, whatever bloodiness waited. She'd come for this, not to tidy supply closets and dress up for parties. She nudged Kat who silently touched Penny's wrist. The three of them raised their hands in unison.

The meeting concluded, Kat smoked while Penny and Audrey paced in the scorching sun outside. Audrey's scalp throbbed with heat.

Penny straightened her wide shoulders. "Look, we're going to be fine."

"As long as we stick together," Kat said. She dropped the butt of her cigarette onto the sidewalk and stubbed it out with the toe of her white shoe.

Penny was already nodding. "No matter what happens, and goodness knows we haven't got a road map for any of it, we stay by each other."

Audrey's throat thick with emotion, she agreed. "We stick together. I need you two—we all need each other."

"No matter what," Kat repeated. "Good, bad, or worse. Everything in between."

"The trio. The unbreakable three." Penny made eye contact first with Audrey and then with Kat.

Oliver stared at Audrey, transfixed.

"I'm sorry." She shook her head as though she might brush off the past. "That will have to be all for today. I'm feeling like a little afternoon nap is in order."

"I don't take naps anymore. Not since kindergarten," he said cheerfully. He was still sitting on the floor, surrounded by her discarded mail and his school papers.

"I meant for myself." She smiled at the young boy with the cowlick, his glasses perched lopsided on his nose. "When you get to be my age, you get tired sometimes." Of course, she didn't really intend to take a nap. As soon as they left, she would be able to read the letters in her pocket. Again, she sensed some past life unraveling around her, that her secret might unspool like a loose ribbon. She'd gone so many years without so much as a hint of suspicion, no one questioning her.

Oliver had started stuffing papers and pens in his backpack. He stopped and looked at her. "But I want to know what happened at—" He struggled to remember the name.

"Stotsenburg," Laurel said. "Me too."

"How do you know all this anyway?" Oliver asked. He grabbed the rest of the papers from the floor and added them to his already-full backpack.

Audrey leaned forward. "Do you know it's actually something of a secret? Maybe not a secret exactly, but you and your mother are the only people I've talked to about this."

Oliver shoved the last spiral notebook in his backpack and he and Laurel stood, both of them stretching like cats.

As soon as Audrey started to stand, her knees locked and she stopped halfway and bent to sit down again. She missed the chair entirely and began to topple to the floor.

Laurel lunged for her and at the last second grabbed her arm. Their eyes met as she pulled her up by the elbow.

"What happened?" Oliver yelled and ran over.

"Are you okay? Here, let me help you sit down." Laurel eased her back onto the chair. "Oliver, go get her a glass of water."

When he was gone, Laurel bent closer. "Do you feel dizzy?"

Audrey shook her head. "I'm fine."

"Here you go, Miss Audrey." Water sloshed over the rim as Oliver handed her a glass.

She took a sip and set the glass down. "Please don't worry," she said. "I simply lost my balance for a minute."

"Did you get hurt?" he asked.

"I promise I'm all right." She patted the side of the chair. "I missed my seat. That's all."

Laurel tugged at the bottom of her t-shirt. "I guess it could've happened to anyone," she admitted.

Oliver scooped up his backpack from where he'd dropped it. "Were Kat and Penny real people?"

"I'll tell you more about it next time," Audrey said. "I got so caught up, I forgot we were going to call them John and Charlie."

"I think we should probably stay for a while and make sure you're doing okay," Laurel said. "Maybe wait until you take your afternoon pills."

"There's really no need, although I appreciate the offer."

Oliver stared at Audrey, his hand outstretched as if to catch her. Once she managed to stand up, he gave a satisfied nod. "You look back to normal."

They followed her to the kitchen where, with perfectly steady hands, she replaced the glass pitcher in the refrigerator.

"I think Kat and Penny must be real," Oliver said.

Laurel wiped a crumb from her son's cheek. "Oliver, Miss Audrey said she would tell you next time, okay?"

"Yes, ma'am. I'm only saying what I think. Like what my guess is."

"They seem like good friends, don't they? I can't imagine going through something like that." Laurel glanced toward her as though expecting her to agree. "At least they had each other."

Audrey looked away, unwilling to have a discussion about friendship when so many emotions, so many memories, flooded her mind.

"Before you know it, Oliver, you'll have a bunch of new friends at school," Laurel continued. "You have to be yourself, that's all, and it'll happen."

"Excellent advice," Audrey said, relieved the focus was no longer on her story. "I hope you listen to your mother." Although his brow remained furrowed, he nodded like he was absorbing what they'd said. For such a small boy, he could look so grown-up, so serious.

"What if you went ahead and took your pills before we leave?" Laurel slid the capsules into her palm and held them out with another glass of water. "At least your coloring looks better."

Taking her time, Audrey swallowed her medicine.

"There's no need to mention what happened to Deanna." She held her hand to her chest until the pills settled. "She'll only make a big fuss. She'll turn any little—"

"I know," Laurel said. "I mean, I can guess." She adjusted Oliver's overstuffed backpack to better fit over his shoulders. She hadn't exactly promised not to tell Deanna who had, after all, asked for a full report later in the week. Even so, Audrey thought Laurel would be judicious.

At the front door, Laurel hesitated. "You sure you're okay? You don't want us to stay longer? If there's anything you need help with—"

"I'm perfectly well. I promise to take it easy."

Laurel spotted her cane in the corner and, when she offered it to her, Audrey grasped the handle and leaned onto it.

On their way out, Oliver turned back and asked what the Japanese planes looked like.

"Next time," Audrey promised. "I'll tell you all about it. You can bring some colored pencils or markers and draw one in your notebook if you'd like."

With her free hand, she touched the pearl necklace at her throat even as her mind returned again to the folded papers in her pocket.

Part Two

CHAPTER 9

Laurel shaded her hand over her eyes and stared up at the Thorpe mansion, imposing as always. The ivory columns, the brick façade layered with what must have been a hundred years of white paint. Beside the front door, bronze planters overflowed with lush ferns. The porch floor had been swept clean.

But something wasn't right. It had been weeks since she took this job, and every day started the same way. As soon as she pulled under the porte-cochere, Audrey would open the front door to greet her, ready to usher her into the high-ceilinged foyer.

Laurel raised the pineapple-shaped brass doorknocker and let it fall against the wood with a thud. Behind her a steady stream of cars hummed past and the wind ruffled the palm trees along Victory Drive. Seconds ticked by. Laurel knocked again, louder this time, and pressed her ear against the mahogany door, straining to detect any hint of movement inside.

Nothing.

It would only take one misstep. After all, Audrey had almost fallen yesterday. A bead of sweat slid down Laurel's spine at the possibility of Audrey crumpled on the floor whimpering in pain, or worse.

She rummaged through her bag, pushing aside wadded-up tissues and her wallet. Something metallic glinted and she pulled it out only to find a long-forgotten tube of lipstick. Frustrated, she turned her bag upside down and dumped everything onto the porch. A Lego robot Oliver had given her, old receipts, her comb stuck to a pack of gum, a ballpoint pen—everything scattered at her feet. She grabbed the jagged edges of a key and lunged at the front door.

Inside, she called out for Audrey. No answer. It was a cloudy day and the foyer seemed more somber than usual. Even the Oriental rug, with its shades of coral and cornflower blue, looked darker than she remembered. The only movement came from the grandfather clock, its brass pendulum lolling back and forth.

Hurrying upstairs, Laurel kept calling until her head spun. The empty house didn't make sense. Nothing looked out of place. The beds were made up in snowy white linens, the dressers and bow front chests free of clutter or dust. In the master closet, Audrey's clothes, grouped by weight and color, hung on slim wooden hangers. She hesitated in front of the ostrich leather jewelry box and then flicked open a drawer to reveal a platinum ring set with a pear-shaped emerald. At least the house hadn't been broken into.

In the master bathroom, she stood by the clawfoot tub and took a deep breath to try to calm down. She took another breath, deeper this time. Not even the faint scent of lavender lingering in the room made her feel any better.

Back downstairs, in the front parlor, the needlepoint pillows on the couch looked freshly plumped, the coffee table books featuring southern gardens neatly stacked. There was no sign of Audrey.

In the rear parlor, the leather couch and loveseat were empty. Same for the antique secretary where they'd sorted through the mail and paid bills. Audrey's calendar—a book covered in turquoise silk and full of thick pages divided by a ribbon bookmark—showed no appointments under today's date. No charity meetings. No doctor's appointments. Nothing. Laurel gripped the calendar so tightly her fingernail left a mark on the fabric.

Audrey wasn't in the kitchen or the dining room, where the crystal chandelier cast diamond-shaped shards of light and shadow across the plaster wall.

Out back, Laurel hurried over to the detached garage to look for Audrey's car. But the garage door didn't have any sort of handle. Without the remote she couldn't get inside.

In the garden, the flower-lined paths were empty. A steady stream cascaded down the antique water feature into a pool at the bottom. Otherwise, the garden was quiet. Laurel didn't know the names of the flowers, but color flared everywhere she looked—pinks, oranges, reds—and a heavy sweetness hung in the air.

The custom-built gardening shed was locked and her key didn't fit. When Laurel stood on her tiptoes to peek inside, she discovered a magazine worthy setup. Audrey's gardening tools dangled on hooks and bags of fertilizer and mulch were stacked in the corner. A copper sink was centered on the back wall. The constant *plink, plink, plink* of the faucet made her want to scream. She couldn't take care of Audrey if she couldn't keep track of her.

Audrey didn't have a cell phone, at least not that Laurel had noticed. But maybe she'd left her a message from somewhere, a restaurant downtown where she met a friend for coffee or a last-minute meeting she forgot to put on her calendar. She patted her pockets and came up empty. Then she remembered dumping out her bag on the front porch.

Everything was still in a jumbled heap by the bronze planters. She swatted away a mosquito and scooped everything back in her bag.

Her phone showed no missed calls. No messages from Audrey or Deanna. She could call the police or Audrey's doctor's office. Or flip through Audrey's address book to find her friends from the garden club. But Audrey would be embarrassed at her involving so many people, especially if she'd only run to the grocery store or to drop off a check for one of her charities.

Laurel dialed Deanna's number and let it ring. If she was being honest, she dreaded what would happen when she picked up. Deanna intimidated her on a good day.

When voicemail picked up, she paused and considered hanging up without leaving a message. But she explained that she was at Audrey's house and—trying to sound casual—said she wondered where she'd gone. She was likely getting herself into trouble.

She shook her head to get rid of Deanna's syrupy southern drawl, so different from the twang Laurel had heard growing up in the mountains of North Carolina—and so artificial sounding compared to Audrey's elegant accent.

For a few minutes, she sat in a wicker chair on Audrey's front porch and stared at the live oaks. Their lacy shadows shifted with the slightest breeze. Downtown, the row houses were elegantly buttoned-up and wedged shoulder-to-shoulder. Here on Victory Drive, the larger mansions had room to breathe. Dense hedges separated their stretches of grassy lawn from the busy road.

Laurel's family lived off the Abercorn Extension in an area called White Bluff. Built in the 1950s, some of the ranches and split-levels looked tidy with neatly mown lawns and sparkling cars parked under carports. Laurel and Clay talked about fixing theirs up—repairing the brown shingle roof, trimming back the overgrown oleander bushes, patching the cracks in the concrete steps—but they never had the money.

She glanced behind her at the polished mahogany front door. She could go inside and start a load of laundry or straighten up a bit, but it felt strange with Audrey gone.

For someone like Audrey, taking off without leaving word seemed out of character. And maybe it was somehow Laurel's fault. The truth was, she'd never been good at much of anything save being a mother. Now that Oliver was getting older, some days he pulled away from her, didn't even want her to pat his shoulder or comb out the tangles from his hair. He needed her less and she didn't begrudge him that, even if it stung.

Thinking about the second baby who never came hurt the most. At home, Laurel couldn't even set foot in the guest room, which they'd hoped to use as a nursery. Somebody else might have found the room comfortable, the windows draped with secondhand yellow toile, the carpet still lined with marks from the vacuum. For her, it served as a constant reminder of what she lacked.

No wonder the job with Audrey seemed like it was dropped straight from heaven into her lap. Caring for people was something Laurel could manage. At least she'd thought so.

Not sure what else to do, she drove around town hoping to find Audrey at one of her usual spots. Her Mercedes wasn't parked by the doctor's office or pharmacy. In the historic district, she checked the area around Bull and Congress streets near Christ Church and watched people—none of them Audrey—strolling around the fountains in Johnson Square.

Laurel and Clay couldn't afford to live downtown, but whenever she wandered around the area, she noticed how ordinary things had been crafted in such extraordinary ways. Limestone seashells at the points of arched windows. Sterling silver doorknobs. Street names carved in script. Downspouts shaped like fish. And on almost every house and gated courtyard, black ironwork draped like jewelry.

Audrey had told her that in the 1950s, anyone who had the financial means moved out to the new suburbs and abandoned the old houses downtown. But a group of women banded together and stepped in to save them from demolition. *Imagine*, Audrey said, *the obstacles they faced.* She was lobbying the museum to feature an exhibition about them during an upcoming season. In the secretary she'd filed black and white photographs of the Davenport House, the women's first success.

The museum seemed important to Audrey, especially given her interest in the recent exhibit about the Philippines, and Laurel went there next. Positioned on the south side of Telfair Square, The Jepson Center was a white modern-looking building with floor-to-ceiling windows along the front.

Inside, the metallic-scented, chilled air felt bracing after the heat and humidity. Laurel craned her neck to take in the lobby's ceilings, which soared multiple floors high. To her left was the gift shop, and along the back of the room rose a wide staircase, the same creamy stone as the walls. Dappled sunlight streamed in through the glass. From where she stood, she couldn't see the exhibits, but banners advertised the Filipino artifacts, a photography exhibit about New York tenements, and something called ArtZeum for children.

A young guide with a discreet nose ring wandered over and asked if he could help.

"I work for Audrey Thorpe," she began. The nod of recognition on his face seemed encouraging. "We might have gotten our schedules mixed up and I thought she might be here."

The guide shook his head. "I haven't seen Mrs. Thorpe today."

"Could she have some kind of meeting?"

"I don't think so, but let's check the schedule to be sure." He led her to a small office where he logged onto the desktop computer.

"She's on the board, right?"

"Yes, we're so pleased to have her support. Without people like her, this museum probably wouldn't even exist." He tapped the screen and shook his head. "No meetings on today's calendar."

"Maybe she's wandering around the exhibit on her own?"

"If someone of her—let's say standing—comes in, all the employees and volunteers get an alert—you know, to make sure we're on our best behavior. And I haven't heard anything about her stopping by."

Someone of her standing. Obviously, Audrey had a full social calendar and countless charity obligations. An impressive house. Lots of money. More than Laurel could dream of. Her family had always struggled, both when she was growing up and now with Clay. Audrey had to realize the difference in their situations. But she'd never once seemed snobbish or made Laurel feel inferior.

"You're lucky to have fallen in with Mrs. Thorpe," the guide said. "Of all people."

On Bay Street, she lucked out and found a parking spot. Most of the waterfront warehouses had been converted to pricey restaurants, their wine lists framed and hung outside by the front door. Laurel had never set foot inside any of them, but surely Audrey would be greeted by name and ushered to the best linen-covered table. If she hadn't disappeared.

She took the steep steps down to River Street where the air smelled like buttery popcorn. All along the cobblestone street, brightly colored awnings flapped in the wind. The seafood restaurants were packed with tourists enjoying a late lunch. No sign of

Audrey. Along the river, cargo ships glided by from the port on their way to Charleston or Jacksonville. The Talmadge bridge, with its cables like silver strands of steel, arched over the water to Hutchinson Island, a shrubbery outpost in the middle of the river home to a convention center and luxury hotel.

When she spotted a young mother pushing an infant in a stroller, Laurel wished she could swim out to one of the ships and let it carry her away to some faraway, easy place. Any place where she didn't feel such a weight. Money worries. Children who grew out of needing her, babies who never came.

By now she and Clay had given up on another child. He didn't really leave her with a choice. But for so long, every month she had let hope gather inside her chest like an approaching wave. Until the crushing disappointment came, like a heavy boulder strapped across her back, the weight only growing heavier over time.

Maybe it was true they didn't have the money for IVF, but she still blamed her husband. *It's not worth the trouble,* he'd said. What she'd heard was, *Laurel, you're not worth the trouble.*

She had always wanted a house full of children. Her time would be spent fixing snacks and wiping runny noses and getting down on the floor to play another game of fairy princess or pirate battle. A row of sippy cups in the refrigerator, a stack of inflatable whales and turtles in the garage. The days were supposed to be full of squeals and high-pitched laughter, sticky hands needing to be washed off, closets swept free of monsters. Not long after she and Clay met in college, they started talking about having a family together.

"You'll make a good mother one day," Clay had said. "You've got what my own mother calls a nurturing spirit."

When he drove Laurel around town in his truck, he draped his arm around her shoulders. Once, coming out of Beaucatcher Tunnel toward downtown Asheville, they'd been in a minor accident. Even though it was only a fender bender, his first reaction had been to shelter her, reaching across the seat to cradle her head.

As soon as she got pregnant, they stayed up late joking about possible baby names, silly ones like Oreo and Dr. Pepper, the snacks they happened to be eating. Laurel had laughed until her stomach hurt. Now every time she saw a baby, she wanted to crawl into bed and pull the covers over her head, to hide in a stuffy, dark place with no jagged edges of disappointment.

Now, as the mother passed by on River Street, the wheels of the stroller rattling on the cobblestones, all Laurel felt was a hole. She laid her hand against her chest, picturing the gap in her heart, the hollow space meant to be filled.

She returned to Audrey's house, maybe to catch something she'd missed earlier.

In the kitchen, she found a small plate and coffee cup in the dishwasher, leaving her to guess Audrey had eaten breakfast at home. Her pill container was missing.

On her way upstairs, she paused at the gallery wall of family pictures. All the frames were in their regular spots, the portraits of society weddings and grinning, rosy-cheeked children like silent echoes from earlier times. Something nagged at the back of her mind though, a sense that another story lurked in the background.

Upstairs, she tried to ignore the unsettling feeling that she shouldn't be snooping around. Every time the old house creaked or a clock ticked, she jumped. In Audrey's closet, she quickly surveyed the clothes, the wooden hangers clinking as she flipped through dresses and blouses.

Next, she checked the master bathroom, noticing droplets of water clinging to the shower door, the plush bath mats still damp to the touch. Audrey must have showered at home before she left. The drawers under the sink held department store cosmetics and expensive-looking bottles of perfume. Cotton balls and hand lotion. AquaNet Hairspray. Bars of bath soap labeled in French. Headache medicine and lavender-scented bath salts. Bandages and ointment. A dusty bottle of baby powder with a Revco price sticker. A package of wipes to clean eyeglasses.

Right when Laurel closed the last drawer, a noise sounded from somewhere inside the house—a creaking. She held her breath and waited for Audrey to call up for her in her Savannah lilt. Maybe it was too soon to feel this way. But she desperately wanted things to go back to normal.

When she didn't hear anything else, she told herself she'd imagined the sound. Ignoring her messy reflection in the beveled mirror, she stood back from the sink. The small porcelain cup to the right of the faucet usually held Audrey's toothbrush. Laurel was sure of it. But the cup was empty. She opened the drawers again and didn't find a toothbrush or toothpaste. The makeup might have been extras, things Audrey didn't necessarily use every day.

According to her watch, she had to hurry or she would be late to pick up Oliver. Another noise drifted from downstairs. Footsteps, a jangling of some kind. Someone else was definitely in the house.

CHAPTER 10

Stotsenburg was an hour's drive from base. Their caravan of Army buses threw up clumps of mud along the way. Audrey tried to steel herself for what they would discover. They had heard reports, of course, and she anticipated piles of smoldering wreckage and debris strewn everywhere.

Once the unit arrived, her nerves so frayed her pulse jumped in her wrist, she saw for the first time what war could really do, what it meant from up close. Pilots who had rushed out to their planes had been flung over the tarmac as the bombs hit. Her gaze skimmed across the grounds. Unrecognizable chunks of metal, streaks of blood, contorted bodies. None of the triage drills could have prepared her for this.

Musette bags flapping against their hips, every nurse in the unit ran toward young men trapped in the rubble, their calls for help so strangled and garbled they might have come from wild animals. Audrey paused to hand a canteen of water to a begging pilot. He grabbed it with grease-streaked hands while she scanned the tarmac for those most in need of help. They were still just boys, as young and sweet as the ones she'd danced with in Manila.

Kat bent to help a burn victim, his skin mottled with blisters and streaked with blood, and her knees buckled. Audrey reached out her hand like she could keep her upright. With a firm set to her jaw, Kat steadied herself and unrolled a bandage. They always told Penny she was the strongest of the group, but Kat could hold her own too.

A few feet away, Audrey lifted a piece of mangled wing to find a pilot whose eyes—both of them—had been sliced by flying shrapnel. He screamed incoherently. He kept screaming as she wiped away dirt from his brow and wrapped his eyes with bandages, wishing she could do something else. Her hairline broke out with sweat as she ran toward the next patient. For a minute, the adrenalin coursing through her veins made her feel like everything was in slow motion. She had the awful idea of pushing the other nurses, a gentle nudge against their backs to make them move faster, as if they all hurried they might make more of a difference, might unwind time itself. She felt for a young man's pulse and found none. Straightening up she let out a groan. With her forearm she tried to wipe the sweat from her brow, wincing as she tripped on his boot on her way to the next in line.

Fire engulfed so much of the base that charcoal gray smoke obscured the setting sun. The runways at Clark Air Field held only bits and pieces, once solid chunks of metal reduced to splinters. Parts of the mechanic bays were littered with debris, others had collapsed. At the officers' quarters, explosions had stripped off the roofs and cratered the walls.

They performed triage for hours, assessing the severity of wounds so they could signal to the doctors who needed the most urgent help and who was beyond any earthly hope. Audrey wrote on the patients' foreheads with felt markers. M for morphine. C for critically injured. F for fatally wounded. Her fingers shook at first, the gesture so oddly intimate, the men's skin crinkling under the pressure of the ink. With time her actions became rote and the shaking subsided.

At nightfall, the air still heavy with humidity, more nurses and doctors arrived. By then Audrey's unit had been moved to the hospital, a series of modest wooden buildings that looked dark and dingy compared to the sparkling modern facility in Manila. Their patients arrived on gurneys into overflowing rooms and crowded hallways.

A radio operator kept plucking at Penny's sleeve, asking when he could get back to the fighting. He spoke with a drawl as sweet as caramel and Audrey guessed he was from the Deep South.

"Soon, we'll get you back out there as quickly as we can," Penny promised. One of his ears dangled against his neck, barely attached.

"He's not going anywhere. There's no use in misleading him," a doctor said, coming up beside them. He'd appeared out of nowhere studying a clipboard, his chiseled jawline smudged with grease or soot and his thick dark eyebrows slanted in concentration. An artist would've drawn him in bold dashes of paint—his muscular frame, the rich chocolate brown of his hair, the ease of his stance, feet spread apart.

Penny pressed her lips together and spoke under her breath as they moved away from the patient's bedside. "I didn't see why I couldn't tell a little white lie. He would've gotten more upset if I told him the truth."

"We were taught the same way," Audrey said. "It's better, if possible, to avoid upsetting the patient." With her arms full of syringes and towels, she fell into step with Penny and the doctor. "You can dispense hope even when there's nothing else to offer." The words sounded artificial even though she believed them to be true.

"Thank you," Penny mouthed and Audrey nudged her with her shoulder, a gesture she meant as a sign of solidarity.

When the doctor stopped walking, they paused too. He ran his fingers through his dark hair as though deep in thought.

"I'm embarrassed—mortified—that I snapped like that," he said.

Penny brushed off his apology.

"It's this day—everything that's happened here," the doctor said. His voice sounded raw, like he'd been talking for days on end without any rest. He was around their age and couldn't have seen anything like this before. "You have no reason to believe me, of course, but I'm awfully sorry. Forgive me?"

"Of course, we understand. We all feel the strain," Penny said.

She jabbed Audrey's arm as though she was supposed to reply as well. When she looked up at him, she was struck by how handsome he was, tall and broad-shouldered with olive green eyes and a faint shadow of stubble. He still held the clipboard with his long, tan fingers. No wedding ring.

"Maybe I'll see you gals around? It might be nice to grab a coffee—if you ever catch a break. I know you're busy." He glanced around the room at the crowd of waiting patients and seemed to catch himself. "I'm not making any sense." He tapped his pen against his mouth and shrugged. "All I mean is, I hope I see you again."

Audrey couldn't help staring at the sculpted lines of his face. It might have been her imagination, but she thought he'd made eye contact with her when he mentioned getting coffee. Before she or Penny could answer, one of the local nurses hurried up to him and pointed at a patient toward the end of the row.

"Keep up the good work," he said. He spoke with such warmth that Audrey wished they'd been able to talk longer. He took the chart and bent to look at it, leaving her and Penny to their tasks.

Throughout the evening, at times when Audrey looked up from her work at a patient's bedside—administering morphine, updating charts, changing bandages—she found the doctor looking in her direction. Although she turned away, she found herself blushing.

They went off-duty around midnight. They didn't have beds, but Penny spread out blankets on the concrete floor and they settled themselves the best they could. Audrey's stomach growled in protest at the meals they'd missed. The hard work, the unspeakable injuries they'd seen, had taken a toll on Kat, who curled up in a fetal position.

"I might be sick to my stomach," she said.

Audrey rubbed her back. "If you are, we'll clean it up."

"We should try to get some rest for tomorrow," Penny said. She had been lying with her arms crossed over her ample chest, but she rolled onto her side to reach Kat. Audrey and Penny took turns rubbing Kat's back until she fell asleep.

Once Audrey closed her eyes, she saw the doctor's strong jawline and wide shoulders, those green eyes. It was pointless, given the circumstances, but it seemed imperative to find him again. If nothing else, at least she might learn his name.

*

Late the next evening, she trudged across the grassy area between the hospital and the outbuildings. She hoped to catch a few hours of sleep before her next shift. So exhausted she barely registered her surroundings, she looked up to find, emerging out of the twilight like a mirage, the doctor falling into step beside her.

She must have jumped because he reached to steady her, his warm fingers light on her wrist.

"You're all right," he said. His voice sounded deeper than she remembered.

Audrey knew what he meant, that she had no reason for immediate fear, maybe that she was in safe hands. Even so, she shook her head in disagreement. His dark hair, cut short but longer than a crew cut, was matted to his forehead with sweat. Several days' worth of blood and grime stained the front of her uniform. The bodies of the injured and dead may have been cleared from the grass where they stood, but the situation was far too horrific to be deemed all right.

"I'm sorry again for how I snapped yesterday," the doctor said.

"It's all too much to take in, what's happened here." Audrey's voice came out in a hoarse whisper. In the growing dusk, the palm trees stirred and clacked in the breeze. His hand lingered on her wrist for a second longer. When he let go, she felt the absence like a biting wind.

"Can I tell you something?" he asked.

She still wished he would reach for her again. A simple, elemental desire. In the distance, barely visible behind the blackout shades, the lights of the hospital burned.

"I've looked for you constantly. I'd almost given up on seeing you again."

Audrey laughed, the first time in days.

"You don't believe me? Or should I not have admitted it?"

"It's not that—" She stopped short of acknowledging she had looked around for him too. "I don't even know your name or anything about you."

"James," he said. "James Strout. From Portland. Maine, not Oregon. Here by way of San Diego. Next—who knows? Maybe an evac hospital in Australia. What else do you want to know?"

"That's a good start, I guess."

"I've been asking around about you already, at least your name. And age. And whether you've got a fellow." His grin made him appear younger, more like a boy than a man approaching thirty. A dark line of stubble traced his jaw all the way up to his earlobe.

"James," she said. "Not Jimmy?" She remembered meeting Kat and Penny for the first time—it felt so long ago—and their quick assumption of nicknames.

She could see, even in the dark, a shine to his eyes. Whatever existed between them seemed suddenly urgent, the situation giving rise to different expectations than back home. Who knew if either of them would still be here tomorrow? Audrey blushed and looked down at her feet. Her sturdy lace-up booties were caked with mud. All the lessons her mother had imparted, the rules drilled into her at cotillion and during her debutante season, and there she stood in a bloody nurse's uniform, unable to recall the last time she had showered or brushed her teeth.

"You can call me whatever you'd like," he said.

As she peered out the car window almost seventy years later, Audrey could still summon the feeling again, the sense that new experiences awaited, that the full shape of her life was yet unformed.

Even though her decision to take this trip was made in haste, she had packed carefully—a small suitcase with neatly rolled light-weight knits, a zippered case of toiletries, the pill container Laurel had filled for her. It seemed like a long time ago, when she'd stood in the kitchen counting out Audrey's few remaining pills into slots for each day of the week. And yet, she realized with a start, it was only yesterday. Before they sorted through the mail, before everything changed. When surprising news arrived or something shocking happened, a line was drawn. Before lay on one side, after on the other.

As soon as Laurel and Oliver left the house, Audrey had snatched the letters from her pocket and read them three, maybe four times, by the light of a lamp. When she finished, she leaned against the table, her mind reeling. She listened to the sounds of the house in the sunny afternoon. The grandfather clock's weighty pendulum swung back and forth, a creak in the plaster as the house settled further, a bird outside calling, suddenly and frantically, to its mate.

Imagine my shock after all these years seeing you so alive, absolutely thriving, so close by.

After all their time apart, as Audrey read the handwritten words she found she could still summon forth the cadence of Penny's voice.

I wonder, discovering this life you've made for yourself, whether anyone in your family or social circle knows the same Audrey I once did. My nephew located your granddaughter online and a boy called Ford Thorpe-Gayton whom I'm guessing is your great-grandson. Are you close? How well did we know each other?

Audrey had no choice but to take action. She needed to defend herself, to tell the whole story. After all this time, Penny deserved to hear it. All those years ago, Audrey had been at a crossroads. She'd agonized over her decision—and kept it secret ever since.

The accompanying cover letter on inn stationary, from Penny's nephew, was of little importance, save for providing contact information. But Audrey returned again and again to the longer letter written in cursive. She unfolded and re-folded it so many times that the fragile pale blue paper would soon tear. It was difficult to interpret, but the more she re-read it, the more she detected a hint of a threat.

If she didn't reach Penny soon, she might reveal what she'd done. Audrey would lose everyone's respect. The money would be, once and for all, the only thing of value she could offer.

She'd known wearing the brooch was a risk. The jade bloom was too unique. And yet what were the chances it would show up so clearly in a newspaper photograph, that the one person familiar with it would still be alive, that she would somehow come across the very page and pause to let its significance register?

Once Audrey was recognized, it would've been easy to learn more. After all, as Laurel had mentioned, her name and face regularly appeared in the newspaper. Anyone who could work a computer could access details about her life—her address, the names of her family members. They could look up real estate records and pinpoint where her granddaughter and great-grandson lived.

Even if she got the chance to tell her side of the story, she could be tainted in her family's eyes. Deanna would see through the charade once and for all. If she knew who Audrey really was—how she betrayed someone she loved, the years of lying by omission, the assumptions she'd let people make—perhaps she wouldn't want anything to do with her.

And if Audrey lost Deanna, she would lose Ford too. He would no longer skip into her kitchen asking for cookies, no longer squeeze beside her in the pew at church, no longer give her a high five over something as inconsequential as a cartoon about crime-fighting beagles on television.

Up ahead, another bridge stretched across the water, which had turned choppy from the afternoon breeze. She'd stopped that morning at the bookstore to place an order and then by the mechanic's shop to have the Mercedes checked on her way out of town. Both were important errands, but they'd put her behind schedule.

She pressed the gas pedal, then let up as she remembered the speed limit. This happened again and again until she grew lightheaded. She resolved to keep her speed steady. At the first sign of dizziness, she would have to pull over.

By now, Laurel would have realized she'd left town. She would no doubt be surprised, maybe even a bit hurt Audrey hadn't asked her to come along. For all her insistence to Deanna that she could take care of herself, Audrey didn't know the last time she'd embarked on a drive this long, or even ventured out onto the interstate, but she needed to do this for herself.

Before long—two days, three at most—she would return to Savannah, to her old life. By then she would be a changed person, someone who had finally seized the opportunity to defend a decision she'd made during the war, as momentous as it was irreversible.

CHAPTER 11

In Audrey's closet, Laurel held still. Surely she was imagining things. But the unmistakable sound of footsteps drifted upstairs followed by female voices in what sounded like casual conversation. Regardless of who had arrived, it would look strange for her to be snooping around. The drawer she'd opened held a brooch with a broken clasp. She scooped it up, tapped the drawer closed, and rushed downstairs.

Voices filtered from the rear parlor—Deanna and another woman—and Laurel paused to listen.

"It's one thing after another," Deanna said. "It's not like I have time to deal with this. Between the shop—did I tell you that shipment was delayed again? The toile dish towels? Sales are way down and naturally the rent's due. And all of Ford's stuff and now this."

"Such a nightmare," the stranger agreed. "It's only a matter of time."

Laurel stepped into the room. "A matter of time before what?"

"Oh, it's Laura, hi, I'm Courtney," the stranger said. She and Deanna wore sheer floral tunics over tank tops and white jeans.

"It's Laurel," Deanna corrected her friend with an almost unnoticeable shrug in Laurel's direction.

She nodded at Deanna by way of thanks. "What do you mean a matter of time?"

"She'll probably need to move her grandmother into some kind of nursing home. Assisted living, something like that."

"Surely not." Laurel looked at Deanna and tried to sound polite. "It's good for her to have a little help around the house, but your grandmother can practically take care of herself."

"Now that she's taken off like this, it doesn't look good, you know?" Deanna shook her head. "I'll need your input, I'm sure. We're probably looking at round-the-clock care."

Deanna picked up an envelope from the desk, glanced at it, and flipped it over before Laurel could read what was written on the front. She'd been in such a hurry to check Audrey's calendar earlier, she hadn't searched the desk to see what other papers might be there.

"I got your message about my grandmother being missing," Deanna said. "I was worried something had happened to her. I tried the house number, but nobody picked up."

"We rushed right over," Courtney added. Laurel couldn't tell whether she was annoyed or exhilarated by the sudden change in their plans.

Deanna glanced at Laurel. "When we got here, your car was outside, but I couldn't think where you'd gotten to."

She held out the brooch. "I was getting this from upstairs. I thought I'd take it to be fixed."

After Deanna stuffed the envelope in her purse, she took the jewelry from Laurel's outstretched hand. "Courtney, what's this made out of? I can't tell if it's real or not."

Courtney ran her fingers over the brooch and picked it up to test its weight. Laurel wished she could snatch it away from her. She should've left it in Audrey's jewelry box.

"Jade, if I had to guess." Courtney tapped her fingernail on the pearl at the flower's center. "I'm pretty sure it's not fake. Hard to say if it's worth anything."

Laurel figured she was cataloguing Audrey's other jewelry—the diamond watch and the cushion cut solitaire she wore on her ring finger, the necklaces made of pearls as big as gumballs, the indigo blue sapphire studs—and assessing where the brooch ranked.

"Probably not much," Courtney continued. "Maybe if it's vintage, I don't know. It's kind of old-fashioned, don't you think?"

By the time she handed the brooch back, a sour taste had settled in Laurel's mouth.

"That's what I thought when she wore it to the museum," Deanna said.

As she slipped the brooch in her bag, Laurel looked again at the secretary, its leather writing surface neatly stacked with papers. The newspaper article someone had mailed Audrey—that was where she'd seen the brooch before. She was mustering up the nerve to ask Deanna if she knew where Audrey was, even though it would make her look incompetent, when Deanna spoke first.

"Given my grandmother's plans, you'll have a few days off. Until she gets back, I mean. Assuming she does get back safely. God only knows."

"I'm not sure I got the plan exactly squared away. I might've forgotten the details." Her cheeks burning from embarrassment, Laurel checked her Timex. Only minutes to spare before she had to leave to get Oliver.

Deanna pulled her thick, dark hair up off her neck and twisted it into a loose knot. "Here, she left a note." Deanna reached in her purse for the envelope, but she flipped it around before Laurel could see what was written on it. Then she read aloud from the note. "Let's see, she's sorry for not giving more notice, but she's leaving town for a couple of days and will be back on Friday. Something she needs to do for herself." Deanna looked up to gauge Laurel's reaction.

"I wonder what she means." Too late Laurel remembered she'd planned to pretend like she knew all along.

Deanna checked the note again. "She doesn't say. But she shouldn't be driving, that's the main thing."

Courtney picked up the brochure from the Jacksonville museum. "It's probably something to do with art."

Deanna nodded so quickly, so energetically, that Laurel realized she looked up to Courtney, maybe wanted to impress her. "She used to do things like that—visit other museums and installations—all the time."

While Courtney flipped through the glossy pictures, Laurel tried to remember how Audrey had reacted to the brochure. She'd at least skimmed it before setting it aside. Maybe she'd decided to go.

"Says she'll be back by the end of the week." Deanna stuffed the paper back in her purse. "I'm sure she'll call with specifics. I'll text you so you know whether to come on Friday."

Ignoring the tone of dismissal in Deanna's voice, she reached for the turquoise silk calendar in a compartment on the secretary.

"Can I help you find something?" Deanna asked.

"I want to check—Audrey might need me to reschedule an appointment or something." She stopped at the month of September. In her cramped handwriting, Audrey had noted various doctor's appointments and charity meetings. On Thursday, she was supposed to attend a lunch for the altar guild. "I wonder if she let them know she'll miss it."

"Miss what?"

"A lunch on Thursday."

"It's probably not a big deal if she doesn't show up. The show must go on and all that. How has she been lately? Any issues?"

Both women looked at Laurel and waited for her answer. The room had started to smell like expensive perfume. Even though she wanted to justify her job, she was reluctant to betray Audrey's confidences. Her check at the end of the month would come from Deanna, but Laurel couldn't help feeling like she was the enemy. She ran her finger along the upholstered chair in front of the secretary, its cool silk fabric embroidered with golden yellow pineapples, remembering how Audrey almost fell. Still, by the time she and Oliver had left the house, Audrey acted perfectly normal. And the same thing could have happened to anyone.

"I'm glad I'm here to help her out. But overall your grandmother manages pretty well. Very good for her age, really," Laurel said. It seemed like a decent compromise.

When Deanna followed her to the door, asking for more details about Audrey, Laurel mentioned needing to pick up Oliver.

"Ford's going home with a friend today. Sullivan, I think. It's hard to keep track. I swear his social schedule is busier than mine."

Laurel couldn't tell if Deanna's laugh was genuine or if she sounded high strung, like she was close to snapping. Hurrying to the car, she tried not to feel like things were spiraling out of control. Audrey didn't need her anymore—if she ever did—and she'd left town without telling her. Of course, she shared her plans with Deanna. She was family. Laurel was an employee, part of the household staff.

Based on what Deanna intimated, even as a fifth grader, Ford led a whirlwind life full of invitations and demands on his time. Meanwhile, Oliver came home every day and curled up on the couch to play video games by himself. Ever since he'd gotten his school-issued laptop, he spent most of his free time making videos—scenes of spaceships launching into a black sky flashing with fireworks, monster trucks crushing smaller vehicles, tigers in the wild stalking their prey, complete with scary-sounding background music.

Laurel checked the clock on the dashboard. Unless she made it through the next three intersections in two minutes, she would be late. Oliver would be waiting with his backpack, which was way too heavy because he never cleaned it out like she asked. She could picture him scrunching up his nose to keep his glasses in place while he counted the dwindling line of cars in the parking lot.

CHAPTER 12

Something flashed in Audrey's rearview mirror and she glanced up to see the reflection of a pickup truck. Her vision seemed distorted somehow and her reflexes lagged a step behind. The truck would soon overtake her.

Without thinking, she jerked the wheel to the right. Lights danced in front of her eyes and her breath came shallow and quick. The tires rumbled onto the shoulder of the highway until she remembered to brake and the car shuddered to a stop. The truck whizzed past, its driver oblivious to her predicament.

As the minutes ticked by, she considered whether she was foolish to think she could make the trip. But she had no choice. Once she caught her breath again, she pulled back onto the highway, determined to make progress before nightfall.

Kat and Penny used to know her better than anyone. Now nobody knew her. Not even her friend Francine, who called the afternoon she received the letters. Because Whit and Tripp were on Audrey's mind, she asked Francine to take her to the cemetery with flowers for their graves. She'd chosen roses in pure white, the color of remembrance.

It'll be cooler up there—a nice break. We'll be back Sunday night. The last words her son, Tripp, had said to her. A client and old friend of his from Atlanta had recently bought a private plane. At the tail end of a hot, sticky summer they invited Tripp and his wife, Joyce, up to Cape Cod for a long weekend. Tripp was sixty-three years old by then, a husband and grandfather in his own right. Yet, in some ways, he would always be Audrey's little boy, his clear blue eyes unclouded by worry, a lightness in his step as he jogged to the car.

He'd stopped by on his way to pick up Joyce and their luggage. Since Whit passed away, Tripp routinely checked on his mother. He brought her blueberry muffins from the coffee shop he frequented and sometimes flower bulbs or gardening magazines. Two dozen pink roses every Mother's Day.

"It's not natural for a child to go before his mother," Francine said.

"Do you know I remember like it was yesterday the first time I held him?"

"Funny how memory works sometimes." She helped Audrey up from the damp ground and led her back to the car. Audrey rubbed the hem of her blouse. For a moment it might've been the worn flannel blanket that the hospital wrapped around newborn Tripp.

"Are you hurting?" Francine asked. "You seem stiff today."

"Always," Audrey said. Francine recommended a warm bath to ease her aches and pains and Audrey was reminded of how, during the war, Kat would stretch out her slender legs and talk about soaking in a bubble bath until all the grime floated away.

Outside the car window, the sky grew darker, the setting sun all but obscured by dense trees. A tractor-trailer rattled by leaving Audrey jostled in its wake. Even when she took a deep breath, it didn't alleviate her lightheadedness. If anything, she felt worse. Her neck popped as she rolled it from side to side, keeping her eyes glued to the road and her foot pressed lightly on the gas pedal. Without another way to solve her problem, she had to get there—in person and soon—before her old friend ruined everything.

Audrey was only marginally concerned about her standing in Savannah society. Reputation was, after all, superficial. Her family was her primary worry. If Deanna was disgusted with her, she might pull away. She would no longer bring Ford by to visit. Audrey couldn't stop thinking about how devastating it would feel to lose her great-grandson's affection. Since he was little, Ford had attended the garden gala with her, gamely shaking hands when she introduced him and beaming at the photographers. When he was six or seven years old, he began keeping a scrapbook, carefully cutting out newspaper articles and magazine features that mentioned Audrey, even in passing. Across the cover in slightly uneven letters, he wrote *Nana Thorpe*, a lopsided red heart in place of the letter *o*.

If she didn't make it in time, she would lose the chance to reveal the reason behind her long-ago decision. And if her secret came to light, any legacy she hoped to leave could be ruined. Despite her insistence on being independent, she couldn't fool herself that she had unlimited time. At her age, every day mattered.

Up ahead, the highway split and Audrey leaned closer to the front window. She couldn't remember the route she'd planned or which direction she needed to take. North, she would guess. But the signs—they passed so quickly—appeared to mention east and west. The highway, I-26, didn't sound right. The brand-new atlas she'd purchased—up-to-date, its pages crisp and smelling of ink— lay on the passenger seat. When she took one hand off the wheel and reached for it, it was out of her grasp. Stretching, she nudged the booklet closer. If she could flip to the page—but a horn blew and the car in the next lane veered sharply away. Trying not to panic, she gripped the steering wheel of the Mercedes with both hands. She must have drifted into the other lane without realizing it.

She stared straight ahead and checked to ensure her car stayed between the lines. Once her breathing slowed, she resolved to be more careful. If she had someone with her, they might help navigate. As it was, she would have to pull over to consult the map. Every second the evening sunlight faded further. In the growing dark, she might not be able to decipher it, but she couldn't afford to get lost.

Forced to make a decision, she swerved left.

An hour later, her stomach growled, reminding her she hadn't stopped for dinner. She would become disoriented if she went much longer without eating. Still rattled from the traffic, she began to doubt that she'd made the correct turn.

With a half-formed plan to check the atlas, Audrey pulled off the side of the highway for the second time in as many hours. She turned the motor off and tried to remember what else to do. There must be some button to push so that lights flashed on the car to render it visible. She couldn't think of what it might be called or where to find it. The switches and buttons along the steering wheel and dashboard were too confusing, their symbols impossible to figure out. The car manual was in the glove compartment, but when she tried to open it, the latch remained stubbornly closed. When she reached to try again, her arthritic fingers wouldn't allow her to grasp anything.

She groaned and slammed her palm on the passenger seat. At her age, some of the smallest tasks, the ease of which she took for granted most of her life, had become insurmountable. Even the language, the expressions people used, evolved and shifted until she was sure she'd stumbled into a foreign country. It was unreasonably self-centered to think this way, but the older she got, the more the world closed itself off to her. Every day, virtually every minute, she fell further and further behind, increasingly outdated and irrelevant.

When the woman from the museum, the stranger, had mentioned the word legacy, it felt insulting at the time. Now the question of how Audrey would be remembered was thrown into stark relief, Penny's implied threat like a menacing slash of red paint across a white canvas demanding immediate attention.

Every time a car sped past, Audrey held her breath, hoping it wouldn't hit her. Her eyes landed on her purse and she wished she'd packed an apple or some crackers, at least a bottle of water. Her powder compact and rose-colored lipstick, the neatly folded stack of tissues, were useless.

She flipped through the atlas but couldn't see well enough to find the right page. Although it was past time to take her evening pills, the container was in her suitcase in the trunk. She knew better than to get out of the car and try to weave her way along the shoulder of the highway. She couldn't stay here all night and yet she was reluctant to start the car again. After a few minutes, perhaps she would regain her composure and muster up the energy to find something to eat and a place to stay for the evening. She hadn't gone as far today as she'd hoped—and if she'd made a wrong turn, she had lost valuable time.

Even so, it would be foolish to try to gain ground in the dark. As desperate as she was to arrive before it was too late, she needed sleep. Any decent roadside motel would work perfectly well.

When he was young, Tripp had a difficult time sleeping in strange places. For the most part, they were content to stay in Savannah. Still, they traveled from time to time—vacations to the mountains to ski, quick trips back to Kentucky to see their families, an occasional business conference in Orlando where, while Whit attended meetings, Audrey would tug Tripp along the edge of the swimming pool on a float. Usually, at least until he was in grade school, Tripp tossed and turned in the fold-out bed in the hotel room. His legs twitched as he dreamed, almost like he was running. In the dark, Audrey nudged Whit, who smothered a laugh.

Look at this, she wanted to say. Look at this good and perfect thing we have done together. She didn't dare say it out loud for fear of waking up their tiny boy who would ask for chocolate milk before the sun came up, his eyelashes crimped from sleep. Even so, Audrey suspected, as her eyes found her husband's in the dark— the air-conditioning wheezing below the window, the elevator door dinging in the distance—that Whit thought the very same thing.

CHAPTER 13

Each night as darkness advanced on Fort Stotsenburg, the three friends gathered in the corner they had staked out in the nurses' quarters. Beset with nightmares, Kat sometimes moaned in her sleep and Audrey and Penny rubbed her slender back until she quieted.

"She reminds me of my little sister," Penny whispered one evening.

Audrey guessed she must have been the best kind of older sibling, reassuring and protective.

Penny kept her hand on Kat's back as she asked Audrey whether she'd heard about Cavite.

Audrey struggled to place the name. Her brain felt clogged and slow. "The naval yard?"

"It's gone now. The Japanese hit it. That's what they're saying. What few ships weren't destroyed will be gone soon anyway, leaving for the Dutch East Indies."

She wrapped her arms around her knees. Clark Air Field gone. The naval fleet gone. They'd already been asking for more ground troops, saying there weren't enough. It was hard not to picture a line of dominoes falling in ominous clicks, one after another.

"I feel it too," Penny said. "We're not headed in the right direction."

"But there's nothing we can do."

"We'll do our jobs. Stick together. Keep our chins up." With one hand Penny patted Kat's back. With the other she motioned Audrey closer to her until Audrey leaned against her shoulder.

Early one morning, an alarm woke Audrey, its blaring so loud her ears watered.

Penny gathered up her thin blanket. "Another air raid, I'm guessing."

"Leave that. Come on, let's hurry." Audrey reached over to Kat, whose back was turned to them, still rising and falling in sleep. "Kat, wake up. I can't believe you can sleep through this racket. We have to go."

"What is it?" Kat mumbled. "Good lord, what now?"

Audrey covered her ears against the noise while Penny explained. Kat rubbed sleep from her eyes and sat up. Her normally tidy curls lay matted and limp.

"Get to the basement." Lieutenant Johnson appeared and pointed the way to the stairwell. "And hurry."

Penny gestured toward the hospital. "But what about the patients?"

"It's not your shift. They're yours when you come back on." Lieutenant Johnson tapped her watch. "We've got a protocol. I'm telling you to get to the basement."

Another nurse hurried by, the rubber soles of her shoes squeaking on the floor.

Kat's gaze followed her. With a sigh, she turned her attention to Audrey and Penny. "Arguing would be pointless." Her voice carried a hint of defeat. "And we can't afford to get in trouble."

So the three of them ran to the basement where the halls overflowed with corpses, the morgue having gotten too crowded. Audrey was startled to recognize the pilot she'd given water, his blond buzz cut caked with blood, his brown eyes now dull and lifeless. Without thinking she stopped running and reached out to gently lower his eyelids.

"I wish I could've done something," she told Kat. Even after she wiped her hands on her uniform, she could still feel his clammy skin on her fingertips.

Kat took Audrey's hands in her own and squeezed. "You would've given him every last drop of water you had. Now don't deny it. You did everything humanly possible."

Audrey shook her head, but she let Kat lead her down the hall. Along with some of the other off-duty nurses, they formed a neat row surrounded by damp cement block walls. She leaned back and let her spine rest until someone barked out a reminder to sit away from the walls. It sounded familiar, but Audrey couldn't remember the reasoning. With a sigh she bent forward and rested her head against her knees. Beside her Penny sat quietly, rocking ever so slightly back and forth. Talking over the sirens was all but impossible. What was there to say anyway? Shoulder pressed against shoulder, feet pulled up, they waited.

For what seemed like an hour, Audrey crouched with her head under her arms expecting more bombs to fall. The musty basement air smelled of sweat and unwashed hair.

Already most of the base had been destroyed—the barracks and officers' quarters burned to the ground, the hangars and machine shops damaged, the oil field still on fire. As the sirens wailed and more people hurried to the basement corridor, it was hard not to envision what might happen if the hospital was struck. The possibility of already-injured men being subjected to further pain felt hideously unfair. And selfishly, she thought of not being able to say goodbye to her parents, of Penny and Kat being ripped from her, of never feeling her stomach flip as James said her name. She'd left her brooch upstairs in her bag and wondered if she would ever wear it again. With her fingers pressed against her scalp, she prayed they would be spared.

By the time the all-clear signal came, Audrey was drenched in sweat and her uniform stuck to her skin. Along with Kat and Penny and the other nurses and orderlies from their unit, she hobbled back upstairs, her legs cramped, to start a new shift. For the rest of the day, they tended to patients, stopping only to gulp down coffee and sandwiches. Every so often, she looked around for James.

He'd walked her to her barracks again the previous night. When he offered his arm, she took it before she could second-guess herself. From a distance, in other circumstances, they might have looked like a courting couple out for a moonlit stroll. They must have talked for an hour, maybe closer to two. The conversation flowed so easily it was as though they had known each other for years. James talked about his younger brothers and where they were stationed, how much his parents worried.

"My mother cooks when she's anxious," he'd said. "By now she's probably got the Frigidaire stocked with soups and dumplings and turnovers, the kitchen counters so full of pies and cakes there's not room for so much as a coffee cup."

"You'll go home to all your favorites one day." It was presumptuous to assume any of them would return home, but the alternative was too unbearable to contemplate.

He grinned. "Roast turkey—with gravy of course—and butterscotch bread pudding for dessert. In all seriousness, I hope she's at least getting some sleep."

"My mother has all but written me off. She thinks it's improper that I'm over here."

"What you're doing is important. It's a sacrifice. One day you'll tell your children about what you've done, everything you've seen, and they'll be impressed."

"It'll make for some good stories at least."

"How many children do you want? I think I'd like a house full of them. With me and my brothers, somebody was always squealing, somebody else cheering. A lot of noise, you know? Makes you feel alive."

"Maybe one day. I don't know about that many though. I'd probably stick to two."

"That sounds more manageable, doesn't it?" James rubbed her hand, which was still looped through his arm. "All of this, what we see every day, it makes you think about what's important. At least it does me. I'm ready to settle down. Soon as I can."

"It's hard to imagine going back to normal after all this," Audrey said. She'd been on dates before—out for hamburgers and milkshakes, to the movies for *A Star is Born* and *Bringing Up Baby*—but never discussed the future in such an intimate way. Even after the war started in Europe, her beaus in Kentucky mostly talked about baseball or horses or bird hunting.

Once they reached the doorway to her barracks, James stopped. He held her elbow and leaned closer. "Everything's going to be all right," he whispered against her ear.

"You keep saying that. I want to believe you."

"You don't?" He blinked and waited for her response.

"You can't be sure. We can only do what we can." She motioned at the destruction around them, barely visible in the dark and yet ever present.

He nodded. His smile had given way to something more serious. "We can only do what we can." He repeated Audrey's words like he was beginning to grasp their significance. He looked down at her. "All the same, you have to find something to hold onto."

She felt the blood rush to her face as she met his eyes. He cleared his throat and she panicked and turned away. It seemed too much at once. After spending all day with patients, she felt as though any new emotion might knock her off balance.

He reached for her, yet she turned away. Without so much as a backward glance she pushed the door open. By the time it clattered shut between them, she already regretted letting him go.

Inside, Penny rushed over from her cot, her hair tied back under a kerchief. She peered at Audrey's face. "What is it? Something's happened."

Audrey tried to wave her off. "You were going to bed."

Penny, who saw through her in one brief glance, gripped her shoulders. "I'll pester you all night if I have to. But only because I care."

"It's that doctor," Audrey said. "James Strout. He's been waiting for me after my shift. I don't know when he sleeps." She shook her head. Saying it out loud, to Penny of all people, made what had happened seem real when otherwise it might have been only her imagination, some childlike wish born of a more innocent time and place.

"Your face—your cheeks are all pink—why, look at you!" Penny clasped her hands to her chest. "Why hadn't you mentioned it? You know we'll keep your secret."

"I don't think anything can happen. It's impossible. At least not here, not now."

"I don't know why not. Anyway this is a better story for your grandkids than meeting at some stuffy old tea party at the country club."

"You're getting way ahead of yourself."

"And you're still blushing." Penny winked. "Wait until Kat hears about this. I'm on a double tomorrow, but she has the night off. You know you won't be able to get this past her much longer."

Audrey stifled a yawn. "You haven't told me about your shift."

"My story involves an amputation so it's not nearly as nice as yours," Penny said.

No matter what she encountered, Penny managed to stay calm. She didn't flinch at anything. And even though Kat called herself the flighty one of the group, she was stronger than she looked. Day after day, Audrey tried to keep her chin up, telling herself not to worry about them but failing miserably.

Sometimes she imagined their trio like Rodin's sculpture of three faunesses, the mythical creatures carved in bronze, their stance fierce and determined, linked together forever. And yet so much could go wrong.

Chapter 14

The evening after she'd told Penny about James, Audrey and Kat were taking off their shoes, ready to rest for a few hours.

Kat held out her legs and poked at her kneecap, which was flecked with dirt. "What I wouldn't give for a bubble bath." She looked so lost in the illusion, so far away, that Audrey expected she could almost feel the warm water against her skin.

"Penny would probably prefer a saltwater dip," Audrey said.

"Lord, yes, if she had the chance, Penny would be swimming like a dolphin." Kat searched through her duffel bag until she found her tooth powder.

"A porpoise, you mean."

Kat shook her head and laughed. When her eyes lighted on something, Audrey looked in the same direction, surprised to discover a bundle of plumeria blooms on her cot.

"What's this?" Kat reached for the coral flowers, their throats striped with yellow.

But Audrey grabbed them first and held them close, startled by the thrill surging through her chest. She felt like she'd been running for miles.

"Who are they from? Wait, don't tell me. Dr. Strout." Kat grinned, certain she was right. Audrey looked around to make sure no one had heard her. Two cots over, a bedraggled-looking nurse from Ohio slept with her knees drawn up to her chest. One untied shoe still dangled from her foot.

"How did you know?"

"I've got eyes, silly girl. I've seen you mooning over each other. I didn't want to jinx it."

"I don't want to jinx it either." Audrey fingered the stems, which had been carefully tied with surgical strips. "That's why I haven't said anything. I don't know if it's real."

Kat stared at the bouquet. "Looks real to me."

Audrey buried her face in the plumeria blooms and breathed in their sweet scent, so much like tropical fruit that her mouth watered.

"They're certainly a bright spot around here." Kat jabbed her finger at the squalor surrounding them, the dirty uniforms discarded on the floor, a can of pork and beans overturned in the corner. The chipped red nail polish on her fingernails looked faintly obscene, a reminder of how different their lives had become, how far they had veered from dances and cocktail parties in so little time.

Kat grinned again. "Didn't I tell you there are lots of potential beaus around here?" She held up Audrey's hair and twirled it into a knot, then positioned the largest bloom at an angle. "Now you look like Ava Gardner."

Audrey fell into bed still holding the flowers. She inhaled their sugary ripeness until, instead of mangled limbs and blood-soaked bandages, she dreamt of a serene paradise lush with plumeria trees.

When she saw James the next day, it was early morning, the sun starting to rise and the expansive Pacific sky tinged with the same rosy pink Degas used for his dancers. Before she could thank him for the flowers, he groaned and wiped his hand over his face, like he could scrub it clean.

"What's the matter? Did you have a rough shift?"

His hand against her back, he pulled her closer. "Seeing you, it's like I can put that all behind me."

"If only for a minute. I know—I feel the same way."

"Remember what I said about someone to hold onto?" James said, slightly louder than a whisper. "I can't stop thinking about it. About you."

Audrey leaned closer until her face pressed against his broad chest. In this mud-strewn place, he somehow smelled like crisp autumn leaves. She took a deep breath and then another. James stroked the back of her head. Maybe the two of them were destined to meet in this war-torn place. It seemed as possible as anything else.

An orderly appeared on the path pushing a cart of supplies and the wheels squeaked as they bumped over the stones. He kept his eyes down, perhaps chagrined at having interrupted their embrace, and once he'd passed, James chuckled, a deep laugh that rose from his chest like a wave. He gripped Audrey's fingers tighter. She followed as he tugged her away from the path and around the corner of the barracks until they reached a small courtyard she'd never seen before. It looked like a shabby, secret garden, a palm leaf-strewn place enclosed by vine-covered walls where air strikes and death couldn't touch them.

"We don't know what might happen." Audrey said. She shook her head even as James brushed her cheek with his lips. "I might never see you again." *Either one of us could die.* "I have a shift to get to."

"Where are you supposed to be right now?" His breath blew hot against her ear. Audrey shivered, pulled away, then leaned closer.

"The mess hall." Her voice sounded muffled as she spoke into his chest, her lips moving against the stiff fabric of his uniform. Already something inside her gave way. She'd meant to protect herself from getting hurt and yet she couldn't shield herself any longer. She didn't want any sort of barrier between them.

He leaned down. "So skip breakfast."

She tilted her chin up until their faces were level. She touched the back of his neck and let her fingers trace his jawline.

His mouth mere inches from hers, he said her name. When he kissed her, there was no hesitation. Audrey stood on her tiptoes to draw closer to him and his arms tightened around her. She wanted more of him, as much as she could get. His warm skin, the firmness of his chest. The huskiness of his voice as he whispered how beautiful she was. The faint pressure of his fingers on her back, tugging her closer still. She wanted to absorb all of it in some intimate way she'd never dreamed to imagine.

"I wish we could stay here forever," James said. His hand pressed against her lower back.

She closed her eyes and leaned against the vine-covered wall and imagined they were the only people in the world. That they could somehow live full and peaceful lives together in the courtyard. James rubbed her back, his long fingers tracing an ever-expanding circle until he brushed her hip and bent to kiss her again.

By the time the hospital grounds came to life around them, the sounds of the shift change muffled by the courtyard walls, Audrey knew they couldn't stay much longer.

James pulled back and framed her face with his hands. "This is real too, as real as the rest of it."

She nodded slowly and let his words sink in until she believed them.

"Real," she said as she traced her finger over his eyebrow. "This too." She touched his eyelid, the bridge of his nose.

He cleared his throat. "I'll wait for you. I'll find you after the war, after all this has passed."

"Where should we go?"

He gestured around them, at the fronds bent over the courtyard walls. "How about some place with palm trees?"

"Good, we'll have choices then. A lot of places have palm trees." She needed to go, but she pressed her lips against his again. She wanted to carry the taste of him with her.

Before she left James standing in the courtyard, his uniform rumpled and his cheeks flushed, Audrey stood on tiptoe and spoke into his ear. "I'll wait for you too."

Two days later, Audrey's unit was packing to leave when Lieutenant Johnson motioned for her from the doorway. Her hair—light brown shot through with gray—was pulled back into a tight bun and her eyes were bloodshot.

"Come with me," she ordered.

Anxious to please the leader of their unit, Audrey followed. They scurried down one corridor after another until they emerged outside the hospital.

Audrey blinked at the early morning sunlight. Anxious to hear what Lieutenant Johnson had to say, she shifted her weight between her hips, which were almost unbearably sore from sleeping on the concrete and then on flimsy cots. She'd hoped to sneak away and look for James to say goodbye.

"You've gotten good marks here," Lieutenant Johnson said. "One of the doctors mentioned you specifically. He pointed you out."

Audrey scanned the lawn, still dotted with wreckage, for any sign of James. It had been a full day since she'd been with him. They'd met in the courtyard again to spend the hour at dawn talking and kissing. An old stone bench stood in the corner and, teasing that it must have been placed there for them, he'd led her to it. After he pulled Audrey onto his lap, his hands lingered at her hips.

Now Lieutenant Johnson told Audrey what a good job she'd been doing. "Exceptional even," she said.

"Thank you for saying so. Everyone's been working really hard. Penny and—"

Lieutenant Johnson nodded. "They look up to you. They all do."

Just then a Jeep pulled up to the curb. A young sergeant sat at the wheel, his hat askew.

"You're being given a special assignment," Lieutenant Johnson said. "Get in. He'll explain everything." She waited on the hospital steps until they pulled away.

As they rode in silence, Audrey harbored a secret—and probably foolish—wish that the sergeant would take her to James. She imagined him coming out of surgery, flicking off his gloves, his face brightening when he saw her. They would have coffee on the veranda. If only for a few minutes, they could put off worrying about the patients inside and instead enjoy one last chance to talk. Perhaps they might plan for when the war ended.

Before Audrey realized it, the sergeant had driven her into the jungle. He hopped out of the Jeep and she waited, batting away mosquitoes, to be told what to do.

"Follow me, ma'am. And watch your step." He pointed at the rutted dirt path.

She scrambled to catch up. The sunlight barely reached through the foliage. The dense silence was suddenly pierced by the chatter of tropical birds high in the treetops.

Startled, she jumped and almost lost her footing.

With a twinge of impatience, the sergeant called out that they didn't have much time.

"Yes, sir. I'm coming," she muttered, and finally reached the clearing. The sergeant, who reeked of body odor, reached to hand her something. A pistol, its black finish dull in the shade.

CHAPTER 15

The night of Audrey's disappearance, Laurel suggested they go out for pizza. *A special treat* she called it when the truth was she couldn't come up with anything to cook. She could barely string one thought after another.

Inside the restaurant, Clay ordered at the counter, his voice low and husky, and they slid into a vinyl booth to wait. The air smelled like oregano and yeast and eighties music drifted from the speakers.

All afternoon Oliver had given Laurel the silent treatment. She wasn't sure if he was still upset that she'd been late to pick him up or if he'd had another bad day at school. He'd never explained what happened the day the school called. He wouldn't answer when she asked—then or now. Either way, his mood only made hers worse.

More than anything, she wished she could make him laugh. When he was a toddler, no matter how upset he was, she could cheer him up by making animal noises, bleating like a sheep or mooing like a cow. Now he sat with his arms resting on the sticky table, his chin propped on his hands.

When their number was called, Clay heaved himself up from the table and returned balancing the pizza. Laurel distributed paper plates and slices oozing with cheese.

"Come on, Oliver. Will you sit up, please?" She tapped the table to get his attention. "Hope he's not getting sick," she said to Clay. "He's been like this all afternoon."

"Mom, I'm fine. I promise I'm not sick."

"Are you still upset that I was late?" She took a bite and winced as the hot cheese scorched the roof of her mouth.

"What do you mean, you were late?" Clay asked. "Picking him up?"

She wiped her mouth with a paper napkin so flimsy it disintegrated almost immediately. Oliver jabbed the edge of his slice with his finger, like an animal he was trying to prod awake.

"Well, I was at Audrey's house, trying to figure out—it was a little different today because I guess she's taking a little trip. So I'll have a few days off."

Laurel tried to keep her voice light. If she showed any sign of worry, Clay would surely say the whole thing was a bad idea. From the start, he'd thought the job was odd—the wealthy old woman in her mansion, Deanna's trust fund paying Laurel's salary. Since they'd arrived in Savannah, and especially once they figured out how expensive Oliver's school would be, Laurel had applied for all sorts of jobs and never made it past the first interview. Clay should've been happy for her when she landed this one. But it was like a reverse snobbishness on his part, an idea that people who weren't like them didn't measure up. He didn't trust them. He'd grown up watching his mother clip coupons and skimp on everything from discount food to hand-me-down clothes and thrift store furniture. When Laurel had met him in college—both of them were on financial aid—he'd driven an old truck with a rusted-out floorboard that stuttered whenever he pressed the gas.

"Where'd she go?" Oliver asked, suddenly interested.

"I don't know exactly. She didn't tell me."

"That's pretty inconsiderate of her." Clay took a sip of tea and rattled the ice in his cup.

She noticed for the first time a smattering of white hairs in his dark blond sideburns. More like Robert Redford every day, she'd have teased if she'd been in a better mood.

"Don't you think so?" Clay continued. "Like the world revolves around her and she can't be bothered to fill you in."

Laurel shook her head. "She's not like that. This is separate from me." Clay's pessimism, the way he so quickly ended up in a negative place, frustrated her. And it had gotten worse lately.

Maybe she landed too far in the other direction. Sure, people messed up sometimes. Her own father left when she was eight years old. Never looked back. He left her mother alone with Laurel and her brother. Laurel used to watch her cry in bed, picking at the frayed polyester bedspread until it came apart and pieces of stuffing drifted to the forest green carpet.

Sometimes she wished her father would move across the country so they could pretend he'd never existed. Instead, he stayed in western North Carolina and ended up with a new family he must've thought was better somehow. They lived in Mars Hill, not too far from Asheville, where he worked at the college tending to the grounds. They had twin daughters who must have turned out more lovable than Laurel and her brother.

Despite his betrayal, she couldn't help thinking people were mostly good, that things worked out how they were supposed to. More often than not anyway.

"Separate from you? That doesn't make any sense." Clay reached for another slice. He'd never lost his wrestling build, or the appetite that came with it. "What kind of person leaves town without telling her supposed—what does she call you? Assistant or whatever."

"Audrey doesn't have to run things by me." Even to her own ears, she didn't sound especially convincing. When she'd first met Audrey, the older woman said she didn't need any help. Laurel thought she'd come around and decided she was of some use.

"She must've had the idea all of a sudden. By the time I got there this morning, she'd already left." Laurel shrugged like the whole thing was no big deal.

"Were you late?" Oliver asked.

"That's not really a very nice question." When she frowned at him across the table, he mouthed *sorry* with a sheepish expression.

Back when she'd first gotten her driver's license, Laurel had driven over to her father's new house. With the engine turned off, she watched from the curb as the family gathered for supper.

Through the white eyelet curtains, she saw her father's new wife setting serving dishes down on the table. Her father wore a t-shirt and athletic shorts and looked like he hadn't aged a day since she'd last seen him. The twins, who must have been in elementary school by then, waited at the table with their chins propped in their hands. Her father must have told a story or made a joke because both girls threw back their heads cackling. A cramp twisted Laurel's stomach and she sped away.

"It was a weird setup to start with." Clay rubbed his eyebrow, the way he did whenever he was concerned.

He was always expecting bad news—and he worried constantly about money. They argued about the cost of IVF, the expenses at Episcopal that weren't covered by Oliver's scholarship, the roof repairs they needed at home. Every heavy storm, rain soaked through the ceiling in the bathroom and pooled in the center of the vinyl floor.

"Did Miss Audrey drive herself?" Oliver asked.

"I'm not sure. I guess so."

"She left you a voicemail or some kind of message, right?" Clay pressed.

Oliver swung his legs under the table and waited for her answer.

Deciding she wasn't hungry, Laurel pushed the paper plate away. Deanna had looked so smug reading the note Audrey left her.

"She doesn't need to explain herself to me." She cleared her throat to cover up the shakiness in her voice. This job helped pay for all the extras at Oliver's school. With his learning disabilities, he needed their special programs, the one-on-one attention, the dedicated tutor. No other school in town came close. She'd checked and double-checked.

"You could've helped drive her or make arrangements," Clay said.

When he reached for Laurel's hand across the table, she wanted to run out into the parking lot and scream straight from her gut.

Instead she half-heartedly brushed her fingers against her husband's outstretched palm. "Audrey's been taking care of herself for a long time." She squeezed Clay's hand before she let go. Oliver frowned like he was deep in thought, maybe remembering how Audrey had almost fallen.

"I'm sure Miss Audrey will be fine," she added. But her certainty was slowly but surely being replaced by doubt. And Clay's not-so-subtle skepticism about what kind of person Audrey might be—that only gave Laurel more to worry about.

On the way home, they drove past palmetto trees and shopping centers, the lighted signs advertising bait and tackle, jet skis for rent, a special on a twelve-pack of soda. It was dark by the time Clay turned into their neighborhood. Even in the shadows, the small ranch houses looked shabby, the yards choked with weeds. Theirs looked worst of all. The trim needed painting and the front sidewalk had buckled from the roots of a nearby live oak. Moss grew on parts of the roof. The gutters overflowed with leaves.

After settling Oliver in his room, Laurel padded down the hall to the master. Without washing her face or changing clothes, she took her library book and crawled under the covers. It was her favorite kind of book, a Tudor historical, but she couldn't concentrate on the story. She had too much on her mind to follow the palace intrigue, the whispered rumors and elaborate conspiracies.

As strong as Audrey was, she lost her balance sometimes. At her age, one fall could mean a shattered bone—or worse.

CHAPTER 16

The trip she'd planned should have taken a half day, but Tuesday evening Audrey was dismayed to realize she'd gotten turned around. The road signs were confusing and the turn she'd taken some ways back had sent her to the middle of South Carolina. She'd frittered away valuable time.

As much as she would've liked to make up ground, it would be dangerous to plow ahead. It was too dark, the roads too unfamiliar. She needed food and rest.

The sign said *motel* and, as tired as Audrey was, she couldn't afford to be picky. She handed over her credit card and the young man from behind the counter graciously carried her suitcase upstairs and unlocked the door. Inside the musty-smelling room covered with dark brown carpet, he placed her bag on the queen-sized bed.

"Hope the room's okay?" He left the key on the pressboard dresser and pointed to a laminated card on top of the television. "All your channels are listed right here. And there should be an extra pillow or two in the closet."

"I'm sure I'll be fine. Thank you." Audrey fumbled in her wallet and managed to pull out a couple of bills for him.

Curious as to how she'd ended up here, she pulled out the atlas she'd brought in from the car.

"Need some help with that?"

He looked over her shoulder and helped trace her route. She'd definitely taken a wrong turn. She'd headed west instead of northeast. Hours out of her way. As soon as possible, she needed to get back on the road and make up for lost time.

She put the atlas away and the young man stopped on his way to the door. "You're sure you'll be okay? Did you need something to eat?" He scratched the back of his neck. "My grandmother gets shaky when she doesn't eat and you remind me of her."

Still lightheaded, Audrey eased herself onto the edge of the bed. "You're absolutely right. I haven't had the chance to get anything to eat."

The young man held up his finger. "I'll be right back."

He returned with a pack of peanut butter crackers from a vending machine, wished her good night, and shut the door with a soft click. She was so grateful, and so hungry, that she scarfed down the crackers without worrying about the sodium content, even though she should be careful because of her blood pressure.

After she finished eating, Audrey undressed, shocked to find her legs had become grotesquely swollen. Frowning, she poked the fleshy part of her calf, so filled with fluid that it might burst. She didn't know if her doctor would be concerned and it was too late to call and ask. The bed felt lumpy, the mattress strangely bouncy, swaying whenever she moved. Even so, she resolved to stay positive. She would rest and get back on the highway first thing in the morning. After all, she'd slept in far worse conditions.

A sudden banging at the door woke her. Confused, Audrey reached for her glasses on the nightstand, only to knock off her car keys and pill container. She sat up, groggy and disoriented, helpless as the container popped open and pills—she couldn't tell how many—fell into a metal vent on the carpeted floor and disappeared. She squinted at the dark brown carpet trying to work out where she was and another knock, more insistent this time, sounded at the door.

Once she managed to find her glasses she shoved them into place.

"What is it?" she called out. Her voice sounded weak, almost feeble, and her head seemed stuffed with cotton. The strange room, with its whining air-conditioning and stale-smelling carpet, spun.

"Can we come in?" a male voice asked.

Audrey reached for her dressing gown but didn't see it. She couldn't work out where she was or why or who was yelling at the door. Pulling the bedspread, a flimsy, polyester thing, up to her chin, she tried to sit up straight. Her shoulders felt weighted down like she was wearing a cape fashioned from rocks.

"There's no reason for so much racket," Audrey said as loudly as she could manage.

"I have the manager out here. We need a moment, Mrs. Thorpe. If you can't come to the door, we'll use the master key."

The Thorpe name triggered something in her. It felt right somehow, a confirmation that whomever was out there meant no harm.

"Come in, then." She wondered if she was making a big mistake.

Two men shuffled inside. Audrey was relieved when they stopped a respectable distance from the bed, lingering near the doorway. A young man who acted like he knew her introduced an older man with a thick mustache as Mr. Rigley, the manager.

"Manager of what?" she asked, the bedspread still at her chin, its musty smell clogging her nostrils.

"The motel, ma'am." Mr. Rigley gestured toward the television, the pressboard dresser where someone had set an ice bucket and two short glasses covered with paper.

She tried to move her legs, but they wouldn't cooperate. The skin on her shins tingled strangely. "I need to get going. I need you to leave, please, so I can get dressed for my trip." She didn't understand why the sun wasn't shining outside, why it didn't look like dawn. The gap in the shiny, cheap drapes revealed gloomy shadows, more like late afternoon.

"I understand and I'm sorry about the inconvenience." Mr. Rigley cleared his throat. "We did wait several hours past check-out."

Audrey didn't know what he meant. She maintained silent eye contact and waited for further explanation.

"I'm afraid your credit card was declined. Joel didn't run it last night, just scanned the number, because our system was down. But now here we are on day two and the room's not paid for. So if you have another card maybe—"

"I've only got the one. I'll have to call the bank. They'll get this sorted out. I have plenty of money."

Mr. Rigley pointed toward the nightstand where there was a telephone Audrey hadn't noticed before.

"What do you mean *day two*? What day is it?"

He blew out air, halfway between a sigh and a grumble. "Just the way we count it based on check-out time. The paperwork says one night so the room ought to have been vacated by eleven this morning. Now we're coming up on four o'clock in the afternoon."

Audrey wanted to ask again what day of the week it was, but felt embarrassed that she'd slept for so long and lost track of time. Her head still ached and when she swallowed, her throat was raw. She had to get to Penny before time ran out.

"It's Wednesday afternoon," the young man whispered. She had to ask him to repeat it louder.

If everything had gone smoothly, she would've arrived at her destination last night. It was only a five-hour drive, perhaps slightly longer because she didn't care for speeding. Her gaze fell on the atlas. That nice young man had gone over it with her. The road signs had been confusing and now her detour meant several hours' delay. Besides that, she'd been forced to stop for the night because of that ridiculous truck barreling up behind her. If she hadn't been so rattled, she could've made more progress. Now she was woefully behind schedule. She had mileage to make up as soon as possible.

Mr. Rigley handed Audrey her purse and she fumbled with her wallet, eventually removing her credit card. Apparently, he was going to stand there and wait while she called the bank. She re-tucked the bedspread securely around her chest, hoping he didn't notice her underthings draped across the chair by the window. She flipped the card over to the back, but the numbers were too small.

The young man who had been standing quietly beside the manager took it from her.

"I'm Joel," he said. "I was on duty when you checked in—not sure if you remember." Without waiting for an answer, he punched in the numbers for Audrey and handed over the receiver, smiling kindly. He set her card down on the nightstand.

She waited on hold for several minutes. When a customer service representative finally answered, she wanted something called a personal identification number to access the account.

"I've got the card right here," Audrey said.

"Yes ma'am, I understand, but for fraud protection purposes, I can't access the account without the PIN."

"I don't have anything like that." She fingered the name imprinted on the card. "This is Audrey Thorpe," she reminded her, careful to sound firm but not imperious. "I've been a customer for many, many years. I'm sure you can appreciate the difficulty here. I simply need your help releasing the hold on the account."

The representative wouldn't budge. She insisted on asking for a PIN, which to Audrey's knowledge, she'd never had.

"In the old days," Audrey explained, "companies knew their customers by sight. This wouldn't have happened."

"I understand you're out of town?" the representative asked, implying that Audrey wasn't making any sense. And perhaps she wasn't. Through the receiver she heard the click of a keyboard. Standing closer to her bed than strictly necessary, Mr. Rigley crossed his arms in front of his chest. Joel bit his lip as though nervous on her behalf.

"I'm checking here to see if you've set up security questions on the account. If so and if you can provide the answers—ah, I'm not finding any. Unfortunately, there are no security questions set up. Once this all gets sorted out, you might want to look into doing that for the future. Is there anything else I can assist you with today?"

"No, thank you," Audrey said. "You haven't helped with anything so it's hardly accurate to ask whether there's anything else."

She hung up and tried to think of what to do. Calling Deanna for help was out of the question. Laurel's number was in her address book back home, but she'd also written it on a scrap of paper in her purse. Once she found it, she dialed the numbers and waited. When someone at a pizza parlor picked up, she stammered an apology and immediately tried once more. Mr. Rigley tapped his foot, waiting. The same gentleman picked up and sighed when he realized it was her again.

She offered the paper to Joel, who stared at her shaky handwriting and suggested switching the last digit from a seven to a nine, only this time she reached a recording that the number had been disconnected. She couldn't spend all day trying different combinations. And truth be told, it wouldn't be fair to ask Laurel for money of all things.

Francine and Audrey were good friends, but she didn't feel comfortable asking her to share her credit card number or do whatever it would take to wire money to this seedy motel.

Mr. Rigley's eyes wandered over the items on the nightstand, discarded from when she'd taken them off the previous night—her gold wedding band, the relatively modest diamond solitaire, and her diamond watch.

No, not the watch. It had been an anniversary gift, a symbol of the life she and Whit had created together. Maybe it wasn't a fairy-tale, as she'd confessed to Laurel, but Whit selecting the stunningly beautiful Art Deco watch, the warmth in his eyes as he wrapped it around Audrey's wrist, meant a great deal.

Trying to avoid the manager's stare, she slid the wedding rings onto her finger and reached for the watch, fumbling as she tried to secure the clasp. Her hands felt stiffly wooden. She couldn't connect the pieces and the watch fell to the carpeted floor with a quiet thud. Audrey remembered the night of the exhibit opening and her jade brooch falling to the floor in much the same way. Doubt pricked at the back of her mind, her head now throbbing with a headache. Perhaps Deanna was right—she couldn't take care of herself.

"You can take it as collateral," she told Mr. Rigley, flicking her eyes to the watch and back up again. "It's more than sufficient to pay for the room."

Beneath the bedspread, she tried to move her legs. Although they responded— she wasn't paralyzed after all—they were so swollen with fluid that she couldn't imagine walking across the room, much less climbing back into the car for another several hours of driving.

"And I'll be staying the rest of the afternoon and tonight," she said. Her tone sounded more snappish than she intended. "I need the rest and at this point it's already paid for."

Time was running out, of course. That hurt the most, the possibility that she might fail at this last important task. According to the cover letter from her nephew, Penny was on her deathbed. Audrey could only imagine how she'd struggled to get her words down on paper.

I wonder, discovering this life you've made for yourself, whether anyone in your family or social circle knows the same Audrey I once did.

"Can I bring you anything?" Joel asked. He looked away as Mr. Rigley scooped up the watch.

On the nightstand Audrey spotted a plastic wrapper. Now she remembered how he was kind enough to bring her crackers after she'd checked in. But she couldn't stomach any more salt. "I don't suppose you have any fruit lying around?"

He turned to follow the manager out. "I'll see what I can do."

He returned with a bottle of water, a banana and an apple.

"How much do I owe you?" Audrey asked. "I'm sure there are a couple of dollars in my purse. Not enough for the room, unfortunately."

"It's all right," Joel said. "Hope you start to feel better."

"Would you do me another favor? Please tell Mr. Rigley that under no circumstances is he to pawn or sell my watch. It's temporary collateral only. As soon as I work things out with the bank, I'll expect it back."

"Of course. That makes sense. I'm sure he'll hold onto it."

Although she wasn't so sure, she couldn't think of what else to do. Already she felt worn out by the afternoon's events, the word *fraud* still ringing in her ears. After Joel left, she took the last of her pills, the ones that didn't fall into the floor vent. She hoped they would be enough to calm the roaring in her head and drain the fluid from her legs.

"I'm not a fraud," she said out loud in the empty room, but as she leaned back against the pillow a quiet inner voice reminded her of the truth.

That morning at Fort Stotsenburg, after Audrey had been whisked away from the hospital in a Jeep, she waited for instruction. She stared at the pistol in the sergeant's hand and willed it to turn into something else, something less menacing. The sun's first rays pierced through the canopy of palms and mosquitoes settled on her bare arm.

"Take it," he ordered and the next thing she knew, he'd thrust the gun at her and she had no choice but to hold it. Her palm registered its coolness, the surprising weight.

"We need you to take charge of the train back to Manila," he explained. "Someone has to be on guard, on the lookout for any trouble. So that's your job. You're going to get everyone there safely, no matter what might happen along the way—more strafing, any irregularities on the ground. Hard to say what you might encounter."

"My job," she repeated as the sergeant's words sunk in.

"You ever shot something like that?" He tapped the pistol, which was still in her hand. Without her noticing, her fingers had wrapped around it.

Audrey shook her head. "No sir, I haven't." For a brief moment, she wished she could spirit herself back home to Lexington. Not long ago, she'd told her mother she would die of boredom if she had to sit through another afternoon tea. She'd thought a meaningful life meant excitement and adventure. She'd assumed she could handle anything.

"Then it's good I brought you out here for target practice. Now let's hurry up. You're on the train at oh ten hundred whether you're ready or not."

Audrey wanted to find James, to tug him into the courtyard and bury her face against his chest, to feel the weight of his arms wrapped around her. She imagined telling him about the responsibility she'd been given. In his deep voice, he would reassure her that everything would be all right. For now she was in this alone. Squaring her shoulders, she looked toward the target.

Later that morning, she boarded the train headed back to Manila, having had no opportunity to say goodbye to James or even to glimpse his chiseled profile from across the operating room. As much as she worried she would never see him again, she worried too about the task ahead of her.

The pistol fit snugly in its holster, which she'd slung over her shoulder. It bumped against her hip whenever she moved. At the last minute, the sergeant had handed her a green army sock filled with extra bullets. She stared at the sock and prodded at the lumps before stuffing it in her musette bag. She tried not to think about needing it, about what that might mean.

Even as the rubble of Stotsenburg grew smaller by the second, replaced by acres of green sugarcane fields, Audrey felt trapped in some sort of odd dream. Guarding a train of injured soldiers seemed impossible. What was next? Would she be asked to hop on board a fighter plane? That would never happen, but it was almost as ludicrous as finding herself with a pistol. She paced the train and tried not to make eye contact with anyone.

As they neared the capital, a nurse from Florida named Barbara unfolded a map and held it out to Audrey.

"San Fernando, Calumpit." Barbara traced out their route. She looked so young and innocent, she could've passed for a teenager. Off duty, she always had her head in a book.

"Malolos," she said as they passed a small town. Squat stone buildings covered in dingy white paint dotted the landscape. "We're in the Bulacan province now."

They were maybe ten or fifteen miles outside Manila when the train jerked and wheezed and came to a stop. Patients gripped the edge of their gurneys. The nurses tending to them looked up sharply.

"It's all right," Audrey called out. "I'm sure we're in no danger." Even though she tried to project confidence, her voice shook. She touched the edge of the pistol, still snug in its holster. She wasn't sure she remembered what the sergeant had taught her.

Through the open windows of the train, the air smelled of the sea, of thick mud and exhaust fumes. Audrey bent closer to check outside when an air raid siren screeched. No matter what might happen she was supposed to maintain order. She turned toward the patients who were growing restless. In the corner, a young man sobbed silently. Across the aisle, a boy began to laugh, softly at first, then a loud cackle, the crazed sound of shell shock. Audrey bent to him and stroked his arm. She made promises she had no ability to keep, that nobody would be hurt, that they would get to Manila in one piece. The siren droned on.

"Look," a pilot cried, pointing out the window. His other arm hung in a sling against his chest.

Audrey turned around in time to catch the silver flash of a Japanese plane, then another. An entire formation of bombers appeared overhead, louder and closer every second. The rumble of their engines drowned out all but the most panicked cries.

"Everyone stay calm." She drew herself up, trying to look intimidating so they would do as she asked. "There's no reason to panic. You only run the risk of further injury." Audrey looked around for Kat and Penny, then remembered they were traveling by separate transport. She called a corpsman over and asked him to stand near the exit, to block it if necessary. Her instructions filtered back in waves. Keep everyone calm and together. The last thing you want is mass panic.

"We'll be going again shortly," Audrey said, even though she wasn't sure if it was true—or what they might find in Manila once they arrived.

The corpsman tapped the window. Outside the planes tilted and rose and began to bank away. Audrey loosened her grip on the pistol.

"False alarm," she said. Throughout the car, heads swiveled toward the window where the Japanese planes were so far away they might have been birds, nothing more than dark specks in the cobalt sky.

The ambulances met them back at Sternberg General in the center of the capital. Quickly, they unloaded the patients who by then had settled themselves. Even the most seriously injured young men, those being sent for amputations or skin grafting, looked calm and resigned to whatever awaited them. Some even slept.

Audrey's hands felt numb as she turned in the pistol and bullets. God willing she would never need them again. When she looked around, stunned to discover how Manila had changed in their brief absence, she realized the date. December 24, the day before Christmas.

CHAPTER 17

Wednesday was Parents' Night at Episcopal, an event that Laurel both looked forward to and dreaded. She hadn't made any friends, but Clay would be with her. They would talk with Oliver's teachers, but they might be pessimistic about his progress.

The evening mostly passed in an overwhelming blur—the sleek media center, the school's motto in Latin hanging between arched windows in the dining hall, the wall of donors carved with last names like Maclean and Exley and Thorpe.

On their way out of the language arts classroom, Oliver's teacher, Ms. Ross, stopped them and asked if she could have a minute. Laurel braced herself to hear that Oliver simply couldn't keep up. They'd heard this kind of assessment before, but it didn't get any easier.

"At the start of the year, your son struggled," Ms. Ross said. "He sat by himself. Sometimes I worried he went the whole day without speaking to any of his classmates. He was so self-conscious."

"I got that call about him being distraught that one day. Do you know what happened?" Laurel asked.

She shook her head. "I'm afraid we never got to the bottom of that. Mainly, I've been concerned about his reading ability, his speech and other developmental delays."

"We were hoping the extra help here…" She wasn't sure how to finish her thought. Clay touched her elbow.

Ms. Ross held up her hand to stop her. "I've seen great improvement. That's what I wanted to share. In these few short weeks, he's made remarkable strides."

"What kind of strides?" Clay asked.

"Before you know it, he'll move up a reading level. It's more than that though. He's coming out of his shell, slowly but surely. Recently, he's been a welcome addition to the class discussions. Honestly, his positivity helps keep the other children on task, and it will serve him well if he can keep it up."

"You mean he actually volunteers?" Laurel asked. "He participates?" He'd never had the courage before.

Ms. Ross led them to a chart pinned to the wall. She'd labeled a yellow sunshine with Oliver's name, an award for classroom participation.

Thursday morning when Laurel took Oliver to school, he stared out the back window.

"Hey, buddy, are things going okay at school? Are you making new friends?"

"Yeah, and I might want to try football or something."

She tried not to let her surprise show. He'd never been into sports, not even when he was a toddler and all the other boys his age wanted to play catch all day. But it was normal for him to change as he got older. As long as he was happy, it didn't matter what hobbies he chose.

"Sure, football could be fun." She pulled up to the front of the line and promised to look up the practice schedule on the website. "Grab your stuff, okay?"

He opened the car door, already looping his heavy-looking backpack over his arm. She didn't see how he could manage to lug it around all day without his back hurting.

"There are tryouts and stuff. I can't just decide."

"Oh, well, that makes sense. It's up to you. I'll find out the schedule." She waved goodbye, surprised the middle school team would bother with tryouts.

*

While Oliver was at school, Laurel took Audrey's brooch to Levy Jewelers on Broughton Street. As soon as she mentioned the Thorpe name, they fixed it on the spot. She tried to pay—surely Audrey would reimburse her—but the young woman behind the counter waved her manicured hands like she wouldn't dream of charging her.

After school, they swung by the grocery store. Oliver promised he'd had a good day at school and begged for one of the free cookies the store offered. Laurel didn't notice he'd pulled out four until it was too late. He shoved them in his mouth and made a silly face. She couldn't resist laughing, which only made him try harder, contorting his mouth and raising one eyebrow.

They'd barely gotten back home when the doorbell rang. Oliver paused with his backpack dangling from his arm.

"Wonder who that could be?" On her way to the door Laurel tugged at the hem of her wrinkled t-shirt. The mail truck idled at the curb and a thin cardboard package lay on the stoop. The return address read *E. Shaver, Bookseller.* "Look, Oliver, this is addressed to you."

He reached for the package. "What is it? Can I have it?"

"Pull this little tab here." She showed him how to open it and he slid out a book.

"Look, Mom, fighter jets and stuff." As he held up the slim volume his voice sounded high-pitched with excitement. The cover read *Great Battles of the Pacific* in a gray font across a dark blue sky. Above the title flew a Navy plane with a white star.

When she shook the box, a notecard addressed to Oliver fell out. The more she studied the spidery handwriting, the more familiar it looked.

Oliver's forehead wrinkled when he tried to read the note. "The writing's all funny."

"You know how to read cursive. Try," Laurel said. He reacted the same way when he read letters or birthday cards from his grandparents. "What do your teachers say to do when something is hard?"

With the briefest of sighs he stared at the writing with renewed focus. "Dear Oliver, I wasn't sure when your school—what's this word?"

He pointed and his mother read aloud, "Project."

"Okay. I wasn't sure when your school project was due. I can help you with it when I get back, but in the, um, meantime—here's a book you might enjoy. It's from Miss Audrey. Look."

He thrust the note at her and she ran her fingers over the embossed monogram. "That was awfully nice of her, wasn't it?"

"And it works out because it's not due until Monday."

"Perfect. You'll have to be sure and thank Miss Audrey. She's supposed to be back tomorrow."

"So I'll see her after school. You can take me, right?"

"Sure thing. Maybe tonight you can do some reading. Jot down some notes. Tomorrow you can show her what you've worked on."

For the rest of the afternoon they sat on the couch flipping through the book. They read about the Flying Tigers and places like Guadalcanal and Saipan. Oliver spent a long time absorbing the pictures.

"This is pretty cool, huh," he said every few pages. His legs were crossed at the ankle, his shoelaces dangling untied.

It was time to start supper, but Laurel realized she'd been patting Oliver's back and he hadn't squirmed away. "Definitely cool, buddy." She rested her hand lightly against the thin cotton of his t-shirt and nodded as he mouthed the printed phrases *island hopping* and *military strategy*, practicing before he ventured saying them aloud.

Chapter 18

Back in Manila, Audrey was shocked at how frenetic the city had become. Gone were the locals leisurely passing through on their bicycles. The boisterous nightclubs were now shuttered, all the shop windows crisscrossed with tape. The bombings, which had started while they were at Stotsenburg, left charred walls, shattered glass, and the acrid smell of smoke. If the rumors were true, the situation would only worsen.

Even on Christmas Day, officers hurried across the base with their arms full of files and gas masks. They hunched over, bracing for impact. At Sternberg General, corpsmen prepared the ambulatory patients for evacuation and tried to make room for extra beds.

On Christmas afternoon, the nurses draped palm fronds across the doorway to Captain Deegan's office. It didn't look much like the garland Audrey was used to, but it struck a festive note. The captain looked up from her typewriter and nodded in approval. Between patients they distracted themselves by talking about whether the mess hall might serve roast turkey and gravy for dinner—or Audrey's favorite, mashed potatoes.

Then word came that the warehouse docks had been hit. Fresh off their shift, Audrey and a nurse from Baltimore named Pauline rushed to a window on the psychiatric ward. With her forehead pressed against the cool glass, Audrey watched flames shoot across the leaden sky until her eyes felt like they too were burning.

The day after Christmas Manila was declared an open city. Captain Deegan, who was in charge of the entire unit, called an early morning meeting. A metal coffee dispenser had been set up in the corner, and Audrey filled her cup with the stale and weak brew.

"The open city declaration is meant to stave off complete destruction," Captain Deegan said. She wiped her hand across her high pale forehead. Her nails were bitten to the quick. Lieutenant Johnson stood at her right shoulder ready to do what she asked.

"Like surrendering?" one of the nurses asked.

"No more resistance. What happens, happens." Captain Deegan's voice sounded deep and in control, no hint of wavering.

"They'll keep bombing, that's what will happen," Kat muttered under her breath.

Even Penny didn't argue.

Later that day, Penny jabbed Audrey's shoulder and pointed toward a nurse named Sue Darby. Unaware that anyone was watching, she tucked morphine into her hair. Her thick victory rolls were a perfect hiding spot for the tablets.

"What's she doing with those?" Audrey asked. Sue was a few years older and went to Radcliffe before nursing school. She'd always seemed whip smart. After the war she planned on applying to medical school.

Penny studied Sue carefully before she answered. "I think she's planning for the worst case. A last ditch escape." She twisted her watch around in a now familiar gesture. She stopped only when the tarnished gold buckle rested where the face should go.

Sue looked up and saw them staring. She shrugged and pinned the last of her hair up. "Going out this way might beat the alternative," she said.

"But you'll get written up—you can't—" Audrey's voice trailed off at the other woman's expression.

"I wouldn't last two days in a prison camp," Sue said. "None of us would."

*

The following week, stern guards kept watch at the city's bridges. Along the roads, temporary checkpoints brought traffic to a crawl. Impatient drivers blasted their horns day and night. Audrey could stomach the road noise, but the air raid sirens, which sounded with increasing frequency, gave her the worst headache she could imagine. The pressure built between her ears until she could barely restrain herself from screaming.

Across the city people withdrew their money from the bank and began stockpiling food, sandbags, and fuel. Newspaper reporters roamed the streets looking for hints about how soon Japan might launch its next attack. From what she'd heard, it could be days— maybe as long as a week if they were lucky.

One afternoon, she stood for a moment in front of the Army Navy Club and fingered the brooch pinned at her chest. They'd once wiled away the afternoon there, getting to know each other over cocktails and finger food. Now the building looked abandoned. Nobody tripped up the steps. No music sounded from inside.

At the hospital, the nurses tried to keep their patients comfortable and settled, even though they might be ordered to evacuate at any moment. They kept their hands busy and their faces bright, determined not to let their concern show. There were more important things to worry about, but Audrey hoped their trio wouldn't be separated.

When they arrived for an afternoon shift right before New Year's Day, Sue announced the Japanese were closing in. "Heard from an officer," she said. "Won't be long now."

When she shook her head, Audrey wondered if the morphine tablets were still tucked inside her carefully coiffed rolls. Some of their patients had already been evacuated to Australia. She didn't know what would happen to the rest.

"How long do we have to get out?" Kat asked. In the past few weeks, her face had gotten thinner and she constantly blew her nose with a handkerchief. Audrey put her arm around her shoulder and wished her friend could get some rest. Kat leaned into her with a sigh.

Sue laughed bitterly at Kat's question. "They're coming at us from both sides. From the north and the south too. Looks like we're trapped here with no way out," she said.

"Surely not," Kat said.

Sue shook her head again. "Rumor is our engineers have started scuttling the transmission facilities. We've given up. We're out of options."

"I heard they're evacuating us to Bataan. Or they might anyway," Penny said. She fiddled with her watch and peered out the hospital window, like she could see all the way to Bataan, the small peninsula sheltering Manila Bay from the South China Sea. Instead, the window reflected a street clogged with retreating convoys. "We've probably got a fighting chance if we can leave this afternoon."

"Nothing but a last-ditch retreat," Sue said. "Straight into the jungle."

Audrey knew she shouldn't dread whatever came next, especially if they could escape Manila before it fell, but she was tired already and guessed conditions would only worsen.

She kept waiting for a letter from James. Whether he was still stationed at Fort Stotsenburg or had shipped out somewhere, she wished she knew if he was safe. In dark moments, she worried she'd never hear from him again.

Meanwhile, she re-read letters from her family, Whit, and other childhood friends. She felt disconnected from the news they shared, both comforted and exasperated at how the world spun right along despite the war raging.

On her break, she watched the sun set across Manila Bay. She shaded her hand over her eyes and squinted at the gradations of color, the ochre bleeding to a hazy plum. Merely weeks ago, she'd seen the same sun rise with James in the courtyard. She'd felt safe then. Despite the war's arrival, they'd convinced themselves that brightness awaited on the horizon. Now with each passing day, her assurance faded.

*

At dusk, the unit boarded buses to the port. Their ultimate destination was the Bataan peninsula where American and Filipino troops had recently withdrawn.

Locals trudged along the road beside them. Some pushed carts loaded with their household possessions. Outside the city center, Spanish-style homes gave way to thatched-roof huts and carabao soaking in water holes.

Once aboard a small steamer boat, Audrey kept her friends in sight. Like the other nurses, her friends bent at the waist to steady themselves as the boat cut a rough route through the oil-slicked, shark-infested waters. Nearby a pair of discarded storage drums bobbed, sinking and reappearing in a hypnotic rhythm.

Audrey glanced back at the walled city she might never see again. An orange glow rose from fires burning at the docks. She was so lost in the moment she didn't realize they had entered a minefield. In the chaotic scramble, she belatedly remembered to take off her bulky shoes in case everyone ended up in the water.

For the rest of the journey, she sat with her shoes on her lap. Over and over again she tied and retied the cotton laces as the boat bumped along. Before long, Manila faded into the distance and only dense jungle lay ahead.

The troops had established a line of defense near the base of the peninsula. Two hospitals would care for casualties. The nurses who'd arrived at Limay before Christmas worked, slept, and ate in thatched-roof wooden structures. But their unit was bound for the new Hospital Number Two near the Real River. Advance troops had cleared out the tangled undergrowth to make space for tents and open-air wards.

It was dark when they reached Bataan. The cool mist drifting off the water had dried into an itchy film on Audrey's cheeks. Men in fatigues worked along the shoreline and carried boxes of supplies on their shoulders. The slopes of volcanoes rose in the distance. Thousands of retreating American and Filipino troops crowded the narrow road, the night air punctuated with the roar of Jeep motors and clanging canteens and scattered conversations in English, Spanish, and Tagalog.

Lieutenant Johnson, her freckled complexion flushed, pointed toward a trail where the tropical forest appeared mostly passable. Their shoes back on their feet, bulky helmets secured on their heads, Audrey and the other nurses followed. With almost painful slowness, she inched down a steep, narrow trail, pushing aside oversized leaves and hoping she didn't step on any snakes.

When Penny tripped on a root, she cried out, then clapped her hand to her mouth.

"Are you okay?" Audrey knelt in the mud to help her up and strained her eyes in the dark to see if her friend could walk. "You're limping."

Penny waved her hand away. "It's only my ankle."

Still trying to figure out how badly Penny was hurt, she straightened. "Do you think you can walk it off?"

"Let's go. We're already falling behind," Penny said.

"Haven't we always said you're the strongest of all of us?" Audrey teased, a feeble attempt to disguise her concern. Penny grimaced in reply but managed to put one foot in front of the other.

With every step, they plunged deeper into the jungle until overgrown vines slapped against Audrey's cheeks and tall, unfamiliar plants, some with fiery orange blooms, brushed her knees. Penny's limping worsened until she leaned on Audrey to guide her around the rougher spots in the trail. Lieutenant Johnson admonished them to keep up.

"She's only trying to help," Penny muttered under her breath.

A nearby stream trickled over slick rocks. It would have been soothing had Audrey been able to push aside her fears about what might be lurking in the dark. A Japanese soldier could easily crouch undetected in the undergrowth, holding his breath to remain still, his sharp knife ready to plunge into her side.

Suddenly something rustled in the vegetation beneath her feet, and she froze and braced herself for a pit viper or spitting cobra, waiting to be paralyzed or blinded by its venom.

Beside her Penny whispered, "It's nothing. I'm sure of it. We should keep going."

She squeezed her eyes closed and prayed and opened them again. Nothing moved. They had no choice but to inch forward.

Every muscle in her body shook as she lifted her foot and took another step, Penny's weight pushing her to one side.

By the time they reached their assigned hospital, Audrey's legs twitched with fatigue. Hours had passed and a dim greenish half-light rose from the horizon. All around them beads of water shimmered and dripped on the vivid green leaves.

Cots had been set up under the acacia and mahogany canopy. Everyone—patients, corpsmen, doctors, and nurses—would be exposed to the elements as they slept. They'd been told to expect wild hogs, rats, monkeys, snakes, and lizards. The advance unit had hung their laundry along thick green vines. A crude sign directed the way to the open-pit latrine. Overhead, burlap hung between the palms offered scant protection from rain and mosquitoes.

"Soon we'll see the sun rise in Bataan," Kat said. "I feel like we've gone back in time, back to the start of the world."

"At least it's quiet." Audrey wished James were with her. If they shared this strangeness, it might become less uncanny.

They found the nurses' quarters, more white cots set up under the moon, surrounded by sweet-smelling eucalyptus and bamboo. Everyone dropped their bags. Kat, Penny, and Audrey stood together, their arms around each other's shoulders as though they lacked the strength to stand alone. Audrey found an extra canvas sack to prop under Penny's ankle, and then she collapsed in exhaustion.

CHAPTER 19

Friday morning, the day Audrey had told Deanna she would be back, Laurel took Oliver to school and hurried over to Victory Drive. Nobody answered her knock at Audrey's door, so she let herself in to wait.

The house was quiet. The decorative trim—Audrey had called it fretwork—on the narrow windows by the front door divided the morning sun into rectangular shadows. She set her purse down and looked around. The more she could do to prove her worth, the better chance she had of keeping her job. She updated the grocery list on the corkboard and ran a load of laundry using Audrey's lemongrass-scented detergent—a far cry from the store brand she usually bought. On the answering machine, she listened to a message from Audrey's friend, Francine, calling to say hello. She made a note for Audrey. The next message was someone from the altar guild. She'd missed the luncheon and they were checking to make sure she was all right.

In the rear parlor, she paused at the secretary. It didn't sit right that Audrey had missed the luncheon she promised to attend. Frowning, Laurel flipped through the brochure from the Jacksonville museum. Beneath it she uncovered the newspaper picture of Audrey taken at the Jepson Center. The newspaper wasn't local, though. She was peering closer to take another look when a key scratched at the front door. She straightened the stack of papers and looked up in time to see Jacqueline, the housekeeper. They'd met before, but she'd forgotten she came on Fridays. She figured it wouldn't hurt to ask Jacqueline some questions.

Laurel followed the young girl to the kitchen where Jacqueline started to fill a bucket with sudsy water.

"I was wondering, did Audrey tell you she was leaving town?" Laurel wasn't sure what she wanted the answer to be.

Jacqueline turned off the water. "What do you mean she left town? That's strange. I can't think of her doing that before." She tugged at the bottom of her athletic shorts, which showed off her runner's build.

"Can you think of where she might have gone?"

"Not really. I've only worked for Mrs. Thorpe for about a year. Part-time while I'm at Armstrong State."

"Audrey missed a lunch meeting yesterday. And she was supposed to be back today. Maybe she'll show up later this afternoon." Laurel's voice trailed off. She didn't want to cause trouble. Besides, she wasn't sure what difference she could possibly make.

"If you're worried, my Grandma Noreen has probably known Mrs. Thorpe for longer than anybody in Savannah. She worked here for a long time." She'd pushed her sunglasses up on her head, but now lowered them back into place. "Honestly, I owe her a visit anyway. Let's go see her." Jacqueline dumped the water out and replaced the bucket under the sink.

As they climbed into Jacqueline's Volkswagen, Laurel's cell phone rang.

"Is this Mrs. Eaton?" a professional-sounding voice asked. Jacqueline started the car and pulled onto Victory Drive.

"Yes, that's me," Laurel said quickly, hoping Oliver wasn't having another bad day at school. He still hadn't come clean about what was bothering him that day she'd had to pick him up early.

"This is Lowcountry Adult Medicine. We have you down as the emergency contact for Audrey Thorpe."

"I can get there right away." Laurel's voice came out sharper than she meant for it to. "We're in the car and—"

"No, oh goodness, I'm sorry. Mrs. Thorpe isn't here. The pharmacist called about her prescriptions. She normally picks them up right away, but Dan has known the Thorpes for ages, so he let us know."

Jacqueline waited in the car while Laurel went inside the drugstore. She handed over her credit card, cringing at the thought of asking Audrey to be reimbursed, and scrawled her name on the screen.

"Can you tell how much time Mrs. Thorpe has before she'll need these?" Pill bottles rattled inside when she held up the crinkly white bag. They'd been on their way to the pharmacy that day when the school called. At least a week ago.

The pharmacy technician peered at the screen. "Based on her last refill, let's see—ought to be any day now."

"What happens if she misses a day?" She remembered Audrey saying she got light-headed sometimes. "How bad would it be?"

"I'm not a doctor, sorry. But one thing you should watch for is deep vein thrombosis. That's a blood clot, usually in the lower leg. Can lead to pulmonary embolism, which blocks blood flow in the lungs."

Of course, Laurel couldn't help Audrey watch for anything. She had no idea where she was.

"Pain or sensitivity, swelling, increased warmth in one leg," the technician continued.

Laurel touched the cool pads of her fingers, wishing she could reach across space to smooth away any heat or tenderness Audrey might be feeling in her legs.

Jacqueline's Grandma Noreen lived in a nursing home, a dimly lit place with sticky tile floors and the smell of bleach in the air. A phone rang unanswered at the nurses' station and down the hall a patient moaned in pain. If Deanna put Audrey in an assisted living facility, it would be nicer. Still, the idea was depressing.

Noreen's room was furnished with a hospital bed, a chest and nightstand, and two guest chairs covered in mauve vinyl. Family pictures, bottles of lotion, and boxes of tissues cluttered every flat surface.

When Jacqueline introduced Laurel as Audrey's personal assistant, she didn't bother correcting her. Stuck in a wheelchair, Noreen seemed happy for visitors.

"I understand you worked for Audrey for a long time," Laurel said.

Instead of responding, Noreen took a sip of water from a plastic cup fitted with a straw. After she'd placed it back on the nightstand, she looked at her granddaughter.

"Did you bring me some lunch?" she asked.

"Grandma, you've already eaten." Jacqueline pointed to a bowl on the nightstand that appeared encrusted with brown gravy. "You might need to talk louder so she can hear you," she told Laurel.

She tried again. "I was hoping you could tell me about when you worked for Audrey Thorpe and her family."

"Oh yes," Noreen said. She clasped her wrinkled hands in her lap. "Every Christmas Miss Audrey sends over a poinsettia and a box of the nicest chocolates—so big all the residents get to share, the staff too. Makes me popular around here, that's for sure."

"Sounds like she's very generous. She left town this week—kind of suddenly. Does that strike you as odd?"

"Well, I always try to mind my own business. Then and now."

"I'm sure you did a very good job for the Thorpes, just like I'm trying to do. I've only worked for her for a few weeks. It's still kind of new."

Noreen shifted in her wheelchair, but didn't say anything.

"Can you think of where Mrs. Thorpe might have gone?" Jacqueline asked.

"Does she go back to Lexington very often? Could that be where she's gone?" Laurel wasn't sure whether Audrey still had family there.

"Not likely. I can't think of the last time she's gone to Kentucky."

Laurel mentally crossed Lexington off her list. It would've been a long drive anyway and Audrey wouldn't have flown, not based on what she'd told Oliver. "Was there a special vacation spot they liked to go to?"

"Not by herself I wouldn't think."

"I just thought, if the family used to go somewhere, she might go back. For the memories or something."

Noreen shook her head. "They traveled to see friends all over. Once in a while Whit had a work trip. But no one place comes to mind."

Laurel decided to change tactics slightly. This was a chance to learn what she could about Audrey. "What do you remember most about her? Back when Audrey and her husband and son all lived in the house?"

Noreen's eyes clouded like she'd been whisked back in time as she described getting the call from Whit's parents. They'd hired her to take care of the house on Victory Drive, which had been sitting empty.

"I got everything all ready for them—draperies hung, the roof repaired, the kitchen stocked with cookware, the best money could buy."

Laurel leaned forward to encourage her to keep talking.

"I wish you could've seen them when they arrived," Noreen continued. "Miss Audrey in a suit and hat, that sweet baby in his carriage and her husband holding her elbow as they came up the front walk. What a pretty picture they made."

"Did she seem happy?" Audrey had admitted her life wasn't a fairytale. Her words echoed through Laurel's memory until she wasn't sure what the confession meant.

"Happy enough." Noreen shrugged. "They kept things a bit formal, of course."

Laurel must have frowned, even though she didn't mean to, because Noreen promised she didn't mean anything by her comment. "We weren't close, that's all. She kept her distance and her thoughts to herself. Miss Audrey treats her staff fairly, but there's a part of her you'll never know. Not really."

The word *staff* sounded condescending, almost insulting. Back when Noreen worked for the Thorpes, times were different. Of course, Laurel was staff now. Audrey might treat her fairly—she would go so far as kindly. But if Noreen was right, then Audrey would never let her in. She would always keep a certain distance between them.

"I wondered what kind of life Audrey had—used to have when her family was still around. I've read about her in the paper, of course. But people can be so different at home." She paused to let Noreen fill in the blanks.

"Oh, I don't know that I ever heard Whit say a cross word to her. And Miss Audrey sure stayed busy. Always has, as long as I've known her."

When Laurel asked Noreen why they came to Savannah in the first place, the elderly woman said she didn't know. Her attention seemed to be fading as she turned to Jacqueline to ask if she'd brought her any dessert.

"Not this time. This weekend I'll bring you lemon meringue pie. I promise." Jacqueline hugged her grandmother goodbye and Laurel thanked her for her help.

On the drive back to Audrey's house, Laurel did some research on her phone. Based on what she found, if Audrey had ever signed a power of attorney, Deanna could take over the estate. She'd have to show that Audrey was incapacitated or unable to make decisions on her own. But Deanna didn't understand what Audrey could and couldn't do. She wasn't with her every day.

"Even if she doesn't have a power of attorney, there's something called a conservatorship," Laurel read aloud from the screen.

Jacqueline stopped at a red light. "That's got the same effect, right?"

"Either way, Deanna could take control of Audrey's money. She would pay Audrey's bills and have access to her bank accounts. It says here the conservator or agent can buy, sell, or lease real estate and personal property." Laurel shuddered to think of Deanna moving into Audrey's house and slipping her grandmother's rings onto her own fingers.

"I clean for Deanna too, over in Ardsley Park," Jacqueline said. "Drives her insane when her friends call her house precious. Which they do, because that's how those women are. You know the type. Deanna hears precious, she thinks poky. She's always talking about how everybody else has a pool in their back yard."

Laurel could picture the neighborhood. Near Episcopal, old-growth trees sheltered the homes beneath them, but the bungalows were much more modest than the wide mansions on double-sized lots where Audrey lived.

"She's in over her head," Jacqueline continued. "Used her trust fund to get that store of hers up and running. Have you been there? Accessories and house stuff, each thing pricier than the one next to it."

When they turned into Audrey's driveway, Laurel looked around the wide front porch to catch a glimpse of the garden. It felt like only yesterday when they'd sat on the steps together. Another time she might have been intimidated by someone like Audrey. But their friendship began that day, she was sure of it.

CHAPTER 20

After leaving Jacqueline at Audrey's house, Laurel arrived at Episcopal early. The day's events flickered through her mind. She vaguely remembered filling out some forms with Audrey, but didn't know she was her emergency contact. She eyed the pharmacy bag on the passenger seat. At least Audrey would have her medicine as soon as she got back.

Jacqueline had promised to text if her grandmother thought of anywhere Audrey might be. Laurel wished she'd pressed Noreen more about where the family used to go on vacations. If they had a special place, then maybe Audrey had been drawn back there. An exclusive resort with rows of cushioned deck chairs overlooking a private beach, a place like Laurel had only seen in glossy magazines. Finding Audrey might be as easy as calling the front desk.

While she waited for the fifth graders to burst from the doors, she darted inside the main office and grabbed a flyer about football tryouts. Oliver's request still surprised her, especially since he'd never shown any interest in sports. But since he'd asked about football, she wanted to be supportive. If nothing else, it might help him make friends.

When Oliver climbed into the backseat, he asked about going to Audrey's house.

"She's not back yet." Laurel handed him the flyer. "Hey, did you know football tryouts are tomorrow?"

"But tomorrow's Saturday. I don't want to go to school on the weekend." He glared at the sheet of paper, crumpled it, and stuffed it in his backpack.

"Well, it's not really school. Not like you have to go to class. And it's your choice. How did today go? Are you learning lots?"

"Pretty good."

"Has Miss Denise been helping you?" Laurel asked, referring to Oliver's academic counselor.

"Yes, ma'am. She's nice. She gets me out of class every afternoon. At one o'clock, I think? We work on strat—" He paused to search for the word. "Strategies and stuff. Hey, when is Miss Audrey getting back? I thought you said Friday."

"Hopefully soon." She pulled into their driveway and turned off the car. "So about this football thing, are you sure you want to? Are any of your friends trying out?"

"Everybody is. Sullivan, Ford, Josh, Anderson." Oliver got his stuff out of the car and nudged the door closed. "Like literally everybody."

In their home office, Laurel waited for Clay to get off the computer. It was already ancient when they'd bought it second-hand and could be infuriatingly slow. Her husband typed until the screen eventually filled with a complicated-looking diagram. The components of a security system, she guessed.

"I looked up some stuff earlier," she told him. "There are all sorts of ways Deanna could force Audrey into a nursing home."

"Audrey asked you to research that for her? So she's back in town?"

"Not yet. But Deanna mentioned that she was looking into a nursing home so…" Laurel didn't know how it worked, but she wanted to do more research. She asked Clay how much longer he'd be.

"Not sure. I'm trying to get some work done."

"When you're finished, I need to check something. I'm not sure what Deanna might try to do."

Clay sighed. "How is this your battle?"

"Because I care about her."

"You barely know her. You don't even know if she can be trusted."

"I could help her. She might need me."

"You really think she's given one second's thought to you since she left? She lives in a different world. You're better off leaving her alone."

What could somebody like you do? Nothing. Besides, she'll never let you into her circle.

"Never mind." She wanted to take a closer look at the newspaper article. She'd set it down earlier when Jacqueline showed up. "I'll swing by her house again. Maybe she's back."

"Again? Come on."

"I won't be long, I promise. I'll be back to fix supper."

Oliver jumped off the couch and bent to tie his shoelaces. "Where are you going? I wanna come with you."

Her son's eyes widened when they walked through the foyer of Audrey's house.

"It's different without Miss Audrey," he whispered.

"I promise it's okay for us to be here." She held up the key Audrey had given her.

Oliver snorted. "I know, Mom. That's not what I mean."

She pointed to the octagonal mahogany table tucked into the alcove where the staircase curved. Oliver's paper airplane was propped against a white orchid, a touch of playfulness against the backdrop of Audrey's expensive antiques—the Oriental rug, the crystal chandelier, the gold fireflies painted on the blue and white flowerpot.

He smiled as he touched the plane. "She kept it."

"I guess she liked it. Pretty cool, huh?" Audrey had said she didn't like to fly. But she didn't explain why.

"I have to go to the bathroom," he said sheepishly. "Sorry."

Assuring him it was okay, she showed him to the powder room and reminded him she would be in the rear parlor. "Remember the room where you started working on your school paper?" He nodded and closed the door.

In the rear parlor, she looked around the room, admiring the bookshelves—full but not overstuffed, the spines evenly aligned—and the tall windows and French doors fitted with wavy old glass looking out onto the garden. Deanna would probably rip out the maze of clipped hedges, tear up the paths, and mow over the beds of brightly colored flowers to make room for a pool.

The glass-fronted doors on the upper half of the secretary reflected Laurel's flushed cheeks. Wondering what was taking Oliver so long, she flipped through the stack of papers until she found the newspaper picture. She'd noticed earlier that it wasn't local. Now she looked more closely. The article was from a recent edition of the *Wilmington Star-News*.

More urgently now, she shuffled through the papers again to find the accompanying letters. She checked everywhere and came up empty. The day before she disappeared, Audrey had seemed distracted by the letters. If she took them with her, maybe they had something to do with her trip.

In the newspaper picture, Audrey wore a pale green dress accented with the jade brooch at her shoulder. She looked thoughtful, staring into the crowd or at someone speaking at the front of the museum's lobby. Her diamond watch glittered on her bony wrist and she held a small clutch-type purse.

Deanna stood beside Audrey wearing a fitted navy lace sheath that showed off her toned arms. She came across as uninterested or tired. The caption read *Jepson Center for the Arts Board member, Audrey Thorpe, and granddaughter, Deanna Thorpe-Gayton, at opening night.*

Quickly, not expecting to find anything, she skimmed the short article, which described artifacts from the Philippines—pottery, copper plates, porcelain. The article was part of a series about Southeastern art exhibits. This one started in Richmond and made its way down the east coast. She couldn't figure out if the exhibit related to Audrey's sudden disappearance—and she had no idea what the handwritten pages might have said. The letter with the crown-shaped logo was shorter, the handwriting large and blockish, whereas the page of personal stationary was covered in tiny cursive.

Audrey didn't mention staying in touch with her friends after the war. Then again, she hadn't finished her story. And it was strange how she'd asked Oliver and Laurel not to tell anybody. If she served as a nurse in the South Pacific, she should have been proud of her past. No reason to keep it secret.

"Oliver, are you doing okay?" Laurel made her way toward the powder room. The door stood open and she didn't see her son anywhere. If he was wandering around the house, if he broke something, she would have to explain it to Audrey. She called out again. No answer.

Guessing he might have gone to look for a snack, she checked the kitchen. The room, which smelled clean and herbal, like fresh rosemary, was empty. At the window she caught a flash of movement outside—Oliver's royal blue t-shirt as he rounded the corner of a hedge.

She found him crouched down trying to pry up a stone the size of his head.

"What are you doing out here, buddy?"

"In the story I'm reading these kids dig up a rock and there's treasure under it. A super old watch with a compass. And they get to go back in time and stuff."

"That sounds pretty cool, but we can't be messing up Miss Audrey's garden."

He held out his hand for her to inspect. It was covered with dirt and one of his fingernails had torn. Laurel wiped off as much dirt as she could manage.

"Let's leave the rock alone and get cleaned up, okay? A few more minutes and then we'll go."

When she turned back toward the imposing white house, the branches of a live oak casting shade along the deep porch, it looked like a place where treasure might be buried. Or at least secrets of some kind. In the historical sagas she checked out from the library, everyone had a secret.

140

"That story you mentioned, was that one Ms. Ross read to the class?"

Her son shook his head. "It's a book I picked out. There's a shelf in homeroom. You fill out a card and you can take whichever one you want."

She tried not to let her surprise show, but he'd never mentioned doing such a thing. He had such a hard time reading on his own. "Did Miss Denise help you with it?"

"Yeah, she taught me little tricks and I'm reading it by myself for fun."

"Good for you." They stepped inside the kitchen and she steered him toward the sink to wash his hands. "Will you tell me how it ends once you're finished?"

"Sure, if you want."

Even though she'd been frustrated with Clay when they left the house, now Laurel wanted to talk to him. Their son, who for years had been behind on recognizing letters and stringing together words, picked out a book. He could read it to himself. No matter how much Episcopal cost, it was worth every penny.

"What about the book? If it rains, it'll get wet."

"What book? The one from school? What do you mean?"

"No, I mean the one outside. Under the rock."

Shaking her head, Laurel followed him back outside.

He led her back to the large bluish gray rock and bent to pull it up.

"Let's leave that alone, okay?"

"I only nudged it, I swear, and it popped up. Like a secret hiding place, you know? It stuck up higher than the rest of the rocks so that was like a clue. And look—check it out."

She followed her son's gaze and peered into the hole until she glimpsed the edge of a maroon leather-bound book, its spine cracked with age.

Chapter 21

Daylight on Bataan revealed an entire community hacked out of the jungle: electric lights strung on palm trees, dangling Lister bags holding purified water, rough roads, a Signal Corps company for communications, a Quartermaster for supplies.

With her injured ankle, Penny struggled to keep up as the chief nurse pointed out the operating room in a portable Quonsett hut flanked by smaller tents for x-ray and laboratory work and dispensary and pharmacy.

The surgical instruments had been packed in petroleum jelly for safekeeping on the trip to Bataan and on their first morning every piece had to be scrubbed with ether, a task which fell to Kat, Penny, and Sue.

Kat picked up a metal case and squinted to read its label. Audrey had noticed the squinting before, but guessed she might be too vain to wear glasses.

Moments later, Kat swayed on her feet.

Audrey nudged her aside. "Let me help. You get some rest."

Kat shook her head. "I'm not tired, honestly. It's the smell that's getting to me, making me a little lightheaded." She tried to bat away a greenish black fly darting around her face.

Audrey picked up a rag and pair of clamps. The ether had a strong smell, something like gasoline. "You'll faint if you're not careful. Let me take your spot."

"Only if we take turns. I'm not letting you do all of it."

Penny found a stack of surgical gowns and pulled it over for Kat to sit on. "First sign of you fainting and we're sending you out of here."

"You're the one with a hurt ankle. You should sit down, not me."

Sue flicked her hair out of her eyes. "For goodness sake, can't you both fit?"

"I'm too big—" Penny started to say, but Kat was already scooting over to make room.

"Now you can stop your gabbing and get back to work," Sue said.

"Yes, ma'am," Penny gave a mock salute and rolled her eyes in Audrey's and Kat's direction.

Sue sighed. "I've gotta go to the latrine. Back in a minute."

"Never mind her, she's just jealous," Audrey said once she'd moved out of sight.

"Jealous of what? This?" Penny pointed at her swollen ankle. "Or this fine manicure?" She flicked off her glove to show her torn fingernails.

"Of us. She's jealous of what the three of us have," Kat said. She leaned her head against Penny's shoulder for a brief moment, took a deep breath, and got back to work.

The first patients arrived two days later, and a steady stream followed over the coming weeks. After mobile units near the combat zone performed triage, the hospitals provided follow-up specialized procedures. Their patients needed wounds sutured, broken bones set, limbs amputated, perforated organs repaired.

Audrey began to worry about Kat. The unrelenting sun had turned Penny's and Audrey's skin the same toasty brown as the shell of a pili nut. But Kat, with her ivory complexion, reddened, blistered, and reddened again. She refused to bathe in the Real River with the rest of them. During the night, she woke constantly, squirming—and sometimes crying—at the lizards darting across her chest. She became convinced that the harmless lime green whip snake coiled beside her cot, which kept reappearing despite Penny poking it with a stick, was a sign of bad luck.

She started sleeping later and later. Every day she was harder to rouse than the last. At sunrise, Audrey and Penny took turns at her bedside. Brushing away the ever-present ants, they tapped Kat's shoulder and poked her arm until she blinked her eyes open, disoriented and groggy.

Without voicing her concern out loud, Audrey began to watch her for malaria's telltale symptoms—chills, fever, and weakness. Between the damp and the mud, Bataan provided an ideal breeding ground for mosquitoes. And the burlap netting draped across their sleeping quarters offered meager protection. Protocol mandated regular doses of antimalarial medicine, usually Atabrine, but they were starting to run out. Already Audrey had seen a strapping young soldier become bedridden with malaria in a matter of hours.

A new shipment of medicine would help, but supplies were slow in coming, especially once the land routes were closed. Plans called for forty thousand men to participate in the siege of Bataan, but the number soon doubled. With each passing day, stores of food and medicine dwindled while the number of patients increased. The *Si-Kiang*, carrying much-needed flour and petroleum, was bombed and sunk before supplies could be unloaded.

"It's Europe First, that's what they're saying," a young soldier told Audrey one afternoon. She assessed his abdominal wound, which the triage unit had sprinkled with sulfa powder. Since he'd come in, he'd been complaining about being left to rot in the jungle. His tag read *Delfino, Anthony*.

"MacArthur's moved his headquarters to Corregidor." Anthony gripped his hands into fists. Audrey wasn't sure if he was more upset by the pain or their situation. She'd heard the same thing, that Manila had been abandoned and a new command center established on Corregidor, the fortified island at the mouth of the bay.

"They're saying he'll go to Australia, at least his wife and son. But we're stuck here. All the rumors about reinforcements—" he shook his head. "I don't see any coming, do you?"

She didn't answer at first. They'd been expecting reinforcements, but none had materialized. While they waited, the Japanese drew closer. The stories worsened every day, mostly fears about another Nanking where the Japanese raped every woman and some of the men they came across.

"It's better not to focus on what might go wrong." She kept her voice light. "Let's think about getting you well."

When Anthony wasn't teasing Audrey about the khaki jump-suits and coveralls the nurses had taken to wearing, he talked about his mother and sister in New Jersey.

"I've got a girl back home too," Anthony said. "She writes to me whenever she can." He pointed at a bunch of white butterfly orchids growing out of coconut husks. "I can't remember if I ever got flowers for Cheryl."

"I'm sure you did, probably a corsage for a special occasion. Why don't you ask her in your next letter?"

"You think the mail boats will get through soon?"

"I'm sure they will," Audrey said, even though she had no business making such a promise. Like Anthony, she wanted mail so badly she could almost conjure up the weight of the thin paper in her empty hands. She constantly guessed what news her family or Whit might share. Or James. Especially James.

"Watch, Cheryl will send me some candy, maybe even some Pall Malls."

"Everyone in your unit will be jealous," Audrey teased.

"You've got a beau, I bet. After the war, you come up to New Jersey with him and we'll double-date. Wouldn't that be some-thing?"

"Don't I wish. But I don't think my parents would approve of such a venture."

Even with what she'd seen in the Philippines, she sometimes fell back into her old ways of thinking. The dutiful daughter, the proper family. Besides, she'd heard nothing from James, a truth that nagged at even the easier days. He was busy, of course. Perhaps he would write soon.

In his last letter, Whit had sounded frustrated at being stuck at home, unable to serve because of his asthma. When things calmed down, Audrey would write him back, although it might be ages before the mail got out. Even in letters she spoke freely with her oldest childhood friend. She never worried about having to sound like a lady who'd been raised with impeccable manners.

In her letters to her parents, on the other hand, she briefly reported on the weather. Sometimes she mentioned various medical procedures she'd helped with. They'd recently set up a new dental clinic for soldiers whose mouths had been disfigured by bullets and shrapnel. Assuming her descriptions survived the censors, Audrey's mother probably viewed them as unseemly bragging.

By the time they took Anthony Delfino into surgery, sheets of rain beat against the flimsy walls and thatched grass roof. Inside, lizards scurried across the bamboo floor. An orderly wheeled in the balloon-like oxygen machine.

"Let's get you patched up," Audrey said.

"If I don't make it, you'll let my mother know, won't you?" Anthony reached for her hand. "You could go find her once this is all over. Tell her I wasn't scared, not even at the end, you know? That would make her proud."

She stared at his flushed cheeks, his big brown eyes framed with thick eyelashes. "Don't be silly. You're going to make it through."

But Anthony asked again and she promised to try. She had no idea when the war would be over or what shape she'd be in herself. Even so, she found a stubby pencil in her pocket and wrote down his family's address. And when he didn't make it through the surgery, when the surgeon called out the time of death in a broken, defeated voice, Audrey touched her pocket to make sure the paper was still there. Even though Anthony wouldn't know the difference, at least there was some small thing she could do.

That night she sought out Kat and Penny, relieved beyond measure when she found them. She sank down beside Penny at the outdoor mess hall and began the tedious process of picking the maggots out of her rice. They were down to half rations—a fist-size lump of rice, sometimes a fleck or two of tomato. With no real hope of fresh supplies heading their way, the soldiers suggested they study the monkeys chattering in the mahogany and banyan trees. Whatever the monkeys ate, they could eat. Wild bananas full of seeds. Lizards and grasshoppers. Python eggs.

"When we get home—" Kat grimaced as brushed away a swarm of flies—"I'm going to wear a pretty dress and red lipstick every damn day." She rubbed the jade brooch she held in her lap. They couldn't wear jewelry on duty, but she'd been carrying it in her pocket like a comforting reminder.

"I can't stop thinking about frying up some of the fish my dad caught," Penny said. "My little sister and I used to complain about it, not getting to have steak or even pork. Now what I wouldn't give for some flounder."

"And Coca-Cola." Audrey's mouth watered as she remembered the almost spicy, caramel-flavored bubbles.

"Did I ever tell you what I want at my wedding?" Penny asked, a grin playing at her lips. "I want the reception in a dance hall. With a fourteen-piece orchestra."

"Goodness Penny," Kat said. "Such extravagance. You'd think you were turning into a social butterfly like me."

As Audrey managed to laugh with her friends, she resolved to push Anthony Delfino from her mind. Otherwise, she would be haunted by his boyish face and unable to think of anything but his family. She had no idea what his mother or sister or his girl, Cheryl, looked like. Even so, she could picture their desperate prayers at the breakfast table, the way they must jump every time the doorbell rang. His hand, when he'd held hers, had been marked with callouses and rough spots.

Kat pushed aside her mostly full bowl. "One day we'll go dancing again and drink gin and sleep on fluffy pillows." She leaned forward with her hand on her stomach. Her eyes shone strangely. "Maybe one day," she said, sounding less sure than she had seconds earlier.

Audrey tried to catch Penny's eye, but her friend stared beyond the thicket of acacia trees.

"Zeroes!" someone called out as what looked to be a squadron of Japanese planes burst over the hills.

"Hit the dirt!" another voice cried, and Audrey yanked Kat's arm and together they sank to the ground, Penny following close behind. The nurses on duty in the nearby orthopedic ward began cutting the patients' traction ropes so they'd have the option to roll out of bed.

Machine guns fired and kicked up dirt and grass. Seconds later bombers filled Audrey's ears with whistling and thundering until she thought her head might explode. She crouched, head covered, and tried to make herself as small a target as possible. Her knees pressed into the rocky ground.

"Please," Penny muttered into her knees, pulled up under her chin. "Please, please, please," something between a chant and a prayer.

Kat said nothing. Between her interlaced fingers Audrey glimpsed her friend sitting straight up. Kat kept her eyes open, her chin raised. *Go ahead*, she seemed to be saying. *Go ahead and hit me.*

CHAPTER 22

Laurel pulled the book out from beneath the stone in Audrey's garden. It had been double-wrapped in plastic for safekeeping.

"What is it?" Oliver asked in a rush of breath. "Do you think there's a treasure map in there?"

"Who knows." She flipped through the pages to find handwritten notes. Some kind of diary or journal. Some dates were underlined, the years in the early 1940s. When Laurel peered closer, the handwriting looked like Audrey's. She noticed the word *Corregidor* and struggled to place it. On the next line, the abbreviation *POW* jumped out from the page. Laurel slammed the journal shut before Oliver noticed the sketch of a frail young woman, her frame so skeletal she must have been near death.

"Hey, let me see that." He reached for the book. "I'm the one who found it."

"Not right now. I need to figure out if it's appropriate."

"I'm not a baby."

"Then don't pout like one, okay?" She tried to make eye contact, but he turned away in a huff. Not sure what else to do with it, she tucked the journal under her arm.

*

That night, as she settled Oliver into bed, Laurel glimpsed the book about World War II planes from Audrey on his nightstand.

"When you saw Miss Audrey at her house that day, she was telling us about the war and the friends she made. Remember?"

"Yeah, Penny and Kat, like a kitty cat."

"I'm guessing they're nicknames. Maybe for Katherine or Kathleen and Penelope."

"They had fancy necklaces."

"A brooch is kind of like a necklace. You pin it to your clothes instead of around your neck."

"Why would you do that? It's kind of silly."

"To look pretty." Laurel pushed her hair back to show him her silver hoop earrings. Clay had picked them out for Christmas several years earlier.

He shook his head like he wasn't convinced and leaned back against his pillow. The side of his mouth was caked with toothpaste, but she resisted the urge to wipe it off, knowing he would hate the gesture.

"Do you think Miss Audrey went back to that Stots—whatever place?" Oliver pulled the bedsheet over his mouth so that his voice sounded muffled and she could see the shape of his teeth as he pretended to chew the cotton. "Did you read what was in that old book that I found in her garden?"

"That's awfully far away." Laurel shook her head. "In the Philippines. Remember how she doesn't like to fly?" She purposefully didn't answer his question about the journal.

Her son popped his face out from under the sheet. "Yeah, but maybe to see her friends. Like if one of them needed her help or was having a birthday party or something."

Laurel plugged in his rocket ship nightlight. She couldn't help feeling proud of Oliver's noble idea of friendship, his conviction that Audrey would do most anything for her friends. Sadly, Audrey's friends might be either dead or in a nursing home—a realization Laurel didn't share out loud. Not many ninety-year-olds got around like Audrey did.

The way she looked at it, this trip was turning out to be a test. If anything went wrong, Deanna would have evidence that Audrey couldn't take care of herself. Worse than that, Audrey could end up in the hospital. And the longer she stayed away, the greater the chance of something going wrong, especially once her medicine ran out.

In their last real conversation, Audrey had talked about the war—right after she got the letters. She'd seemed distracted, maybe because she'd recognized the handwriting.

Oliver grasped the edge of the quilt, once sunshine yellow, now faded. His fingernails were ragged from digging in Audrey's garden. The journal he'd found was further evidence of Audrey's interest in the war. She'd made a scrapbook of sorts, but then buried it in the garden to hide it.

"Honestly, wherever she is, I wish Audrey had asked me to go with her." Laurel lingered in his doorway, the overhead light turned off and a soft glow shining from the nightlight.

Her son nodded. "Because you're her friend now and you could help her."

"I think so anyway." When she turned around, Clay stood in the hallway, his mouth set in a firm straight line.

You barely know her. You don't even know if she can be trusted.

"Big day tomorrow, Oliver. Get some rest before tryouts," her husband said.

When they'd been in bed for a while, Laurel nudged Clay awake. "I'm wondering if I should do something about Audrey. She should've been back by now."

Clay groaned. "She's not your problem. Look, we've got enough to worry about. What's the expression, don't go borrowing trouble?"

She breathed in the familiar spearmint smell of his mouthwash and considered his words. This wasn't what she wanted Oliver to learn. She didn't want him thinking it was okay to be an island. To slough off responsibilities even for people you'd grown to care about.

"It would be so much easier if you left it alone, Laurel." Clay rolled over, apparently finished with the conversation.

Close to midnight she still hadn't fallen asleep. Without turning on the light, trying not to make a sound, Laurel pulled on her robe and slipped into the home office. The only sound came from the refrigerator humming in the kitchen. *It would be so much easier if you left it alone.*

She flipped through the journal again and noted details about the prisoners of war on Corregidor, a rocky island in the Philippines with an underground network of tunnels.

She set it aside and logged onto the computer. The clunky keyboard had a tendency to stick and part of the screen display flickered in and out. But with a few clicks, she found a website listing Army nurses stationed in Manila around the time of Pearl Harbor. Audrey had talked about her friends the day before she left. And she asked Oliver and Laurel to keep it a secret. Maybe something from her past prompted her to leave town.

No matter what Clay said, she couldn't sit around waiting for Audrey to come back. Not if she might be lost or sick or need help. Of course, she hadn't known Audrey for long and there was only so much she could do. But Laurel figured Audrey agreed to a caregiver in part because she took pity on her. During their time together, Audrey had been nothing but gracious and kind. And wherever she was, whatever she was up to, she didn't know Deanna was talking about a nursing home.

Laurel didn't know how to find Audrey, not yet anyway, but she figured Oliver was right about what friends would do for each other.

Part Three

CHAPTER 23

Thursday morning, Audrey woke up in the motel room somewhat restored. Although her legs were painfully stiff, she could at least pull herself out of bed.

According to the atlas, she'd managed to drift hours out of her way, west instead of north. She couldn't afford to lose any more time. But she had no medication left, a problem which she would need to remedy before getting back on the road.

At the front desk, she found Joel, the young man who'd helped her before, and convinced him to take her on a few errands when his shift ended. She didn't trust herself to drive, especially not in an unfamiliar South Carolina town, lest she veer further off course and waste more valuable time.

At the bank, she explained the problem and handed over her driver's license and recited her mother's maiden name. She returned to the car with a thousand dollars, more than sufficient to settle the outstanding motel bill and fund the rest of her trip. It might be dangerous to carry so much cash around, but she would be careful.

Their next stop was an urgent care center. After a long wait, the nurse led Audrey to an exam room and asked her to disrobe. She tried to argue.

"I simply need a prescription refill," she explained.

The nurse took her pulse, temperature, and blood pressure. She looked concerned as she wrote down the numbers.

A young doctor—olive skin tone, thick eyebrows, astonishingly handsome—listened to her heartbeat with a stethoscope. Audrey couldn't help but be reminded of James. It might've been only yesterday that they spent the morning in the courtyard. She hadn't realized then that she would never again feel such possibility, the sense that anything might happen.

The young doctor with the aquiline nose and straight white teeth was lecturing her about being more careful. Given her age and medical conditions, he didn't think she should travel alone. He made her promise she wouldn't drive until her primary care doctor authorized it.

After what seemed like hours, she emerged from the concrete building with aspirin, eye drops, and, most importantly, a limited refill of her prescriptions. Joel waved from his car and hopped out to open the passenger door. It was late afternoon and she needed to resume her journey before the sun went down.

Back at the motel, she packed and settled up at the front desk, where a woman in her late forties sat on duty, chewing gum and watching a talk show on the television behind the counter.

When Audrey asked for her watch, the woman acted like she didn't know what she was talking about.

"Mr. Rigley took it yesterday as collateral," she explained. "I had a small issue with my credit card. I suppose I should've called to let the company know I was going out of town."

The employee stared as though Audrey was boring her. "Yeah, well, you'd have to ask Mr. Rigley about it. And he's not here."

"I'm sure he put it in the safe." Joel appeared out of nowhere. She'd assumed he'd gone home for the day.

"I don't have the combination," the woman behind the front desk said. "He's the only one and he's not coming in until later."

Outside the lobby, the afternoon sky deepened into a burnt orange. "I can't afford to wait," Audrey said. "I'll get it some other time."

After Joel carried her luggage to her car, she peeled off a hundred-dollar bill and handed it to him. His eyes widened and he drew himself up straighter. This was what money did, of course. This young man who'd been so kind, who helped her because she reminded him of his grandmother, now discovered he'd made good use of his time, and that realization stripped away some of his innocence.

Perhaps money was the only thing of value she had left to offer. Ignoring the doctor's warnings, the promise she had no intention of keeping, she started the engine and headed north. She reached behind her glasses to wipe away the gathering tears. There was no reason to be so emotional. She'd spent countless hours on community service and donated a lot of money. She'd made a life in Savannah, one that looked good, close to perfect, on paper. Once she explained herself to Penny, her friend would understand. Audrey would tell her everything, the way she should have a long time ago. Then she could return to Savannah where her old life would be waiting.

By the time she crossed the border into North Carolina, night had fallen. Especially now that she'd gotten this close, she felt compelled to keep going. According to the letters, her friend was sick, possibly close to dying. Her nephew had come to see her one last time. Audrey didn't have much time to make amends.

In ordinary circumstances, a woman in her condition wouldn't go to the trouble of exposing an old friend's secret. But Audrey knew something of Penny's strength. Given the warning tone of her note, her resentment had simmered all these years. She might be capable of a great deal.

Imagine my shock after all these years seeing you so alive. All these years later, Penny recognized the brooch in the newspaper picture—the unusual hibiscus bloom carved from jade, the tiny pearl at its center a pinprick of luminescence like a beacon from another world. Handmade by a Filipino artisan. Only three like it in the world. Penny must have been surprised to see it.

I wonder, discovering this life you've made for yourself, whether anyone in your family or social circle knows the same Audrey I once did. The road signs passed too quickly for Audrey to make them out, especially in the dark. She tried to stretch her legs, but it proved impossible.

At the next exit, she pulled into a filling station. Mosquitoes batted against the streetlights. She heard a hideous screech as the car scraped against the concrete barrier. When she got out to examine it, the back left wheel was scuffed with bright red paint from the curb. At least the car was still operational. By her calculations she had a little over fifty miles to go. Unless she got lost again, and assuming her eyes managed to function in the dark, she would make it before ten o'clock.

After she got some much needed rest, a new day would dawn—a day she'd never imagined would arrive. She would tell Penny everything and watch her face carefully for the signs of acceptance, of forgiveness, that might settle there, relaxing her wrinkled skin until it almost resembled the fresh innocence of her youth.

CHAPTER 24

After a few false starts, Laurel found an Army Nurse Corps unit that arrived in Manila in September of 1941. Among its members were Kathleen P. Brooks born in 1918 in Knoxville, Tennessee, and Penelope M. Carson born the same year in Wilmington, North Carolina.

With a growing sense of getting somewhere, Laurel wrote down *Wilmington*. The newspaper clipping Audrey had gotten in the mail was from there too. Same, she was pretty sure, for the return address printed under the crown-shaped logo.

Audrey's maiden name was Merrick, but when she entered *Audrey Merrick*, the search results came up blank. Puzzled, Laurel tried again with only *Merrick*. This time a listing for Merrick, Helen A. appeared on the screen. The A could stand for Audrey. A farfetched idea sparked at the back of Laurel's mind. Maybe Audrey wasn't who she claimed to be. She'd seen a story like this on TV. Somebody came back from the war—she couldn't remember which one—and assumed another person's identity. They fooled everyone for years. Then again, maybe this listing was Audrey's and she'd decided at some point in her life—for a perfectly innocent reason— to go by her middle name. Or it was a simple misspelling. Next time she went to Audrey's house, she would check the family Bible to make sure she had the right name.

Pleasantly surprised to find the real estate records for Tennessee and North Carolina online, Laurel checked Knox County first, but didn't find any property under Kathleen Brooks' name. Of course, she might have gotten married, and who knew where she went to live after the war. Assuming she made it home alive.

Next, Laurel tried New Hanover County, where Wilmington showed up as the county seat. After she typed Penny's name in the search box, she waited. When a Penelope Carson turned up at an address on Oleander Place, she let out a silent cheer.

She and Oliver had once marveled over satellite images from around the world, a fleeting afternoon Laurel hadn't thought of again until now. If she tried hard, she could almost feel it again, the weight of his slender body on her lap, his hair prickly under her chin.

It took forever to load, but the satellite image of Oleander Place eventually revealed a cluster of one-story patio homes with bright white trim and rock-lined paths leading to their front doors. A tidy, modest place where an elderly woman might live. She jotted down the address. Another string of searches turned up a phone number, which she added to her notepad.

She needed to get some rest but felt too wired to sleep. She logged onto her email account and sent brief messages to her mother and brother, wishing them a happy weekend and promising to call soon.

When she clicked back to the satellite image of Oleander Place, Laurel tried to imagine Audrey ringing the doorbell and her old friend, Penny, ushering her inside. In the morning, she would call the number to see if Audrey was there—and if she had enough medicine to last for the rest of her visit.

Deep down, Laurel worried she was getting ahead of herself. Audrey had been talking about her old friends the last time she saw her, but that might have been a coincidence. Since Friday had come and gone with no sign of her, she might already be finished with whatever she planned. Something could've happened to her on the way home. Laurel couldn't search all the highways between Savannah and Wilmington by herself. When someone went missing on TV, their loved ones checked the local hospitals. But there were probably hundreds of hospitals along the route.

On the interstate map online, Laurel traced I-95 winding up through South Carolina. Audrey might have taken 95 all the way to North Carolina, then headed east onto 74. Or she could've turned east sooner and gone on 17 up through Georgetown and Myrtle Beach. If she bought gas or food with her credit card, there would be a record online, but only by providing the number. She closed her eyes against the bright screen and stretched her stiff neck.

Driving to Wilmington—close to a five-hour drive—seemed risky without more to go on. Even if she found Audrey, she might be embarrassed or upset that her caregiver had chased after her. Their tenuous friendship would be ruined.

Early Saturday morning, Laurel looked up from the desk when Oliver appeared in the doorway rubbing sleep from his eyes. His hair was matted on one side and stuck up on the other.

"What are you doing on the computer, Mom? Could I maybe have some eggs? With those sausages, you know the long skinny ones I like? Not the flat kind."

Her knees popped as she stood up from the desk. She couldn't imagine what her body would feel like at ninety. "Link sausages? I'll see if we have some. How did you sleep?"

"Good. What were you doing?"

The last thing Laurel wanted to do was worry him, especially the day of football tryouts. He looked so puny in his t-shirt and shorts that it was hard to see him as a football player. But she wanted to support him, to want whatever he wanted.

"It's a little silly," she said, walking with Oliver toward the kitchen. "But I was trying to find out where Miss Audrey went. Kind of making a game out of it, you know? I had trouble sleeping last night."

"Did you find her?"

"Not yet. Do you remember how she almost fell that day at her house? I worry a tiny bit about her being somewhere on her own." Laurel stopped short of saying anything about Deanna or what she might be planning. He was too young to understand. Besides, she didn't want her son focusing on the ways people betray each other, how selfish they could be.

"If you found her, you could make sure she doesn't fall."

"Exactly. That's what I was thinking."

Oliver hopped onto a stool at the counter and swung his legs back and forth. "What if she had a car accident? Could you help her then too?

"Hmm. I'm not sure. I guess it would depend on how bad— you know, we probably shouldn't worry about her so much."

"She is pretty old though. Way older than my grandmothers."

Laurel agreed and rummaged through the freezer to find the sausages. The shelves were stacked with boxes of vegetables she'd bought on sale. "I don't see any sausage, Oliver. Sorry. I'll get some at the grocery store."

After she poured him a bowl of granola, she called the number for Penelope Carson in Wilmington, but a recording said the number had been disconnected. She crossed out the number with her pen. She wasn't sure what it meant—maybe the number was outdated—but it made the next step more uncertain.

In case Deanna was right about where her grandmother had gone, Laurel looked up the art museums in Jacksonville—The Museum of Contemporary Art and The Cummer. Acres of historic gardens surrounded The Cummer, but the other one matched the brochure Audrey had gotten in the mail. Would she leave town with no notice to wander around an art museum? It seemed inconsiderate or selfish, and Audrey had never struck her as either.

She called the main phone number for both and left a message. A man from the Cummer called back right away. He'd heard of Audrey because he grew up in Savannah, but he hadn't seen her. While they were on the phone, he checked with the woman who provided private tours and confirmed she hadn't either.

After Laurel rinsed out Oliver's cereal bowl, she worked up the nerve to text Deanna.

Any word on your grandmother? She hit send before she could second-guess herself.

Nope. Deanna's reply came almost immediately.

I have her Rx. She'll need it soon. Maybe Laurel was providing Deanna with more ammunition about how Audrey couldn't take care of herself. Still, she should let her know.

Sigh, Deanna's text read. Laurel waited for more, but the screen stayed blank.

Think someone should call the police? Or go looking for her? Maybe check credit card records?

I'll add it to my list, Deanna typed. *Will text later re next week's schedule.*

Laurel slapped her phone against the counter as Clay appeared, a bath towel draped around his neck. He took the carton of orange juice out of the refrigerator, looked at the expiration date, and tossed it in the garbage. She filled him in on the high points of what Deanna had said, still fuming at her callous disregard for her grandmother.

"Yeah, but isn't it up to the Thorpes to decide what to do? If they think she's fine—" Clay's voice trailed off as he rubbed his eyebrow.

"What about her medicine?"

"You think they don't have pharmacies wherever she went? Come on."

"She might not think of it. I think I need to go look for her. For now, I'll get Oliver to tryouts."

Once Oliver was dressed, she slipped on her flip flops and ushered him out of the house.

"Come on, let's go. I can't wait to see you out on the field," she said as she unlocked the car.

"Wait, you're not watching me, are you?"

"Well, I thought I would, yes." Laurel got in the car and checked the rearview mirror to make sure his seatbelt was fastened.

"No way." He kicked the back of her seat. "It would be way too embarrassing. Can you just drop me off? Please?"

"Maybe if you ask nicely. And please stop kicking my seat."

Mothers in tennis skirts and fathers in khakis, all clutching coffee cups, milled around the parking lot at Episcopal. A boy around Oliver's age darted between Laurel's car and an SUV. Weighed down with padding, his shoulders looked bulky and artificially wide.

"Hey buddy, were we supposed to bring a helmet or something?"

"I don't know," he said as he got out of the car. "They probably have everything here."

Laurel climbed out after him. "I want to at least watch the first part."

With his arms crossed over his chest, Oliver peered at her through his glasses. He blinked and looked away. "Sorry, Mom. I want to do this by myself."

She let a few seconds tick by, wishing she could wrap her son in some kind of protective armor, and finally said, "Fair enough." As he trotted off toward the field, it took all of Laurel's strength not to follow. Before he was out of sight, he turned around to wave and called out that he hoped she would find Miss Audrey.

"Is your son a big football fan?" A tall man introduced himself as Neal Gayton. Laurel recognized the name as Deanna's husband.

"I'm not sure, to be honest. My husband watches it on TV. Oliver hasn't shown much interest until the last week or two."

"It's good for them to try new things, right?" Neal squinted in the morning sun. His pink golf shirt was tucked into his khakis, cinched with a canvas belt embroidered with nautical flags.

In the t-shirt and shorts she'd slept in, Laurel couldn't help feeling self-conscious.

"Ford's grandparents have season tickets at Georgia," Neal continued. "They get him a jersey every year for his birthday. He's growing but not fast enough to need a new one every year." He shook his head and laughed.

"His grandparents—do you mean your parents or Deanna's?"

Some emotion she couldn't place crossed his face and he paused to gather his words. Before he answered, he dug his sunglasses out of his pocket and put them on.

"Mine," Neal said eventually. "Deanna's parents passed away. I forget you're new. You weren't here then. Ford was only five. He doesn't remember it, not really."

"Both of them at once? What happened?" She hadn't focused on it before, but Audrey never talked about Tripp visiting. Every time she mentioned him, it was something in the past.

"It was a plane crash. One of those tragedies you'd never expect to happen."

For a minute the parking lot spun. No wonder Audrey had said she didn't like to fly. The sun beat down on the back of Laurel's neck. Down at the field the children were squealing and calling to each other.

"Deanna's parents were killed instantly," Neal said. "It's a shame Ford never got to know them, not much anyway. He can barely remember them."

Laurel shivered, imagining the tangle of smoldering wreckage. Audrey's son dead. He would have been older—probably in his sixties if her math was right—when he died. But Laurel couldn't help remembering the day she and Audrey stood by the gallery wall of pictures. The young boy in horn-rimmed glasses had left his mother in such a violent and sudden way.

Neal cleared his throat, clearly uncomfortable, and ran his hand along the back of his neck before changing the subject. "Hey, so, I happened to overhear something about you looking for Audrey?"

Not sure how to answer, she glanced around the parking lot for Deanna. She hadn't exactly forbidden her from looking for her grandmother. But she acted like there was nothing to worry about, nothing they could do. Audrey would show up again whenever she felt like it.

Neal adjusted his sunglasses. Everything about him from his legs to his hands looked stretched out and lanky. Most of the Episcopal dads looked like overgrown frat boys. Something about Neal—his gentleness, the way he radiated intelligence—reminded her of her father. The way he was before he left them.

That first morning waking up without Laurel's father in the house, without the smell of his coffee drifting from the kitchen or the sound of him grunting as he stuffed his feet into his work boots, she felt a cold shock in her lungs like she'd plunged into the French Broad River.

At eight years old, the loss struck her hard. After bedtime, when she should've been asleep, Laurel had wandered the upstairs hallway in her flannel pajamas, the cuffs frayed because she chewed on the fabric when she was anxious. First, she stopped by her mother's room, then her brother's. Making sure they hadn't left but were safely in their beds. Even now she could still remember the lint-like fabric of those pajamas, the way the loose threads sometimes got stuck in her teeth.

"To tell the truth," Neal said, his voice low like he was confiding in her, "I've been a little worried about Deanna's grandmother ever since the museum."

"I heard she had a hard time that night, but at least it was short-lived."

"I sort of wonder if the exhibit upset her somehow."

"Y'all were looking at Filipino artifacts, right?"

"Yeah, really old pottery and copper plates, things like that. I can't think of why Audrey wouldn't like it, but as soon as I said hello, she started backing away. She acted very confused—or disoriented is probably a better word. She definitely didn't know who I was, at least not at first."

"I'm sure that upset Deanna." It was true Audrey hadn't confided in Laurel about the plane crash. But she trusted her enough to share her connection to the Philippines—maybe not about the hidden journal, but at least the fact that she'd been there.

"The police could put out a bulletin, I guess. A silver alert or whatever it's called?" Laurel wondered out loud, remembering how highway signs sometimes flashed notices about missing children or elderly adults.

"Maybe." Neal gave a short nod. "It's hard to know what to do. I could mention it to Deanna."

Laurel must have reacted visibly to his suggestion because he smiled.

"My wife means well," he said. "Besides her grandmother, she's stressed about the shop, about making sure Ford has what he needs, all that."

Laurel tried to put herself in the other woman's shoes, to give her the benefit of the doubt. "I've seen her with Ford at school," she said finally. "You can tell she's a good mother."

"When it comes to Audrey, they've never been all that close," Neal said. "Now that she's struggling a bit, Deanna charges ahead so she feels like she's doing something, checking it off her to-do list."

Laurel shifted her weight between her hips. People kept talking about the distance they felt with Audrey, but, despite the difference in their circumstances, Laurel had thought they were getting close.

"What do you think she'll do about it?"

"Personally, I think with a little help—like from you, for instance—Audrey will probably be fine. I don't think it's time to ship her off yet, do you?"

"Not at all." She repeated the phrase more forcefully, hoping Neal understood how strongly she felt. "Not at all. Audrey would be furious to hear us even mention it."

A whistle blew from the direction of the fields. From the parking lot, she could barely make out Oliver's small frame, his t-shirt with Lego robots marching across the front and back.

She couldn't imagine how Audrey got through losing her son. That would be devastating for a parent of any age.

When Neal fiddled with his keychain, Laurel turned her attention back to him.

"So is it okay for us to drop the kids off?" She pointed toward the field. "Or should I stay to watch?"

"We're all swinging back by later. The kids will be fine. They don't want us here anyway. At least Ford doesn't."

"Yeah, same with Oliver," she said.

Laurel waved goodbye and headed for her car, but stopped when Neal called her name.

"I was thinking, Laurel, you'll make sure Audrey has at least another garden club gala in her—better yet, four or five? I'd hate for her to give that up. She looks forward to it all year."

"I'll do my best. Maybe she'll still be hosting it when she's a hundred."

He raised his hand to wave. "I like the way you think."

Chapter 25

Go ahead and hit me, Kat had seemed to say, the Japanese firing not far from the hospital grounds, kicking up dirt and grass all around them. But she'd emerged unscathed and Audrey helped her up from the dirt.

"Are you feeling sick? Dizzy?" she asked. Kat shook her head. She reeked of sweat and Audrey couldn't understand why she was so reluctant to bathe in the river with the rest of them. The murky water was better than nothing.

Not long after they cleaned up the mess—pajama tops and blankets blown into the treetops, precious vials of medicine broken and spilled, case records shredded—the Japanese broke through the Allied line.

Once Bataan saw constant fighting, the daily routine at the hospital disintegrated into a never-ending nightmare. The unit had so many badly wounded patients waiting for surgery that the orderlies lined them up on sawhorses, head down to prevent shock, until their turn. Mud-covered bayonets and rifles piled up in the corner. The chaplains never got a break. Their whispered last rites—*through this holy anointing may the Lord in his love and mercy help you with the grace of the Holy Spirit*—became as familiar as the black and gold mynah birds squawking in the trees.

Audrey worried it was only a matter of time before they ran out of room for the dead bodies. She worried the rain would drone on forever, that she would never get dry, that she would never hear from James, that something was wrong with Kat's mind. She worried they would all rot, sinking into the jungle floor in a foul-smelling, disintegrating heap.

They ran out of quinine, sulfa drugs, morphine, blood plasma. Before long they took to eating raw camotes, a kind of wild sweet potato foraged from the jungle. The starch made her stomach distended and bloated, but at least it was something to gnaw on.

One afternoon a Filipino staff sergeant said the narra trees, which were now blooming, might yield honey if they were lucky. *Luck*, Audrey repeated to herself, wishing she'd retrieved her brooch from her trunk. She squeezed the bright yellow petals and dabbed one against her tongue. Nothing, not even a drop.

One morning Audrey woke up with blood under her nails from where she'd scratched her scalp during the night. Penny noticed and checked the part of Audrey's hair.

"Lice," she said. "I've got it too. Sorry to say there's nothing to be done for it but scratch."

The Voice of Freedom radio station reported Singapore had fallen, then the Dutch East Indies. General MacArthur fled for Australia.

Despite the red cross marking the grounds, the Japanese bombed the other hospital on Bataan, scoring a direct hit on the wards. When she heard that over a hundred patients and personnel were wounded or killed, Audrey kicked the radio into silence.

The soggy air of Bataan reeked of wet mud and exhaust fumes. Penny got the worst of it when she was assigned to clean the outdoor latrine.

"All week?" Kat's pale face blanched at the thought.

"You've just come off a night shift," Audrey said. "Doesn't seem fair."

Penny rolled up her sleeves. "Someone's got to do it. If they take me off, they'll put Sue Darby on."

"So let her do it," Kat said. "At least this once."

Penny shook her head. "Haven't you seen her? She's been sweating non-stop the last couple days. Shaking too."

"Dengue fever?" Audrey asked.

"Maybe. Anyway, she's in no shape to be out there." Penny scooped up the pail and scrub brush. "Pray I don't see any snakes. That's what I'm most worried about."

"But the smell alone—" Kat gagged.

"You're not helping," Audrey whispered.

"Sorry." Kat bit her lip. "You're right. Do you need us to come with you?"

Penny turned down their half-hearted offers of assistance and headed out. Audrey and Kat should've gotten some rest, especially since they were on duty that night. They were on their way to their cots when Audrey realized, counting the days on her fingers, that it was Penny's birthday. She hadn't even mentioned it. Instead of celebrating, Penny was dodging the ever-present rats and lizards while scrubbing a crude toilet carved of mango wood. Audrey gave up on the idea of getting some rest and told Kat they should think of something nice to do for her.

When Penny got back, her face flushed red in the afternoon heat, Audrey helped her clean herself up the best they could. Then Kat presented her with a canteen.

"Taste it," she said with a wink.

Penny unscrewed the lid and raised her eyebrows.

"We remembered it was your birthday," Audrey said.

"And I batted my eyelashes at that boy from Birmingham," Kat said. "You know the one who's been out on patrol? There's an abandoned sugar refinery in Pilar."

"Go ahead." Audrey pointed at the canteen.

Penny shook her head but took a tentative sip. Kat clapped when she saw the smile spreading across Penny's face. "Molasses? It doesn't seem possible." Penny's thick fingers gripped the canteen. "I'd forgotten this kind of sweetness ever existed."

After another sip she passed the canteen around, wanting Audrey and Kat to taste for themselves. Even though the sugar made Audrey's teeth ache, she could imagine drinking the whole thing, and letting the smoky molasses coat her tongue and throat. She pressed her lips together and held the canteen out to Kat.

When Audrey and Kat came off their shift the next day, the rain had stopped, but the rhythmic sound of dripping droned steadily around them. The monkeys in the trees swung from branch to branch, and showers of rainwater gushed from the slick green leaves. Audrey wrung what moisture she could from her coveralls, already looking forward to a few hours off duty. Her muddy shoes squelched in the mud and she'd developed an itchy fungal rash between her toes. She couldn't think of the last time her feet had been fully dry.

Kat grabbed Audrey's arm and pointed toward a clearing up ahead. A rustling sound grew louder and a skinny Filipino soldier appeared. He wore too-big GI trousers cinched at the waist and the sleeves of his shirt were rolled up despite the mosquitoes. In his arms, he held a little girl, no more than three or four years old, her black hair half covered by a faded yellow scarf. Her cheek was caked with mud, as though she'd been sleeping on the jungle floor. She stared at them, blinked, and jabbed her thumb in her mouth.

While Kat tried to comfort them, Audrey ran for an MP. Her shoes kept slipping in the mud and, by the time they returned, she was wheezing and out of breath.

The MP said the toddler's parents were killed in a recent bombing.

"What will happen to her?" Kat asked. Her hand clutched her chest.

The MP sighed as he took his leave. "Above my pay grade."

"They'll put her in a facility somewhere, I'm guessing," Kat whispered. She and Audrey had paused at the edge of a bamboo grove. "You know what we did for birthdays in the children's home?"

"You don't really talk much about what it was like growing up there."

"A sheet cake on the first of the month. Sometimes our hall mother remembered to list off everyone with upcoming birthdays. Sometimes she didn't. Either way, she sliced us all a paper-thin piece."

"But that's so pitiful."

Kat shrugged. "Tasted pretty good at least."

Audrey swallowed against the lump in her throat. "One day our children will celebrate their birthdays together. We'll live in the same neighborhood. Everyone will come over for music and games."

"If you and James get married—" Kat managed a weak smile—"you might not want me and Penny down the block."

"I don't even know. I haven't heard from him."

"You will. Surely."

"Anyway, whether I get married one day or not, I mean what I said."

"About the birthdays? You're awfully kind." Kat still sounded distant, like she knew something Audrey didn't.

"More than that. I mean we'll take care of each other. We'll be like family." They'd made a promise when they volunteered for Stotsenburg. *We'll stick together no matter what.*

"During the war, of course," Audrey said. "We already agreed to that. But after too." She placed her hand over Kat's, a promise on top of a promise, the way an artist paints in layers to create depth.

Chapter 26

In the parking lot at Episcopal, Laurel listened to the thwack of children tossing footballs, their high-pitched squeals. Half nerves, half excitement. She pulled up the Georgia Bureau of Investigation website on her phone and scrolled through until she found information about silver alerts. What she read made her wish she'd never mentioned the idea to Neal.

The alerts were usually for missing adults who were cognitively or developmentally impaired. There was no way the word impaired could be applied to Audrey. Even if she occasionally got confused, it was short-lived. And since she'd kept her time in the Philippines a secret, it made sense the exhibit might have upset her.

She could at least make the drive to Wilmington. Audrey might need her help.

Anxious to pack, Laurel pulled out of the parking lot. More than anyone, she knew what Audrey was like during the last few days before she left town. It might have been the first time in her forty-two years that Laurel was this perfectly suited for anything.

Clay wasn't home when she arrived, which was just as well. She texted him about her plan and asked if he could pick up Oliver at tryouts. Moving with a sense of purpose now, she packed her clothes and toothbrush and hurried back to Audrey's house.

On her way upstairs, she stopped at the gallery wall of framed pictures. The story of the Thorpe family told in images of glamour and privilege. Still, she couldn't shake the feeling that something was missing. She scanned the wall more carefully but discovered no noticeable blank spaces. The pictures were hung in neatly measured rows, their narrow gold frames perfectly aligned.

She grabbed a carrier bag from a fancy-sounding boutique from a hook inside Audrey's closet. She picked out a change of clothes for her—a white blouse in crisp poplin and navy linen pants with a drawstring waist, sensible underwear, and comfortable-looking slides made of soft Italian leather fitted with Velcro straps.

In the bathroom, she tossed in an extra pair of glasses and small bottles of various toiletries. It was hard to know what Audrey might need when—if—Laurel found her.

On her way out, Laurel paused at the bookshelves in the rear parlor. She pulled out the oversized white leather Bible to see how to spell *Merrick* and if Audrey's first name might be listed as Helen. On the front page, a family tree was printed in brown, its branches made to look like brushstrokes. Unlike the weathered journal stuffed in her bag, the Bible smelled like bleached wood and sharp ink. There were lines for several generations and space to fill in more if needed. But all the lines appeared blank. Not a single name had been filled in. A proper southern family like the Thorpes would take every opportunity to show their lineage. She would've expected Audrey to complete the family tree over the years as people were born and died. Not sure if the blank page signified anything, she replaced the Bible on the shelf.

She sped down the downtown streets sheltered by moss-covered live oaks, barely noticing the tall, stucco townhouses with their gas lanterns and wrought iron. The roads here—Macon, Broad, Habersham, Charlton, Tattnall, Liberty, Broughton, Bay—were flat and straight and orderly. A contrast to the winding roads back home in North Carolina, which twisted around steep inclines.

Halfway through South Carolina, Laurel called to see how tryouts went. Clay sounded tired, even slightly bewildered.

"It was ninety-five degrees out there," he said. "And Oliver, from what I saw, he didn't do anything but sit on the sidelines. Literally."

"Can I talk to him?" She looked ahead for the next exit, trying to figure out how soon she could get back to comfort her son.

"Hey mom, the coach said I didn't have to."

"Have to what?"

"Try out. It looked, I don't know, everybody was running and smashing into each other."

"I thought you wanted to. It's okay if you changed your mind—" *But it's good to try new things. Even hard things.*

"Yeah, I changed my mind. Totally."

Oliver sounded so convincing, so sure of himself, that Laurel struggled with the right response. He should be willing to try new activities, but she didn't want to force him. Soon enough he would face all sorts of peer pressure—maybe he was already.

"Hey, have you got Miss Audrey yet?"

"Soon, I hope. Be good for your dad, okay?"

As she eased the car back onto the highway, something hardened in the pit of her stomach. An uneasy worry that she might be making a mistake. Audrey was hiding something—and Laurel was going out on a limb for her.

Several miles down the highway, Deanna called to say she'd gone by Audrey's house to pick up the mail and check the answering machine.

"There was a message from her credit card company, something about an attempted use of her Visa at a motel in Swansea," Deanna said. "They stopped it because of potential fraud."

Laurel tried to place the name but came up short. "Where's that?"

"Middle of nowhere, South Carolina."

"You don't think her card was stolen, do you?"

"Possibly," Deanna admitted. "I don't know what we're going to do with her. Seems like we definitely need to call the police at this point."

"Actually, the thing is, when I mentioned it to Neal, I didn't know what it involved. Turns out a silver alert is for people in much worse shape than Audrey. She's really doing pretty well, especially for someone her age."

"If you're not careful, you'll talk yourself right out of a job."

"Well, I'm on my way to find her."

"On second thought, why don't you come back to Savannah? I've set up a meeting with Spencer Howerton—do you know Spencer?"

Laurel shook her head even though Deanna couldn't see her.

"I've had to get a lawyer involved. I didn't know what else to do. He's looking into what we should do about my grandmother and he set up an emergency hearing on Monday morning. If you could tell him what you've observed, the difficulties she's been having, it would be a huge help."

"Are you trying to kick Audrey out of her house?"

"Of course not." Deanna sighed. "I don't know what it'll come to. I'll do whatever is best for her, of course. But with her needing around-the-clock care—"

"She doesn't. I don't think that's true."

"Well, she left town suddenly without clearing it with anyone. Don't you think that's odd? Especially for someone her age?"

Maybe Deanna was already rehearsing her story in her sugar-laced drawl. *Look, we got her help and she still left town and got herself into a mess, even when she was about to run out of her medication. She needs constant supervision. Bless her heart, she certainly can't be trusted to manage her accounts or stay in that big house by herself.*

Laurel had seen stories on the local news about elderly people with dementia or Alzheimer's who wandered off. One older man spent hours in the hot sun in a stranger's car. He found it unlocked and climbed in, thinking it belonged to his son who died in a training exercise at Camp Lejeune some ten years earlier. When the police found him, the old man had wet himself. But mostly he was upset his son might get back to the car and he wouldn't be there waiting. That man looked pitiful, all the light gone from his eyes.

No matter what Deanna said, Audrey wasn't like him. Not by a long shot. She might need a little help, enough that Laurel felt compelled to go looking for her. But she wasn't impaired.

Beyond the interstate bridge, Lake Marion stretched wide, a peaceful grayish blue. In the distance, boats sped away from the shoreline.

"I'm not coming back this evening," Laurel said. "I'll be back as soon as I find Audrey."

"Where do you think she is anyway? Jacksonville? How in the world are you going to find her?"

"I think maybe Wilmington. I don't know. It's better than sitting around waiting and worrying."

"Why would she go there? Regardless, I really need you here. Let the police do their job, and help me figure out what to do next."

In her mind, Laurel saw the bills from school and their dwindling bank account. But then she pictured Audrey wandering by the side of a busy highway, confused and lost.

"I only want what's best for my grandmother," Deanna said.

"Me too," Laurel said.

"Look, you're going off on a wild goose chase. What's the point? Even if you find her—which let's be honest, is highly unlikely, do you really think she'll clasp you to her bosom and coo all over you? That's not exactly my grandmother's style."

Laurel didn't know what to say. So she muttered goodbye and Deanna hung up.

Some fifty miles or so down the highway, she noticed a sign for Sumter and, underneath, a smaller sign for East Sumter, Mayesville, and Cherryvale. None of them sounded like the town where someone tried to use Audrey's credit card. Maybe she'd never taken this route at all. But she couldn't let go of the idea that Audrey had chosen to be with her friend.

The next hundred miles passed effortlessly. Before long Laurel saw a big sign in the shape of a sombrero, the phrase *South of the Border* in bright colors. She crossed into North Carolina, her native state, although the flat coastal plain looked nothing like the twisty mountain roads of home.

Audrey could have stopped for the night because she was tired or not feeling well. Deanna didn't mention whether the Visa charge actually went through. If not, she would've had to pay with cash. She had trouble seeing numbers on screens and her fingers fumbled over small buttons, like the ones on an ATM, but maybe she had enough in her wallet. The only problem was that Swansea didn't look to be on the way to Wilmington.

No matter what had already happened, she needed to find Audrey, nurse her back to health if need be, and hurry her home to stop Deanna. They would convince the lawyer, or a judge, that Audrey, with Laurel's occasional help, could take care of herself.

We're a team, she imagined telling the grandfatherly judge, who would see through Deanna's slick exterior to the ugly greed coiled inside.

Laurel's thoughts carried her through Rowland and McDonald, the flat expanse of trees interrupted only by billboards advertising fast food and boiled peanuts, and east onto 74 toward Whiteville and Lake Waccamaw.

By the time she reached Wilmington—passing signs proclaiming "Home of the Azalea Festival"—Laurel felt more certain than she had about anything in a long time. The afternoon sun had slipped away, replaced by a gradually deepening dusk. Branches of live oaks formed arches across the streets like they did in Savannah, the same knots of Spanish moss dangled overhead. Her knees bounced against the seat with pent-up energy. She followed the directions to Oleander Place, a neighborhood surrounded by a low wall of pink stone, the streets one cul-de-sac after another, arranged around a gazebo like petals on a flower.

The houses were modest, but relatively well-kept. Penny's house was a compact patio-style model with a one-car garage. In the gathering dark, Laurel could make out the cheerful yellow paint and glossy burgundy door. She imagined Penny and Audrey inside eating a late supper.

Or if Audrey wasn't feeling well, maybe she was already in bed, the blanket pulled up to her chin, her legs swollen and aching. She would have no idea that Deanna had called a lawyer. If Audrey knew, she would be in her rosemary-scented kitchen on Victory Drive, a sheaf of creamy white linen paper in front of her, gripping a fountain pen, ready to map out a counter-attack.

Gravel crunched under the wheels as Laurel eased the car to a stop. The house was dark but she rang the doorbell anyway. The chime reverberated behind the door. She listened for footsteps but heard nothing. Her mind flashed to the day she'd found Audrey's house empty, the piercing worry about where she'd gone.

She knocked on the door until her hand came away sore. At a creaking sound nearby she whirled around to find a man on the small porch of the house next door.

"Something I can help you with?"

Wondering how to explain herself, Laurel pointed toward the house she was still sure belonged to Penny. "I'm looking for Ms. Carson."

The older man's mouth twitched under his mustache. "Carson, you say? Well, sweetheart, the place is rented out now. Short-term in the summer, mostly tourists. Only a few minutes to the beach from here. There's a website, but I don't know how to find it."

She shook her head, her exuberance quickly fading. "I don't need to rent it. I need to find Ms. Carson. Do you know if she's still around somewhere?"

"Some relative of hers set up the website, best I recall. She wasn't doing well when she moved out. She's old, you know, much older than me. Seems like she already had her ninetieth birthday a year or two ago. Wonder if she's passed on by now?" He shrugged. "Sorry I can't be of more help."

"Is there a nursing home or something like that around here?"

"Sure, a number of them. Couldn't guess how many. Lots of retirees around here, they fall or get sick, that's where they end up."

"And you don't know where she might be?"

"Wouldn't know where to start, I'm afraid." A voice called from inside his house and he lifted his hand in a wave. "Phyllis has my program paused. Better get back to it."

Laurel waved back, her spirits falling as she sunk to the top step of the porch, its plywood warm against the back of her legs. She flicked a fallen leaf off the step, then realized it made no difference. The porch was speckled with leaves and twigs, a state she'd failed to notice earlier. Maybe nothing she did would ever make a difference.

Wherever Audrey was, it wasn't here. Tracking her down seemed all but impossible now. Not only had she left town with no explanation, she'd also been hiding things, leaving Laurel to wonder if she was worth all this trouble. Even after all the time she'd spent with her, in some ways she didn't know Audrey at all.

CHAPTER 27

Wilmington appeared as a constellation of lights across the Cape Fear River. Lights blinked on the metal bridge too, a distraction that sent Audrey veering out of her lane. The flash still pulsated in her eyes as another driver blared his horn and she maneuvered back across the line. She fixated on a glowing white steeple and let it guide her over the water and onto narrow streets lined with oyster bars and Queen Anne houses.

Most of the houses had been turned into inns and Audrey looked for the one where Penny's nephew, Bill Branson, was staying. Since he'd written to her from the inn, the stationary included its address beneath the embossed logo. In neat blockish handwriting he'd printed his phone number and information about the hospital where she could find Penny.

She drove past a late-night coffee shop where young people milled around, smoking and drinking, their merriment punctuating the night air and mingling with the forlorn call of a ship from the nearby river. She and Penny were like them once, friends who clinked glasses in a toast, who made each other laugh. They made promises they intended to—and could not—keep.

And what of James? Audrey had made a promise to him too. The last time they were together she'd sworn she would wait for him after the war. Yet she had to let him go.

Finally, she spotted the inn up ahead and managed to squeeze the car into a spot on Princess Street. Feeling pleased with herself, Audrey retrieved her luggage and checked in at the front desk. Given the difficulties of the last few days, she didn't bother with her credit card, instead paying with the cash she'd gotten from the bank. The lobby hummed with cool air-conditioning, the air heady with the scent of late summer gardenias, their milky white blooms clustered in a short crystal vase.

She felt like she'd arrived—not simply that she'd made it to Wilmington, but that she'd achieved some greater victory. No matter what her granddaughter said, she could still manage to take care of herself. And, even more importantly, she'd seized this chance to finally explain herself to one of the dearest friends she had ever known.

The young woman behind the desk carried Audrey's luggage up to her room, which was on the second floor overlooking the river, its steady flow barely noticeable in the dark, the day's ships now silent and past. In front of her, a four-poster bed beckoned, its matelassé coverlet turned back to reveal cool white linens. The next morning she would be reunited with Penny.

Once the sun rose Friday morning, Audrey massaged her legs, still swollen with fluid, and forced herself out of bed. By the time she finished bathing, she was exhausted, but dressed herself in navy slacks and a pale pink silk tunic. Her neck was bare of its customary pearls because she couldn't manage to fasten the clasp.

It took what felt like an eternity to navigate the steep, unfamiliar stairs, pausing every few seconds to catch her breath. When her legs wobbled beneath her and threatened to give way, she gritted her teeth in focused concentration, as if by force of will alone she could make it—not merely downstairs, but across town to Penny's hospital bed.

As soon as Audrey's foot found purchase at the bottom of the staircase, she breathed a sigh of relief. On the polished sideboard she noticed a porcelain bowl filled with fresh apples, bananas, and oranges, silver platters of muffins and other pastries, and carafes of coffee, iced water, and orange juice. She filled her plate, retrieved her medicine from her purse, and settled onto the couch.

By the time she finished eating, a crowd had gathered around the food and a young woman scurried around replenishing the platters. Audrey took the letters from her purse. Penny's was written on pale blue stationary, the paper so thin as to be almost see-through. She'd read it so many times she'd come close to memorizing Penny's words.

For now, she turned her attention to the letter from Penny's nephew.

My aunt asked me to mail this to you. I'm in town to see her one last time. She's ill and not expected to live long.

She adjusted her glasses to read the phone numbers he'd printed at the bottom, his cell phone and the hospital. But a guest phone was nowhere to be seen—not on the side tables, which held oversized lamps with bases of green celadon and tasseled pulls, or on the small entryway table near where she'd checked in last night. The gardenias in the crystal vase were beginning to look a bit wilted, the slightest hint of brown darkening the white petals.

Trying to recall if there was a phone upstairs in her room, Audrey glanced toward the curved staircase with its steep climb. If Laurel was with her, they could pull up a map to the hospital on her cell phone and they would be there in no time. No matter. She found a stack of maps beside one of the lamps and unfolded it to find the hospital marked with a blue "H." She traced the route with her finger, two, three times until she was certain she could find it. She put the map in her purse and pulled out her car keys. Her stomach felt pleasantly full, her eyes remarkably clear. It wouldn't be long now.

Outside the sky spat rain. Trying to hurry, she climbed in the car and unfolded the map on the seat beside her. Between the gingerbread-looking houses, raindrops puckered the river's surface, the gray hulk of the *USS North Carolina* stalwart in the distance.

Thirty minutes later, after a wrong turn or two, Audrey peered through the windshield wipers at the concrete building in front of her, bypassing the emergency entrance and outpatient surgery toward visitor parking.

Inside, her voice cracked as she explained to the sixty-something woman at the front desk that she'd come to see Penelope Carson.

"She's an old friend," Audrey explained needlessly. "Her nephew gave me the name of this hospital." She rummaged in her purse for the letter he'd written.

The woman sighed and tapped at her keyboard. "Three twenty." She handed Audrey a visitor's badge. "Elevator to your left."

By the time she reached the elevator doors, she'd forgotten the room number and had to go back and ask again. This time, with another sigh, the woman scribbled it on a sticky note. She probably wished she could pin it to Audrey's blouse like she was a small child traveling alone on a long journey.

Clutching the paper in her now clammy hands, Audrey rode the elevator upstairs and navigated the maze-like hallway until she stood in front of the door marked 320. Across the hall, the nurses' station crackled with life. A phone rang and a nurse slammed a file drawer closed as she darted to answer it. Audrey swallowed and tried to take a deep breath, but it hitched in her throat. She tugged her purse strap higher on her shoulder and raised her hand, trembling ever so slightly, to knock.

Chapter 28

Although Audrey had known Penny's voice would sound different, that it had almost certainly grown tremulous and weak with age, she couldn't help expecting to hear the clear, ringing tone she first heard almost seventy years ago. She knocked again, waiting, anxious to hear a greeting called out, an invitation to come in. She glanced at the metal door handle, the need to turn it making her palm itch with anticipation.

The nurse appeared beside her. "Three twenty's empty, dear."

Audrey shook her head. That couldn't be right. What if, after all this, she was too late? "I'm here to see Penny—Penelope Carson. They told me—" She held up the paper with the room number.

The woman read it. "Sometimes the visitor desk records aren't updated immediately. They should be, but they aren't."

"Where is she?" Audrey cleared her throat, embarrassed at how desperate she sounded.

The nurse frowned. "Are you family?"

Yes, Audrey wanted to scream. We were supposed to stick together like sisters. She squeezed her eyes closed against the glare of the fluorescent lighting.

Then she remembered the letter. "Wait, I have her nephew's phone number."

The nurse stared at her, not unkindly, but as though she didn't understand. "I'm not authorized to give out information about a patient's condition unless you've been specifically identified by the patient. In writing."

"Do you have a phone I could use?"

"Certainly." The nurse took her elbow and guided her to a cubicle down the hall, barely large enough for a built-in shelf with a telephone and thick paper directory. She thanked her and closed the door, then adjusted her glasses and held the letter out as far as she could, trying to decipher the numbers. Her hips ached from walking across the tile floor and she wished for a chair or any decent spot to rest for a minute.

When she explained who she was and why she was calling, Penny's nephew, Bill Branson, thanked her for coming.

"I'm afraid my aunt doesn't have long. They moved her to a hospice center late yesterday."

Audrey held her breath. Penny was still alive. That was the important thing. She repeated it to herself. She was alive. While she had the chance, she had to look Penny in the eye and make her understand.

"Where is this center? Can I come right away?"

He gave Audrey directions, but couldn't promise what state Penny would be in. "She sleeps most of the time. She wasn't this bad when she wrote to you, but it changes. She's gone downhill."

The center seemed to be a straight shot, a few miles down the highway and she could think of nothing but getting there, arriving out of breath at Penny's bedside in time to grasp her hand and tell her that she never stopped being her friend. Audrey loved her as a sister. She'd never stopped.

Her foot pressed the accelerator. Strip malls and chain restaurants whipped past the window, palm trees swaying in the breeze. The rain had stopped, but the sky looked dark and heavy. Up ahead, Audrey saw a building that might be the one she was looking for and she leaned forward as though it would help her arrive more quickly.

She registered the intersection too late, the traffic light glowing red as she barreled through. Audrey braced for impact, imagining a tractor trailer heading toward her, the driver cursing as he pumped the brakes, knowing there was no time to stop. Her wipers screeched against the windshield and she flicked the wand to stop the noise only to find she'd turned on the turn signal, its blinking suddenly so loud it made her heart jump in her chest.

She eased her foot off the gas pedal, shaking, not daring to look anywhere but straight ahead. Just as she told herself she'd emerged unscathed, lights flashed in the rearview mirror. A police cruiser had appeared out of nowhere. She had no choice but to pull over.

When the officer approached, she rolled down the window. "I'm trying to get to the hospice center. My friend—one of the closest friends I've had in my life—is dying," Audrey said.

The young officer appeared unmoved. Audrey couldn't fathom how he could possibly be more than eighteen or nineteen years old. "License and registration, ma'am."

She fumbled for the registration and, flustered, handed it to him along with her change purse.

"License?" he asked, giving Audrey back the change purse as though it might detonate any second.

"I apologize." She took it from him and managed to find her driver's license, which she handed over. "Everything is up-to-date and in order."

He held up a finger and promised to return momentarily. Seconds ticked by. In the rearview mirror, she saw him squinting at a computer on the passenger seat. Driving at her age was not a crime. She passed the same driving test they administered to everyone else.

But when the officer reappeared, he read off a list of infractions. She ran a red light. She was driving erratically, failing to stay in her lane.

"I'm not from around here, you see. And with this rain—" Audrey motioned outside, where the swollen sky, pregnant with more rain that wasn't yet falling, mocked her.

"Running the red light is what I'm most worried about, ma'am. Do you realize you could have caused a serious accident? When is the last time you've had your vision checked?"

Could he take her license away? Forbid her to drive even the short distance to the hospice center? If Deanna found out—

"My eyes are fine, Officer."

He asked for an address and Audrey told him where she was staying. He wrote it down on his notepad but seemed unsatisfied. Ordering her out of the car, the officer explained she would have to walk a straight line to demonstrate her awareness and lucidity.

He stood with one hand at his hip, as though ready to grab his nightstick in case she made a run for it. A laugh almost bubbled out of Audrey's chest until she remembered the seriousness of her predicament. She needed to convince him that she was capable of driving, that he should let her back in the car without any sort of citation. Then she could go see Penny.

Her legs wobbled, but she concentrated on placing one foot in front of the other. One foot, then the other, wishing she had her cane even as she willed herself to stay upright without it. She blinked back the moisture in her eyes. She didn't dare reach up to adjust her glasses in case the movement threw off her balance. Audrey imagined Penny rising from her bed, raising her hand in a wave from the window, a light breaking on her face as she recognized Audrey and understood she had come.

Trying to peer ahead to see how close the hospice center might be, Audrey tilted her head. Worried she'd thrown off her balance, she hesitated before taking the next step. The officer pursed his lips. Not wanting to appear unstable, she tried to speed up, but without warning her right ankle turned and she lurched sideways, biting her lip to keep from crying out.

She was forced to leave the Mercedes on the side of the road. The wheel cap she'd scraped at the filling station made it appear run-down and abandoned. *Rode hard and put up wet*, Audrey heard her father say, something she hadn't imagined in years.

The officer was kind enough to drive her to the hospice center, but he took her car keys and handed her a citation he ripped from his pad. She was too embarrassed to look at it very closely. Instead, she stuffed it in her purse.

Penny's nephew, who had been waiting inside, asked the officer if there was a problem. Audrey couldn't make out their hushed conversation, so she stared at the framed artwork—mediocre marsh landscapes, the colors too muddy, the brushstrokes uneven—to avoid meeting their eyes. Although her ankle throbbed with pain, she could walk on it.

She remembered Penny's face, the grimace she made as she hobbled to her shift in Bataan on her injured ankle. It healed within a matter of weeks. In that small way, luck was on Penny's side.

By the time the other hospital on Bataan was bombed—destroyed completely the day after Easter—Penny could walk normally. Those days the three of them were covered with rashes from the dampness. Kat cried out in her sleep, scratching until she bled, and Audrey grabbed her hands to hold her still. They kept hearing reinforcements were on their way, but no longer believed it.

Meanwhile, Audrey waited for a letter from James, hoping he was safe, wondering if she was naïve to hold onto his promises. She wrote to him just as she wrote to her family and Whit, but she never knew what made it through.

Once the officer left, Mr. Branson, his face scruffy with day-old beard, his sixty-something eyes bloodshot and tired, led Audrey to the corner of the lobby by the window. Outside, rain began to spatter against the pavement, and steam rose with a hiss.

She tried to tap down her impatience. "Can we please see Penny now?"

"As it turns out, it's not a good time. I'm sorry. The doctor is with her now and then they're switching her room. I didn't know all this when you called earlier. I'm heading out myself, back to the inn for a quick shower. I can give you a ride if you'd like."

Audrey glanced toward the bank of elevators. "If I could pop my head in—I won't stay long."

"Not today, I'm afraid. What's this about anyway? I presume you're an old friend?"

"Yes, I'm a very old friend. And I've come all this way. I really need to talk to her, to set the record straight. It's important."

Mr. Branson stared at Audrey like he was trying to figure out something, the same way Ford looked when struggling with a math problem. "She was shocked when she came across your picture in the paper. She demanded a notepad immediately and asked me to look you up. It's been a long time since I've seen her that focused on something."

"But you put down the information about how to find her. You must know she needs to see me."

"She said you probably wouldn't come. You'd have better things to do."

"And yet here I am."

Mr. Branson stared at her. "Here you are."

Audrey let him lead her to his truck. He had to help her up, a humiliation she resolved to ignore. On the drive back to the inn, they passed her car on the side of the road and Audrey looked the other way and tried to pretend everything was normal.

Once inside, Mr. Branson held her elbow and guided her up the staircase, which suddenly seemed three times as long as before. By the time they arrived at her door, Audrey was out of breath.

"Look, I'm sorry you came all this way. Is there someone I can call?" he asked.

Audrey shook her head even as Laurel's name came to mind. "I need to rest for a bit. Will you let me know when I can visit your aunt?" She couldn't fathom leaving without seeing or talking to Penny. On the other hand, finding her so close to death might be unbearable, especially if she wasn't able to understand what Audrey had to say. She shook her head again. There was no right answer.

"We'll see how it goes." Mr. Branson continued up the staircase to his room on the third floor. "No matter what, even if you talk to her at some point, I can't have you upsetting her, okay? She was rattled when she wrote to you. I'm not sure what got her so worked up. Do you want to tell me what this is all about?"

Audrey was silent. Mr. Branson waited a moment and then resumed his climb until he disappeared.

Seeing Audrey's picture had clearly set something off in Penny. It reawakened that old fiery strength of hers, and this time, she'd lashed out. Putting herself in her friend's shoes, Audrey could imagine so many years of rancor layered upon each other like hardened shale, a wall destined to topple at the slightest nudge.

She ate dinner in her room, took her medicine, and went to bed. Tomorrow Penny would be settled in her new room. She would have to convince Mr. Branson to let her visit.

Saturday morning, Audrey ate breakfast downstairs again. The wilted gardenias had been replaced by day lilies. The thickly sweet scent was almost sickening. She called Mr. Branson, expecting to be able to visit Penny first thing. But he asked that she wait until the afternoon.

"She's had a difficult morning," he said.

She waited for him to elaborate, but he didn't. "I'll be able to see her this afternoon, won't I? What time?"

They settled upon three-thirty, a time which seemed far too late, and agreed to meet in the inn's lobby.

When the designated hour arrived, Audrey powdered her nose, dabbed on some lipstick, and went downstairs.

The air outside smelled of briny saltwater and sweet rich coffee. Worried about the time, she scurried around looking for her car. She breathed heavily, hobbling up one street and down another. Although she thought she'd parked on Princess Street, she couldn't find her car anywhere. As she continued wandering around, she reached for her purse for a tissue to wipe off her forehead, only to discover that in her haste she'd left it in her room.

Back at the inn, Audrey paused in the air-conditioned lobby to catch her breath. Something about the well-appointed room pricked her memory. She was supposed to meet Mr. Branson here in the lobby at three-thirty. Now, with all the time she'd spent looking for her car, he must've given up. He'd left without her. Audrey gripped her arthritic hands into fists until she felt her nails dig into her skin. The futile gesture left her sapped of any remaining strength.

She limped up the staircase until she finally reached her room. At least she could retrieve her purse and call Mr. Branson. Perhaps he would come back for her. She took her key card from her pocket and swiped it through the slot on the door, but the light stayed red. She flipped the card around and tried again to no avail. Finally she had the opportunity to see Penny and yet she'd made one error after another. She glanced at her wrist, only to find it bare, her watch still back at the motel in Swansea. Yet another insult.

Three times she tried the key card, faster, then slower, willing the light to turn green. All she saw was red. She tried the knob and it remained locked. The door wouldn't budge. Audrey couldn't think why the inn would have installed these devices when old-fashioned keyed locks would've been more reliable.

She couldn't keep up anymore. The world moved too quickly, leaving her at least a step behind. Now she'd gotten a traffic ticket and lost the use of her car. As soon as Deanna found out, she would hire a lawyer, if she hadn't already. This would be the beginning of the end. Audrey would lose her independence. She would have nothing left. Penny would die without hearing her story.

Her gaze on the carpeted floor, she hobbled toward the staircase. If she could make it to the front desk, they would provide her with a new key. Then she could climb into bed and try to forget she'd ever embarked on this foolhardy trip that hadn't accomplished anything except make her situation worse.

Trying to favor her still hurting ankle, she inched her way down. She'd almost reached the bottom of the staircase when she heard voices in the front room. Peering over the banister she discovered the police officer who had pulled her over talking to the inn's manager, a middle-aged woman wearing a Lilly Pulitzer sundress.

Perhaps he'd come to bring back Audrey's car, although she wasn't sure what good it would do. She was too weak and flustered to drive, too tired and unsure of herself.

As Audrey turned from the banister to descend to the next step, she heard the phrase *potential silver alert* and the manager looked up, her eyebrows knitted with concern. Everything in Audrey's journey had led to this. Deanna would win and she'd made a fool of herself.

Tears pooled in her eyes, clouding her vision, and she hesitated, one foot in the air. In one hand she still held her key card, although now she had no intention of asking for help. She took her other hand off the railing to wipe her eyes, a movement which sent her pitching forward until she missed the last step and landed on the rug below with a shriek.

CHAPTER 29

The police officer rushed over with the inn manager not far behind. Breathing hard, Audrey sat in shock, unable to move. What had she done? They spoke in a frenzied flurry of words she couldn't quite make out. The manager knelt beside her on the floor, her bright sundress creasing at the hips, and introduced herself as Valerie. She looked Audrey over until she brushed her away.

The officer bounced on his feet. "EMS can get here pretty quickly."

Another guest, a teenaged girl in a tennis dress, approached the staircase and stopped abruptly at the sight of Audrey on the floor near the first step.

"I can come back later," she said. Her hoop earrings swayed as she turned to leave with the indifference of youth. Audrey tried to calculate how many years had passed since she was her age, blithely convinced no harm would come to her.

Shaking her head, Audrey took stock of what hurt and what didn't. The inn's manager, Valerie, and the officer watched her intently. Her wrists worked fine. She felt a twinge—nothing serious—in her back. When she rotated her neck, she noticed a familiar stiffness but no pain. She tried to shift her legs, a simple movement that made her cheeks flush with warmth.

"Don't move anymore," Valerie said. "I'm calling 911. You could've broken your hip."

"Happens a lot at this age," the officer added.

Her cheeks burning hot, Audrey tried again to straighten her legs. The left knee of her slacks had ripped.

"Can you not do that, ma'am? Like the woman said, it's best if you stay put until EMS gets here."

"I don't want EMS. There's no need," Audrey said.

"There's already a history of you disappearing and all. It's best for you to get checked out."

"We didn't know she was missing," Valerie said. "I would've called right away if I'd known."

"Just came in. I wasn't aware of it myself when I pulled her over yesterday. But I recognized the name."

"I'm perfectly entitled to leave town and go wherever I please. I have a driver's license." Audrey looked up at them from the floor. Although her legs were shaking, they didn't hurt.

"What's the nature of your trip?" The officer didn't mention the citation he'd given her or the fact that she might not have a driver's license for much longer. "Is this your final stop?"

Audrey nodded and tried to assess her condition. The ankle she'd rolled earlier looked more swollen. As soon as she tried to rotate her foot, pain shot through the joint.

"Should I call 911?" Valerie asked again. "I'll run to my office. Wait, what am I saying? There's a phone at the front desk…" Her voice trailed off as she scurried away.

"I'm used to bumps and bruises at my age," Audrey said. "There's no reason to clutter up the lobby with emergency personnel. Imagine what the other guests will think, the disruption it will cause."

Valerie appeared to have heard her because she paused, the receiver in her hand. The officer motioned her over.

"I'd feel better if someone was looking after you," Valerie said. "Was it a family member who reported her missing? A man—Mr. Branson, I think—stopped by the front desk earlier. He'd been waiting for you." Looking increasingly agitated, she kept glancing back and forth between Audrey and the officer. Perhaps after work she would go home and vent to someone—a partner, a friend—about her difficult day.

When Whit used to tell her about demanding clients, he chuckled in a way that told her he wasn't seriously bothered. Since their families had set them up with trust funds, he didn't need to work, but he went into the office as a way of meeting people. Perhaps it was an excuse to have some time to himself, to cultivate an aspect of his life at least marginally of his own design, especially since so much had been thrust upon him.

The officer flipped through his notes. "Granddaughter." He stared at Audrey as if he expected her to say something.

Pressing her lips together, she didn't respond.

She was anxious to get up from the floor, but didn't want to put any weight on her ankle. With each passing second, she became more resigned to the fact that the officer would call Deanna. It was this possibility more than any bodily pain that brought tears to her eyes. To be humiliated like this, to have given Deanna such ammunition—there was no excuse for it. Her own foolishness led her to this moment. Audrey wasn't who she thought she was. She couldn't take care of things like she used to. Worst of all, she had no one to lean on, no one who truly knew her. With her fingernail, she rubbed the paisley design on the carpet, pressing the blue fibers into the red and letting them spring back up. The officer stood off to the side murmuring with Valerie.

Through her tears, Audrey detected movement and Valerie and the officer swiveled their heads toward the foyer. She blinked and willed her eyes to focus.

As the vague shape of a person materialized, time seemed to come to a standstill. From her position on the floor, she craned her neck forward. The person drew two, then three steps closer until Audrey was struck with a flare of recognition so startling it buzzed in her veins.

CHAPTER 30

Saturday afternoon, Laurel sat in the driveway of Penny's old house and flipped through the journal Oliver had found. After all her driving, her neck and hips ached like her joints were lined with gravel. She could only imagine what it was like for Audrey, all the aches and pains she managed to smile through, the world moving so fast she could barely keep up.

She still hadn't heard from the Museum of Contemporary Art. For all she knew, Audrey could be down in Jacksonville drinking freshly squeezed pineapple juice before her private museum tour. Even if she was right and Audrey had come to visit Penny, Laurel had no way of finding where she might be.

Out of options, she turned the car south toward home.

When her cell rang, she almost didn't answer. The battery was drained and she didn't feel like talking to anybody. But as the chime sounded again and Clay's name appeared on the screen, her maternal instinct kicked in and she pulled off the road. At least she could find out how Oliver was doing.

"I got Dad's phone," her son said. "He's been on the computer ever since we got home from tryouts," her son said. "But it's not working right and he's frustrated. Hey, did you find Miss Audrey? Did she have a car crash?"

"I'm not sure where Audrey is, buddy. I tried looking for her, but she could be anywhere. And she might not need my help, to be honest. So I'm coming home and I'll see you soon."

"Okay." Uncertainty crept into Oliver's voice. "Dad said we have to run a bunch of errands and clean up the house."

She'd left the sink full of dirty dishes, the counter piled with mail, the sour smell of dirty laundry drifting from the hamper. Oliver's school papers were scattered across the dining room table, his backpack stuffed with junk.

"I thought you were going to look for Miss Audrey," Oliver said.

"I tried." Laurel's voice trailed off.

One day her son would understand the lengths people might go for each other. She remembered him flipping through the World War II book Audrey had sent—an awfully kind gesture on her part. Whatever she was going through, whether she'd planned this trip or left on impulse, she had thought of Oliver as she set out. Maybe, at least in the ways that mattered, Laurel did know her.

After he blew a kiss through the phone, Oliver hung up. While she waited to turn back onto the highway, still unsure which way to go, Laurel pictured him back at the house. He was probably wearing one of the Lego or Star Wars t-shirts he loved, his hair a little messy, making a video on his laptop or poking around in his too-full backpack. Then she realized her son may have had the answer all along.

Minutes later, a woman in a bright sundress stepped in front of Laurel and blocked her path with a polite smile.

"What can I do for you? Checking in?" She tilted her head toward the inn's front desk.

When she'd called him back, Oliver had found the envelope from Audrey's mail in his backpack, the same backpack he stuffed everything in, no matter how often Laurel asked him to clean it out. That day when she'd sorted Audrey's mail, Laurel had handed the discarded envelopes to Oliver and asked him to recycle them in the pantry. Instead, he'd stuffed everything, his school papers and Audrey's recycling, in his backpack. When Laurel explained what she needed, he described the inn's crown-shaped logo and—in a surprisingly confident voice—read the return address out loud.

Now Laurel tried to peek around the woman in front of her.

"Sorry, we've had a small incident," the hotel employee said. "We'll get everything cleared shortly. If you come this way, I'm happy to check on our room availability."

Without responding, Laurel sidestepped past her to discover Audrey in an undignified heap on the carpeted floor. The older woman stared like she couldn't quite believe what she was seeing. Then she began to nod, a sort of confirmation Laurel felt deep within her chest.

She didn't say anything but closed the gap between them and dropped to her knees beside Audrey. The older woman still smelled of lavender and Laurel took a deep breath of the familiar comforting scent.

"You came," Audrey said, her voice almost in a whisper. "You found me."

"Are you okay?" Laurel started to say how worried she'd been. But Audrey seemed so fragile that she didn't want to make her feel guilty.

Audrey tried to pinch the rip in the knee of her pants closed, but it gaped open again once she let go.

"We'll get that fixed," Laurel said. "Or find another pair." In Audrey's well-stocked closet back home, she probably had six or seven identical pairs, some with the tags still attached.

A police officer introduced himself as Will. The inn manager had gone behind the front desk where she was frowning at the computer screen.

Laurel turned back to Audrey. "Are you hurt?"

"My ankle might be the slightest bit tweaked. I twisted it when the police pulled me over—maybe yesterday? Then I fell down the stairs just now."

"We'll get it looked at. I bet they'll give you some ice packs, maybe some prescription pain reliever. It could've been much worse," Laurel said even as she noticed how swollen it looked.

"I've made such a mess of things." Audrey's chin quivered while she appeared to study the patterns woven into the carpet.

Laurel tried to imagine how her trip had gone and what she'd been up to. Had she really been pulled over by the police?

"Oh, it's not so bad," she said. "Besides, I'm here now. Let's go get your ankle looked at." It wasn't enough that she'd found Audrey, that they were sitting on the floor together, the older woman's head pressed against her shoulder. She needed for Audrey to be all right—and if she wasn't, to be able to take care of her.

Laurel helped her get to her feet, but Audrey winced when she tried to put weight on her right foot.

"Think you can make it out to my car?"

"I can look for a wheelchair somewhere," Will offered, but Audrey declined with a firm shake of her head.

"I'll need you to sign a release of the missing person report." Will held up the clipboard. "And proof that you're a relative or legal guardian."

She glanced at Audrey. "Missing person report?"

Audrey mouthed *Deanna*.

"This part might be my fault," Laurel said. "I suggested it earlier. Only because I was worried about you. Before I knew what it meant. Once I looked it up, I told Deanna we didn't need to."

"Well, she didn't listen. What's new about that?"

"So are you able to sign or—?"

"I'm her caregiver." Laurel held up the bag from the pharmacy. "I have her prescriptions."

"I'm afraid that's not sufficient," Will said.

"But I'm her emergency contact. Doesn't that count for something?"

"It's not a designation. Legally or officially."

"We'll have to call Deanna. Just tell her you're visiting an old friend," Laurel said. She held up her car keys in an attempt to hurry Audrey along.

Audrey raised her eyebrows, perhaps impressed at how much her caregiver had already figured out. Once they got Deanna on the line, Laurel and Audrey both spoke at once.

"I found her—"

"I'm perfectly fine. No need to worry."

"What in the world? Where have you been all this time? You've had us so worried. Are you sure you're fine?" Deanna's voice seemed to crack and Laurel wondered if she might be about to cry.

"Visiting an old friend." Audrey paused. "It's taking a bit longer than I'd anticipated. I ought to have called so you didn't worry."

Once they reassured Deanna that all was well, she agreed to release the alert and Will said they were free to go.

"Now let's get you to the doctor," Laurel said. She would tell Audrey about the upcoming hearing—and she needed to get some answers from her. But first she needed medical attention.

At the urgent care center, Laurel paced around the lobby. As soon as Audrey's ankle was taken care of, they needed a plan for Monday's hearing. Deanna's lawyer would argue that Audrey couldn't take care of herself. Her sudden unexplained trip wouldn't help matters, especially given her injury. The woman at the front desk lent her a phone charger and Laurel found a voicemail from Friday she hadn't noticed. It was from a law firm where she'd applied for a receptionist job before she started working for Audrey. Since she had nothing better to do, she called the office manager's cell.

"We offered the position to another candidate, but it fell through at the last minute," she said.

Unsure why the doctor was taking so long, Laurel glanced back at the door to the exam area. A man was signing paperwork at the front counter, his young son pumping the hand sanitizer dispenser and squealing in delight when the foam overflowed.

"I like dealing with people. Helping them." Of course she could be a receptionist. Direct people where to go. Offer them coffee or water. Laurel tried to ignore how fake her voice sounded, how empty and pointless the idea felt.

"We'd like you to come in for an interview first thing Monday morning."

Laurel couldn't possibly turn down an interview, especially when her future with Audrey was so uncertain. Audrey might end up in a nursing home, or she might need a caregiver or nurse with actual training, someone who could do much more for her. It was hard to imagine going back to Savannah and picking up where they'd left off, like nothing had changed. Anyway, once they got back to Savannah, their focus needed to be on the hearing.

"Any chance I could come in later in the week?" Laurel kept pacing around the waiting room. At his father's urging, the little boy took a seat, leaving behind the sharp scent of sanitizer.

"The office manager is at a conference the rest of the week. The other candidates are coming in first thing Monday morning."

"Sorry, but I don't think I can make it Monday morning." Laurel spoke quickly even as she tried to convince herself she wasn't making a big mistake. Especially after she'd gone to such trouble to find her, she couldn't in good conscious skip the hearing Deanna's lawyer had arranged. She asked about coming Monday afternoon, but the office manager didn't sound very encouraging. She'd probably already crossed Laurel's name off her list.

When Clay called, she braced herself for a lecture about how helping Audrey wasn't the best use of her time. Instead, he stayed quiet while Laurel explained how she'd found her.

"Will you let Oliver know she's all right?" she asked. "He's been worried about her too."

"Yeah, sure. Of course. Hey, listen, I guess—I mean it's good you're there with her. She's probably glad to see a familiar face."

"Thanks."

"I hope she'll be okay. I never meant otherwise. You know that. I worried another disappointment, I don't know, might make you depressed."

Willing herself not to cry, Laurel gripped the phone tighter. Not depressed. It hadn't gotten that bad. Only a dark cloud hovering. The deep-down ache of not having another baby, like a punch to the gut whenever she thought about it. Oliver shifting away from her, not needing her anymore. The feeling of utter uselessness, like she might always be drifting, aimless, not much good to anyone.

"I want to protect you," Clay added. "It's hard to know what to do."

"I get it." Even though she didn't need his pity, she figured he meant well. "But I promise I can take care of myself." No sooner had the words left Laurel's mouth than she began to doubt them.

CHAPTER 31

Evening had fallen by the time Audrey was released Saturday night, armed with a prescription painkiller and anti-inflammatory, her sprained ankle encased in a compression wrap and stabilized by a brace. Outside the urgent care center, the heat had let up, but the cool breeze brought with it stony gray clouds.

On their way to Laurel's car, Audrey leaned on her arm.

"Now that you've gotten what you need, we should head back as soon as possible," Laurel said. "Deanna's lawyer has scheduled a competency hearing for Monday morning."

"I'm too tired to think about something like that," Audrey said. Her ankle still throbbed and now she had a mounting headache. The walk to the car seemed interminable.

Laurel helped her into her seat and pulled the seatbelt across her chest. Then she walked around to the driver's side. Before she started the car, she held up her phone. "I need to send Clay a quick text. It's crazy, but I had a call about this other job interview."

Laurel's demeanor was casual, almost flippant, in the wake of this confession.

"Wait, you're leaving me?" Audrey asked. Embarrassed at how shaky her voice sounded, she leaned her aching head back against the seat.

"No. I mean Deanna surely won't let me stay after all this." Laurel looked up from her phone. "But no, I haven't been looking around, not since I've been with you."

Still annoyed at the possibility of her caregiver—her friend—leaving, Audrey searched Laurel's face for some sort of sign that they understood each other. The younger woman's cheeks were pale, her eyes bloodshot and tired. After she put her phone away, she started the car.

That day when they'd first met, Audrey had been struck by Laurel's wide-eyed innocence. Like a Pre-Raphaelite angel, she'd thought then. The resemblance remained, never mind that Laurel wore an outfit she might as well have slept in, cotton shorts paired with a t-shirt the same dusky mauve that Cezanne used to paint autumn leaves. It still surprised Audrey that she had come all this way, and that she'd done so for her.

"I thought we could trust each other," Audrey said finally. She meant the statement as a confirmation. They could rely on each other. But Laurel only raised her eyebrows and she wondered if she'd gone too far. Her headache was so intense that she saw spots.

They pulled into the parking lot of a small deli with a striped awning.

"Wait here. I'll be right back." Laurel's voice sounded strained and she didn't meet Audrey's eyes when she got out of the car. Her back hunched against the first drops of rain, she hurried to the entrance.

When she returned, she handed Audrey a bag with an egg salad sandwich and two bananas. Audrey ate a few bites of the sandwich and unpeeled the fruit. Laurel must have remembered that bananas helped her potassium levels. She was considering how best to move past any unpleasantness when Laurel swiveled toward her, the car keys still in her hand.

"If you must know, I passed up the job interview. It was a good one too, a receptionist at a law firm. Imagine how easy that would be, how straightforward. Nobody running off suddenly. No secrets."

"Fair enough," Audrey said.

"Anyway, Deanna clearly didn't want me leaving town to look for you. So I probably should be looking for another job instead of staying here."

"I hadn't thought of that possibility, the difficult position I put you in. But obviously we'll work something out."

"Like I said, I turned it down. I'm here. We'll get you ready for the hearing at least."

The smell of ripe banana filled the car. When Audrey took a bite, the sweet fruit lodged in her throat. Laurel handed her a bottle of water and she drank until she could speak again. "I didn't know what to think when you mentioned another job."

"Clay called earlier, and I forgot to tell him about the interview. He was being nice for once, and even a little sweet. The job didn't come up. I texted him about it because I—" Laurel's voice broke and she shook her head in an apparent effort to gather herself. "Because I wanted him to know that other people see potential in me. They don't pity me." She lifted her chin ever so slightly and Audrey found herself surprised at the pride she felt. Even though Laurel wasn't happy with her, her eyes shone with a brightness she hadn't noticed before. It suited her.

"I've wanted to help you, Laurel. But not out of pity."

"I know. I mean, I thought so. But the last few days, I've been running around, not sure what to do, whether to call the police." She jabbed her finger in Audrey's direction. "Losing sleep, picturing you dead in a ditch somewhere."

"I assumed the note I left would be enough. I'm sorry I've made you worry."

"It's okay if you wanted to come up here to visit your friend. But I can't think of why you didn't tell me. I would've come with you. Or at least known you were safe."

"You don't understand."

Laurel snorted. "That's nice. After everything I've done for you."

"I only mean—"

"If I don't understand, it's because you haven't let me. You haven't told me enough. You haven't explained yourself."

Seconds ticked by. Audrey wasn't sure what to say. She'd never imagined them having this conversation. She stuffed the banana peel and sandwich wrapper in the paper bag.

"I feel like there's something I'm missing," Laurel continued.

"I'm in the dark." She reached into the backseat and tossed a journal onto Audrey's lap.

Audrey pushed the bag aside to examine the book closer. As soon as she recognized it, she closed her eyes and opened them again. Her fingers trembled as she flipped quickly through the pages, the scribbled notes about what happened to the prisoners of war on Corregidor. Swords and blood, stomachs distended with hunger, the ground littered with bones and teeth.

The food she'd eaten churned in her stomach. She slammed the journal closed. When she turned to toss it onto the backseat, pain shot through her ankle. The book landed with a thud and she turned back around, breathing heavily.

"How did you get that, Laurel?" She imagined the younger woman peeking into her closets, rummaging through cabinets and drawers, digging up stones in the garden. "Have you searched every inch of my house? To what end might I ask?"

"Trying to figure out where you'd gone," Laurel snapped. "I looked in your closet to see if you'd packed clothes. I drove around town looking for your car. For God's sake, we didn't know what might have happened to you or if you'd even left town on your own accord. You see stuff on the news."

"I'd hidden the journal for a reason," Audrey said, even as she struggled to explain a reason to herself. She supposed she never wanted anyone to ask about the war or wonder why she was interested in Corregidor. "It was not in plain sight. There's no way you casually happened across it."

"It was an accident. Oliver was playing outside, digging around, and I guess he noticed the loose stone."

At the reminder of that sweet, quiet boy with his big, kind eyes, Audrey's heart softened. "Did he look inside?"

"Not the journal, no. I took it away from him. But he did get the World War II book you sent." When Laurel lowered her voice, her tone sounded less stiff. "He wanted me to come looking for you, did I tell you?"

Audrey wasn't surprised. Like his mother, Oliver had a big heart. Without saying where they were going, Laurel pulled the car back onto the road. Her accusation that she'd been selfish still rang in Audrey's ears. She'd earned the right to be selfish, at least this once. Because when it mattered the most, she made a choice that changed everything. Laurel couldn't guess at the truth.

Saturday night, Laurel, who muttered something about leaving Audrey enough room on the bed, settled herself in the armchair with her legs bent beneath her. Audrey didn't see how she could be the slightest bit comfortable, but when she handed her the throw blanket from the foot of the bed, the younger woman merely draped it across her shoulders and tucked her chin against her chest with her eyes already closed.

In the morning, over an early breakfast, Audrey asked to go to the hospice center where Penny had been moved.

Laurel shook her head. "We should head home to get ready for tomorrow's hearing. If we don't show up, Deanna will get what she wants."

"Laurel, my friend is probably dying, and I came all this way to see her." She didn't even want to check with Mr. Branson first. If they showed up, perhaps they'd have a better chance of getting in to see her.

They argued back and forth, debating whether to deal with Penny or Deanna first. Eventually, much to Audrey's relief, Laurel relented.

When they arrived, Penny's nephew didn't look surprised to see them. He introduced himself to Laurel and said they could go back to Penny's room.

"You need to understand though, she might not be responsive. Sometimes she's heavily sedated," he said. "I'm going to get some errands out of the way." He pointed down the hall toward the elevator. "Take your time."

In her ankle boot, Audrey began the laborious process of hobbling down the tiled hallway toward Penny's room. Laurel, who stayed behind in the lobby, called out to be careful, then bit off the rest of her warning.

Audrey stopped and turned around, offering a sheepish smile, an apology of sorts. Now that the time had come to see Penny, she wanted Laurel with her, a desire she never would've expected. But it was there all the same, lodged beneath her rib cage.

"Would you mind coming with me, Laurel? I know it's a lot to ask."

If Laurel came with her, then no matter Penny's condition or reaction, at least Audrey wouldn't be alone.

Without hesitating, Laurel took her elbow. Together they turned the corner and located Penny's room. Audrey took a deep breath and, after knocking, they went in, not bothering to wait for a response.

Penny's shriveled body lay still, a morphine drip at her side. Its faint trickle provided the only sound in the room. The air-conditioned air smelled of citrus cleaner and the musty undertone of illness and decay.

As Audrey stared at her old friend, she realized she wouldn't have recognized her if they'd passed on the street. Penny's shoulders were still broad, but they lacked her former swimmer's strength. Her hair, what was left of it, was white.

But Audrey couldn't look away and the more she studied her, the more the old Penny came into focus. Despite the ravages of time and illness, her facial features—that wide forehead, the thick eyebrows—might still have belonged to a sunny peasant woman painted by a Dutch master.

She managed to keep her hand steady as she reached for the bed, tracing her finger along the white sheet. Beneath the fabric, Penny's foot twitched. Audrey flinched and yanked her hand away.

"It's all right," Laurel said. "You're not going to hurt her."

Audrey let her words sink in. Laurel didn't know, of course, how much they meant. When she touched the sheet again, Penny didn't stir. Audrey's eyes traveled the length of the bed, tears gathering each time she blinked. Penny appeared emaciated and pale. Her face was gaunt, her lips papery thin and colorless.

"This isn't how I expected her to be," Audrey said.

Behind her Laurel cleared her throat. "Do you need to sit down?"

She didn't answer, but Laurel pulled up the visitor's chair and gently nudged her into it. Her ankle stuck out in front of her, immobilized in the brace. For a minute, she rested her head in her hand.

Penny's bedside table was cluttered with a stack of newspapers, a bouquet of red carnations, and a plastic water pitcher. By now, given her condition, the newspapers likely went unread.

"How long has it been since you've seen her?" Laurel asked.

"A long time," Audrey said, not sure she wished to elaborate.

"It's good you're here now."

"Since the war. That's how long it's been. One of my oldest friends. And now she's dying."

"It's important then, this last chance. It's good you came. If she wakes up—she might already know you're here. Maybe she senses it."

Audrey raised her head slowly, glanced at Laurel, and reached up to pat the edge of the bed.

"Penny, I never wanted to have to choose between you. I never dreamed of such a decision." She waited for a response, but the body on the bed didn't move. Penny's eyes stayed closed. "I loved you like you were my own sister, as much as any one person can love another." Again, she waited and Penny didn't stir.

Down the hall, the elevator doors dinged. Penny's room was otherwise silent until Laurel whispered, "Do you want to go back to the inn? We could come back and try again later once you've gotten some rest."

"It looks like I'm too late." Saying the words out loud was as shattering as a blow to the chest. Audrey wasn't entirely sure she could find the strength to stand up.

"I'm sorry." Laurel wrapped her arm around her.

"I took such a risk coming here—and, worse yet, I caused trouble for you, Laurel. You dropped everything to come all this way."

"It's what friends do," Laurel said. She spoke with assurance, a confidence in her voice Audrey hadn't noticed before. "We look out for one another."

We look out for one another. It's what friends do.

The weight of the words, half of which Laurel could only guess, settled in her mind. She was right, of course. In the best and worst of circumstances, that was what friends did.

Penny might have been too far gone to hear what she wanted to share, but Laurel had come all this way. Audrey gestured toward the chair by the window until she understood she was asking her to sit down.

"I shouldn't have gotten my hopes up," Audrey said. "I wanted Penny to understand and that's not possible. I have to accept it. Even so I keep thinking—I'm probably running out of time myself." She held up her hand against Laurel's protest. "When one gets to this point, my dear, certain sentiments crystallize. I have this idea now, a need to be understood by someone who might truly know me. Perhaps Penny can hear more than we realize. Or she might not. It doesn't matter. What you said about friends settles it. I want to tell you anyway."

"Tell me what?"

"About the secret I've kept since the war."

Part Four

Chapter 32

Laurel settled in the chair by the window in Penny's room. Then she reminded Audrey where she'd left off with the story, with the three women volunteering to go to Stotsenburg. Audrey shook her head, not out of regret, but amused at how she'd already shared more than she ever expected.

And yet she wanted to tell Laurel much more—enough for her to understand who she was and how she'd gotten here, to this lonely place where nobody truly knew her.

Laurel listened carefully as she described the scene at Stotsenburg. She raised her eyebrows, intrigued, at the mention of her time with James and the plumeria bouquet he'd left for her. Throughout the tense journey back to Manila, she gripped her thighs until Audrey explained how she relinquished the pistol.

Lying on the hospital bed, Penny remained still, her breathing shallow.

Laurel's phone blinked. She muttered Deanna's name and turned it face down.

"My story doesn't match up to what Deanna has in her mind," Audrey reminded her.

"I don't know why you've never told her—" Laurel stopped herself. "But it's up to you, of course."

"In its own way, the truth might be a sort of leverage over my granddaughter." She mulled this over for a minute, then decided Deanna would be dealt with later.

The dense jungle of Bataan came next. Days and nights of rain, eating bowls of watery rice, lizards skittering above their heads, the loss of Anthony Delfino and countless other patients, falling asleep, exhausted, to the sound of creaking bamboo and more rain.

Audrey guessed surrender lay ahead. She'd noticed an officer shredding a stack of maps, had seen troops setting fuel tanks on fire and destroying engines. Every day artillery shells burst overhead. The peaks of the Mariveles Mountains were all but obscured by smoke. Leaving for the island of Corregidor, the one remaining spot where American troops maintained control, seemed their only hope.

By that time, they had run out of dressings and were using strips of old white uniforms instead. They boiled rope for sutures. Audrey's hands were raw and blistered, her feet much the same. During raids, they dropped everything and jumped into foxholes. To equalize the pressure in her ears, she kept her mouth open, flinching when the stench of her own breath reminded her of the gangrene ward's putrid odor.

Three days after Easter, the unit was ordered to join a convoy evacuating Bataan for Fort Mills on the island of Corregidor. In a daze, she climbed on board an open-sided bus that would carry them to the port. The bus held two long seats and a middle railing to hold onto. Along the bumpy road, the driver skirted charred remains of Jeeps and trucks. On their way out, the troops had scuttled anything of value. The air still smelled like burning metal.

Around a sharp bend, emaciated-looking soldiers appeared. They raised their hands toward the bus windows and begged for food. Audrey, who had nothing, not even a grain of rice, to give them, wished she could shut her ears against their cries. Some of the young men were barefoot, their feet so swollen from beriberi they could no longer fit into their boots. In the distance, the advancing Japanese troops called out *Banzai*. As the bus bounced and swerved over ruts in the road, she held onto the railing to keep from falling.

When the sky rumbled with what sounded like thunder, Audrey ducked as shells arched overhead. Across the aisle she noticed Kat doing the same thing. Penny was sitting down the row. The back of her neck looked flushed and beads of sweat trickled behind her ear. Was it her imagination or did her friend shiver? Chills were the first sign of malaria, followed by dizziness and extreme weakness. Just yesterday a once hearty nurse from Indiana had collapsed like a rag doll. Penny reached back to wipe the sweat off her neck. Almost as if she could sense Audrey staring, she turned around and flashed a weak grin in her direction.

Kat glanced up too, returning Penny's smile. It was probably because she looked forward to the relative safety of Corregidor, but Kat seemed stronger. Even though they had nothing but rice to eat—and scant portions at that—her appetite had returned and she'd even gained some weight. Audrey imagined gathering her close the way a mother hen shelters her chicks under her wings. Perhaps in the underground tunnels awaiting them they might find some bits of carabao, the water buffalo that roamed the islands, sprinkled in with the rice.

Lieutenant Johnson had filled them in before they left Bataan. Corregidor was an island in Manila Bay, which everyone called The Rock because of its rocky beaches and limestone cliffs—or because it was a stronghold, the last territory in the region still under U.S. control. Kindley Field boasted a small airstrip and anti-aircraft artillery batteries along the rugged coast. The island's most distinctive feature was hidden underground—an elaborate maze of concrete tunnels built by the Army Corps of Engineers some ten years earlier as a bombproof bunker. Audrey recalled the first time she'd heard of The Rock. With no foreknowledge that it would become their last retreat, back then she'd thought it sounded bleak.

"Imagine an underground village, both for storage and personnel. Twenty-five lateral tunnels branching off the main shaft," Lieutenant Johnson said. "The main tunnel, Malinta, is wide enough for trucks to drive through."

"It's awfully hard to picture," one of the nurses said. "But I'm hoping for something more than rice, that's for sure."

"Rock and concrete sure sound better than a foxhole," someone else said.

The first few weeks on Corregidor passed in a confused haze. At first, having electric lights seemed a luxury. No worries about a blackout since they were beneath solid rock.

Since they spent every minute underground, Audrey lost track of night and day. Red lights blinked to warn of air raids, each blast releasing clouds of dust and particles of concrete that clogged everyone's chests. Before long, Audrey couldn't recall how it felt to take a good, deep breath, as deep as she wanted. She worried the dust was steadily settling in her lungs, filling up the tiny air sacs until one day she would suffocate.

One night as she tried to fall asleep, the triple-decker bunks crowded with nurses, she tapped her fingertips against her sternum. Inside her chest cavity the bronchi split into smaller branches, the same as the tunnels in Malinta. If only she could sweep her lungs clean, same as the dust-filled hallways.

Over the coming days, the three friends scurried around the maze of corridors like anxious rats, looking for their assigned patients, for the chief nurse, for food and water, for each other. At times, Audrey expected the concrete walls, so constantly battered by the Japanese forces, to cave in and crush them all. On the worst days, she had to force herself out of bed to make it to her shift on time. As she twisted her dirty hair up off her neck, she reminded herself of the promise they'd made. They would get through this together. After the war, she and Kat and Penny might end up in different parts of the country, but they would write letters and visit when they could. They would stay friends, bound by what they'd shared together.

Now that uniform protocol wasn't strictly enforced, they wore the matching brooches every day. Regardless of what happened, they would stay together and help each other through to the other side. The promise shone in front of Audrey when she was so tired she could barely keep her eyes open. It sounded in her ears like a distant hymn, blocking out the wails of pain and the shrill sirens warning of more to come.

When near the end of April they heard about two planes coming to rescue a chosen few, the news meant almost nothing. The chief nurse scheduled a meeting at the mess hall where she called out the names on the list. Audrey didn't stay. Instead, she snuck back to her cot and tried to catch a few minutes of rest before her next shift.

A young nurse named Barbara came in crying. When Audrey asked what was wrong, she said she wanted to be on the list so badly she would've cut off her own arm to make it happen. But her name wasn't called. The nurses on the list had been abroad the longest. They were the sickest and weakest, the oldest.

"We're stuck here," Barbara said.

Later that day those who could take a break from their work gathered at the mouth of the tunnel, squinting at the last of the evening's natural light, by then foreign to their eyes. Audrey gulped in the fresh air, relieved her lungs could manage it. She'd almost forgotten what the outside world smelled like, the reassuring vagueness of it after being stuck underground while assaulted by the stale scents of mildew and diesel exhaust fumes. Even the temperature, despite still hovering in the low eighties, offered a temporary reprieve.

Since trunks and footlockers were too much weight for the PBY planes, the departing nurses had packed their belongings in duffel bags. As dusk deepened, the women lined up, their bags zipped and ready. Audrey wondered what it would be like to leave with them, to return home to hot meals and long showers, to a place of restful sleep and safety. At home, the war touched people in only indirect ways—worries about their loved ones, the minor inconvenience of gasoline and meat rationing. Once, Audrey's biggest concern had been escaping her nanny's watchful eye to walk down to the river with a beau.

She'd finally gotten a brief letter from James, several weeks old by the time it arrived. Although she assumed her response would be similarly delayed, Audrey was simply glad he was still alive. She'd held the thin airmail paper to her nose and tried to detect his scent. Remembering the coral plumeria flowers he'd left on her cot, the way he'd kissed her with such urgency, she closed her eyes. Then she began to read, devouring every word. James reported that he was working long hours at an evac hospital in Australia. It was difficult work, but the thought of seeing Audrey again—of holding her—gave him at least some measure of strength. She clasped the letter to her chest, already composing her response, and held it out to read again until she had memorized each loop and curl of his handwriting.

Whit was still in Lexington. Audrey guessed he spent most of his time outside with his family's horses, their ebony manes whipping in the hay-scented wind. Kentucky was a different world now and she wasn't sure she would ever return. At this point in her life, after what she'd seen and done, she could no longer imagine sitting at her mother's formal dinner table making small talk about racing or gardening, worried about her posture and whether her fingernails were neatly filed.

At the mouth of the tunnel, the crowd shifted and inched forward. Someone called out that the planes were arriving and Audrey craned her neck to see them, the roaring dark shadows against the purple and gray evening sky. General Wainwright, who'd taken over after MacArthur left for Australia, appeared and began shaking hands. His cheeks looked hollow, his limbs gangly, his eyes etched with deep wrinkles. Most everyone was crying and hugging one last time.

Audrey stayed dry-eyed until she glimpsed a familiar brunette head. She pressed forward to get a better look. Something—fear or perhaps it was already anger or jealousy—pounded in her chest. By the time she made it to the front of the crowd, she choked back sobs.

Kat looked straight ahead, her mouth set in a determined line as she prepared to leave. In those early days in Manila, she'd pursed her lips to apply her bright red lipstick and wrinkled her nose as she pressed the powder puff against her skin. Now Kat's face was bare. She kept her eyes trained forward and slung a duffel bag over her shoulder, its strap nearly obscuring the jade brooch pinned to her uniform.

CHAPTER 33

At Penny's bedside, Audrey looked more slumped and tired by the second. When Laurel handed her a glass of water, her hand shook as she gripped the glass.

Kat had taken the easy way out, leaving Audrey and Penny behind without even saying goodbye. Obviously, Audrey had been through a lot, but she hadn't shared the secret she'd mentioned. There was still a chance Audrey wasn't who she claimed to be. Somehow she ended up in Savannah, an awfully long way from where she grew up. For years she'd lived the life of someone in high society with plenty of money, museum boards and charity galas, a mansion filled with antique furniture and high thread-count linens. It wasn't a fairytale, she'd said once.

"Laurel, do you still have the journal? Did you bring it with you?"

She dug through her bag until she found the leather-bound book. Since she'd already flipped through the pages, she had some idea of what they held—notes and newspaper articles about nurses and doctors serving in the Philippines who were taken prisoner by the Japanese. Laurel had always assumed prisoners of war meant soldiers, not doctors and nurses. One of the newspaper interviews taped in the journal mentioned how some of the prisoners lost teeth because of malnutrition and poor hygiene. Laurel ran her tongue over her teeth, thinking about how Kat wasn't only selfish. She was lucky too. Even if her escape meant leaving her friends behind, at least she got out. Laurel handed the journal to Audrey, who stared at its cover and pressed her finger against the rich maroon leather.

"Have you seen what's in here?" Audrey asked.

"A little. Enough to get the general idea."

Laurel wanted to ask if she and Penny were there, if they were taken prisoner after Kat left. Otherwise she couldn't think why Audrey would have collected the articles.

"It must have been hard." Laurel pointed at the journal. "I get grouchy if I miss a meal. Never mind practically starving to death. Not sleeping. Not knowing if the next bomb will end everything."

"Perhaps hoping it would—end everything, I mean."

Laurel might never be able to forget the gaunt figures from the articles she'd read, the vacant looks in the nurses' eyes. And those pictures were taken after the prisoners had been released. They should've been celebrating. Even though most of the nurses were young—in their twenties—they looked middle-aged, their faces creased with worry even when they tried to smile or cheer for the cameras.

When Audrey handed the journal back, she let out her breath like she was relieved to be rid of it. "I don't think the guilt will ever go away."

Laurel waited, but Audrey didn't explain what she meant. If she'd been taken prisoner, she shouldn't have felt guilty about it. She flipped through the pages of the journal again. Over the years Audrey had collected newspaper interviews with nurses who were captured by the Japanese on Corregidor. With Audrey silent, perhaps even dozing, beside her, Laurel started reading, sinking deeper into the chair by the window. One after another they described the claustrophobia, the pitiful rations, the constant bomb raid sirens. As the nurses lost weight, they rolled up their waistbands and reported to shifts around-the-clock. Many came down with malaria. Plagued with extreme vertigo and weakness, they shook with chills even as they applied dressings to their patients' wounds. Those who lost all feeling in their extremities took on other duties.

In early May, the United States surrendered. Over the tunnel radio, the nurses learned about the flag being lowered and a white sheet taking its place. The Japanese turned off the ventilation system and the air grew even more rotten than before. At night, the enemy soldiers slid off the nurses' rings and watches while they pretended to sleep, too afraid to protest. Since they'd heard about the gang rapes at Nanking, they knew the soldiers could do much worse. They squeezed their eyes shut and tried not to shudder in disgust when unfamiliar skin brushed theirs, letting out sighs of relief once the thud of heavy boots, the jangling of swords, faded into the distance.

By July, the prisoners were moved to a camp at Santo Tomas where they were allowed to plant fruit trees.

"I should've been happy about the pineapple and mango trees," a nurse named Rose said in a magazine interview. Laurel fingered the straight edges where Audrey had cut out the paper. Wondering if she would ever understand her, she looked up from the journal to find Audrey dozing off beside Penny's bed.

"But the idea that we'd be rescued soon—that went out the window with them telling us we could plant those trees. Do you know how long fruit trees take to produce? It depressed me more than anything," Rose had said.

"I don't know where or when, but my grandmother said she once ate boiled slugs and canna bulbs," another nurse told the interviewer. "Carabao stew was a real treat."

At Santo Tomas, they waited in line for everything—for rations, to shower, to receive their allotted squares of toilet paper. Most of all they waited to be rescued.

"Every day we hoped we'd get word of help coming. We waited and waited," another post said. The whole time, all those harrowing days and months and years, they kept serving as nurses, caring for the wounded and sick internees.

The nurses were rescued, but not for nearly three years. After spending so long in captivity, they had lost half their body weight,

most with permanent damage to their intestinal tracts. They'd forgotten what a pillow was for, how to use forks and knives. Every
time someone tapped them on the shoulder, they jumped.

I don't think the guilt will ever go away. Laurel tried to work
out what Audrey had meant. Someone with the Thorpe name and
connections might have found a way to avoid the hardships others
had endured. Weren't wealthy, privileged people all about calling in
favors? Clay's earlier words echoed through Laurel's mind, his spec-
ulation that Audrey might be somebody who let her money carry
her, who didn't think about—or care about—other people.

Of course, Audrey wasn't a Thorpe back then. Maybe she was
so desperate to get off the island that she called up her childhood
friend, Whit. He or his father might have convinced someone in
power, a senator or general, to pull strings and get her out. Once
she returned home, she could've married Whit to return the favor.

Frustrated at the possibility, Laurel slammed the journal closed.
At the slapping sound Audrey woke up, startled. From her bed,
Penny twitched and opened her eyes.

CHAPTER 34

Audrey looked from Laurel to Penny and back again. "Did you see that?"

Laurel rose from her chair. "Try to talk to her."

Audrey cleared her throat and said Penny's name. At the sound, Penny blinked—her eyelids like worn parchment, her eyes a muted green. She held up her hand like she could stop Audrey from talking, a gesture that to Laurel's surprise made Audrey tremble.

"Do you think she can hear us?" Audrey asked.

"Maybe she wants to hear the rest."

"Penny knows this part already."

"But there's something she doesn't know, right? I thought you said—"

Penny opened her eyes wider and, even in her weakened state, looked directly at Audrey like she knew exactly who she was. Laurel patted the gentle ridges of Audrey's spine.

"My letter—" Penny faltered, then gathered herself to continue—"brought you out of hiding."

Her voice sounded reed thin and raspy, her tone so accusatory that Laurel assumed Penny must be delirious.

"About the letter," Audrey began. Even though she seemed determined to press forward, her chin raised ever so slightly, she stopped, apparently at a loss for words.

"I saw you in the photograph," Penny said.

"The brooch." Audrey tapped her finger on her chest. "I know."

Penny tried to touch her own chest but dropped her hand back to the bed.

"Let me explain, Penny."

Penny made eye contact with Laurel and looked back at Audrey. "Your granddaughter? She looks nothing like in the paper."

Neither Audrey nor Laurel bothered correcting Penny's misunderstanding. With every word out of her mouth, she sunk deeper, spent and exhausted.

"Tell her how you left, too," Penny said.

"Where?" Laurel asked. "Corregidor?"

"I can explain—"

Penny grunted, cutting Audrey off. With great effort, she lifted her head. "Yes. The Rock." Bitterness made her voice louder. "She. Left. Me. There." She let her head fall back to the pillow and closed her eyes.

Laurel had begun to pace. "This is why you married Whit, right? It's what you meant when you said it wasn't a fairytale love story. His family somehow got you out."

"That's not true, Laurel. If you'll listen—"

"Why else did you keep your time in the war a secret? It's like you've been hiding."

Audrey raised her eyebrows and gave a short nod of confirmation. "I hid from everyone I'd known in the war. Including James."

At this confession, Laurel could only stare at the older woman and wonder how she'd ever thought she knew her. Desperate to get out of the room—away from Audrey—she fled.

She made it to the parking lot before letting out a frustrated groan. An orderly pushing an elderly man in a wheelchair looked up, but she waved him off. Around the corner, she found a small koi pond surrounded by metal benches. Relieved to find the area empty, she collapsed on a bench and pulled her knees up to her chest.

This was what it all came down to. She'd wanted so badly for Audrey to be someone worth admiring, for Clay to be wrong when he said Laurel didn't know her. If Audrey broke one of the most serious promises she ever made, then she wasn't who Laurel thought.

We stick together. No matter what.

Audrey had betrayed someone she claimed to care about, maybe even loved. Just like Laurel's father abandoned his family. Laurel had gone to all this trouble for her—and she had yet to be paid a cent. In the meantime, she'd turned down another perfectly good job opportunity. She pressed her forehead against her knees.

If they didn't have the money for Oliver's school fees, he'd have to start over in public school. No more special programs tailored for his needs, no more dedicated tutor. He would get lost in the shuffle, left behind the other students who were quicker and smarter and more mature. And it would be Laurel's fault.

Not that he'd ever hear about it, but she couldn't bear to consider what lesson her son would take from all this, what kind of example it provided. Don't worry so much about other people. They aren't worth it. When things get hard, you can abandon everyone, even your family and friends. Slough them off like dead weight.

Digging in her purse for a tissue, Laurel's fingers hit something smooth and cool. The jade brooch she'd taken to be fixed. The koi fish opened and closed their mouths, gliding smoothly around the pond and blinking up at her.

"I could mail it to her," Laurel said in their direction. She didn't need to have any further contact with Audrey. She could chalk the whole thing up to a job that didn't work out.

The mention of mail, though, reminded her of the book Audrey had sent Oliver. He'd flipped the pages with such eagerness and paused to study the pictures of P51 Mustangs, the Japanese Zeroes.

So Audrey had made a small gesture of goodwill. Nothing but a polite nicety. It didn't need to mean anything.

Before she could think better of it, Laurel called Clay to fill him in.

"You should probably hear what Audrey has to say," he said. "I thought you trusted her."

"You're the one who's always looking for a snake in the grass, Clay. I figured you'd tell me to cut my losses and come home."

"Sometimes there is a snake in the grass. It's not a bad thing to be cautious."

She stared at the brooch in her hand, remembering how Audrey told her and Oliver about it when her own family didn't know. "I'm not sure I can tell who's trustworthy."

Her husband sighed through the phone. "You see the good in people. It's not a bad thing. I've never said that was wrong."

But caring about people meant being vulnerable. It meant disappointment and light being snuffed out. Jagged edges. Blank nothing where there ought to be fullness.

"Truth is, we should all be more like you," Clay said.

Laurel didn't answer. She stood up from the bench, the brooch still in her hand, her father's face flickering in her mind. The childhood memory of his suitcases lined up by the back door, his quilted jacket flung on top while he rummaged for his car keys. Nothing good had come from caring about him. He left anyway.

"Listen, before you go, Oliver wants to say hi," Clay said.

Oliver promised he'd finished his school report, then asked what was going on with Audrey.

"She's seeing an old friend," Laurel explained. "Getting some things off her chest. Do you know what that means? Sort of like telling the whole story so there aren't any secrets. I think that's what's going on with Miss Audrey and her friend, Penny."

"Yeah, so then she can feel better." Oliver sighed. "Secrets and stuff can make your stomach hurt."

"What do you mean?" Laurel paced around the pond and waited for him to answer. "Are you keeping a secret, buddy?"

His voice shook as he confessed he only wanted to try out for football because everyone else was doing it. Once tryouts started, he realized he'd made a mistake.

"And what about that day at school? When you were upset?" Laurel tried to find a connection—if there was one. She braced herself, worried he was being bullied. Maybe he would finally admit it. If Ford took after his mother, he could be responsible. He seemed like a nice enough kid, but Laurel had no idea what he was like when grown-ups weren't around.

Oliver said the chaplain that day had talked about honesty. "It was right after I'd started telling Sullivan and all those guys that I liked football the best, then basketball, then baseball. I said me and my dad tossed the ball outside all the time. I tried to say I was just like them."

"So you figured out it was sort of dishonest? How you weren't being yourself?"

"Yeah, saying that stuff made me feel bad."

"I'm relieved you're okay. But lying—"

"I know. Look, I won't ever do it again."

Trying not to laugh at his earnestness, Laurel considered explaining that everyone lied sometimes, but settled for saying it was good to listen to his conscience. Before she hung up, she asked about Ford, why he left school early that day too.

"Um, I don't know," Oliver said. "He had some kind of rash or something. I don't think he wanted me to tell."

Laurel left that alone, her mind circling back to Oliver's confession. He was ten years old, trying to fit in at a new school the best way he knew how. The more she thought about it, the only thing that surprised her was how he came clean so quickly.

On Laurel's way back inside, Oliver's voice, his lingering innocence, sounded in her head. She asked to see Audrey in the hall.

As soon as she limped through the doorway, Laurel held out the brooch.

Audrey took it and fingered the clasp. "Was this the broken one?"

Laurel shouldn't have been surprised that she had so many pieces of jewelry she couldn't keep track of them all. She crossed her arms over her chest. "I took it to be fixed."

Resigned to make a clean break, Laurel turned to leave. It would be easier this way. Better than dragging things out. "Good luck with the garden gala," she called over her shoulder. Her voice betrayed how tired she felt, the lack of good sleep having caught up with her. And now the disappointing realization of what kind of person Audrey really was—it was too much to handle.

"You're not taking me home? You haven't even heard my side of the story."

With a sigh, Laurel turned back around to face her. "You drove yourself here. Can't you figure out a way to get home?" She intentionally avoided glancing at Audrey's ankle brace. It was more convenient to pretend she wasn't hurt.

Audrey shook her head. "The ankle is one thing, but they've also taken my car. It's humiliating."

"Who took your car?"

"The police. I couldn't decipher the form he gave me, it was typed in such small print."

Her resolve to make a clean break already weakening, Laurel shuffled on her feet and her flip flops squeaked on the tile floor.

Audrey turned the brooch over in her hand and pressed her fingertip against the jade surface. "I'd like you to have this," she said and tried to give it back to Laurel.

"Why?"

"As a thank you for coming after me. You'll get paid too, of course."

"Deanna said if I didn't come back to help her—"

"Never mind her. I'll pay you myself."

Figuring it was the least Audrey could do, Laurel paused. The brooch was something else though. Audrey had no reason to give it to her. She hadn't done anything to deserve it.

"It's yours, Laurel. The brooch isn't simply—it's not quite a matter of payment. It's a token of our friendship."

"Friendship."

"Back when I first got the brooch, it symbolized not only good luck, but also friendship. It does now too. Keep it, please."

Audrey gently closed Laurel's fingers over the brooch. Their eyes met and Laurel dropped her gaze to the floor.

"You might as well listen to what I have to say." Audrey turned back toward Penny's room. Laurel let her go, her quiet words echoing in her mind. The brooch felt heavy in her hand. Solid. Full of meaning. She didn't need to stay and listen to the rest of Audrey's story. But Laurel knew—picturing her father's tired profile, the way he couldn't bring himself to say goodbye—that she wasn't the kind of person who left.

Her fingers traced the hibiscus bloom carved from jade, the tiny pearl at its center like a promise. The door to Penny's room swung almost closed but not all the way and through the crack she watched Audrey resume her place by Penny's bedside. She picked up the story at the same spot Laurel remembered, which told her she hadn't missed anything. Audrey must have known she would be back, that Laurel wouldn't give up on her.

CHAPTER 35

After Kat boarded the plane for home, Audrey couldn't get her out of her mind. When her shift ended, she lay down to sleep, drained, her bones aching from exhaustion, but sleep wouldn't come. Behind her closed eyelids spun images of her friend. She remembered Kat as she'd been when they first met, her waist cinched with a patent leather belt, her hair in crisp curls, her red lipsticked mouth. On that first evening at the Army Navy Club in Manila, they'd been mostly carefree young women embarking on their first of life's adventures. The scent of bougainvillea and salt water on the air, they had sipped gin from crystal tumblers and admired the manicured tennis courts and swaying palm trees.

Her hands clenched into fists, Audrey tossed and turned on the flimsy cot. She wished for a pillow to rest her head. For a moment she imagined slapping Kat. Wouldn't it be satisfying, her eyes widening at Audrey's audacity, her high cheekbones reddening?

At the same time, she knew she should feel immense relief for her friend, who was headed for safety.

No sooner had the thought drifted across her mind that another took its place. Kat should have shared her plan. She should have said goodbye.

*

Later Audrey found Penny at the mess hall just as the lights flickered.

"Not again." Penny flung her muscular arm toward the ceiling. The electricity, powered by diesel generators, kept going out as Corregidor sustained direct hits from the Japanese bombers overhead. For now, the lights stayed on, a small mercy despite the hailstorm of artillery shells hammering above them.

Penny stood up from the table. "A few bites of mushy rice." She added her empty plate to a teetering stack. They'd long since given up on any meat.

Penny took her hand from her pocket and showed Audrey her jade brooch. "I don't even want it anymore," she said with the air of a confession. "I can't believe Kat would leave like she did, without even explaining herself to us. She owed us that at least."

"Maybe she was ashamed?"

"It's not like we would've begrudged her leaving. Part of me would've been happy for her," Penny said. Her scowl didn't quite match her words.

Audrey imagined Kat, her porcelain skin scrubbed clean and rosy with good health, with a full plate of piping hot food in front of her. She deserved every good thing she had coming. Penny's hand drifted back toward her pocket, but without thinking Audrey reached out to stop her. She took the brooch and pinned it to Penny's chest, the cloth of her unwashed uniform stiff against her fingertips. "Remember what you told us? That the jade carries good luck and healing. It will shield and protect the wearer."

"Do you really believe that?" Already the war was changing her, turning Penny's toughness into something brittle.

"What else do we have? Besides, what does it hurt?"

"Where's yours?"

Back in their barracks, Penny waited as Audrey retrieved her brooch. Another bomb hurtled closer. The room shook and overhead the ceiling rained pellets of plaster. As her friend ducked her head, Audrey did the same. She closed her eyes against the mud-streaked concrete floor. Only when the all-clear signal sounded did she open them again. Penny took the brooch from her hand. Her mouth pressed in a straight line, she concentrated on pinning it carefully between Audrey's breast and shoulder.

That night, shells struck Corregidor in a constant barrage. Audrey's shoulders ached from hunching over, her nerves so frayed that when a rat ran through her legs she screamed and swore at it. An hour into the shelling, the chinstrap on her helmet snapped off and she tossed the whole thing aside. Let a wall crash down on her, a chunk of concrete strike her head. What did it matter anyway? Every few seconds more shells. Two hours. Three. Four. Five.

Audrey was mopping up blood in the operating room when Lieutenant Johnson appeared in the doorway. Her eyes were red-rimmed with exhaustion and her already petite frame had shrunk to the size of a child. While Audrey waited to be assigned a new task, she noticed the lieutenant had cinched her uniform with a rope to keep it on. It hurt to look at her.

"I don't know if Kathleen confided in you—" Lieutenant Johnson's voice trailed off as she seemed to reconsider what she'd planned to say.

Not sure if she wanted to hear any sort of explanation, Audrey raised her hand to stop her. "Kat made her decision. It had nothing to do with me." Kat didn't owe her anything. Perhaps in her mind, a promise made in peacetime meant next to nothing once war arrived. Whenever Audrey thought about Kat being gone, about never seeing her again, she felt as though her insides, the innermost parts of her, had been battered and bruised. Still, she couldn't afford to dwell on what had happened, the trio now reduced to two. "I've got a lot of work to do here," she said and turned her attention to the floor.

Lieutenant Johnson frowned as she turned and left. Audrey dipped the mop into the bucket and water sloshed over the top. She was so hungry that for a minute she imagined the mop's yarn strands were potato fingers like their housemaid used to make back home, glazed with egg and sprinkled with salt.

In the distance, the squeak of rubber-soled shoes stopped. Then the sound started up again, uneven because of Lieutenant Johnson's limp, her knee swollen like a grapefruit from a bad fall.

When she re-appeared, Audrey brought the mop to rest beside her hip and waited.

"I'm telling you this only because I know how close you are," Lieutenant Johnson said.

In her head, Audrey corrected her silently. She and Kat had been close. Not anymore.

"It's a law as old as battle. Not law, maybe, but code. A soldier never leaves another soldier behind."

"I don't understand," Audrey said. Leaving others behind was exactly what Kat had done.

"She had no choice but to leave. What I'm saying is Kathleen would've been sent home regardless. Now the question is what you'll do."

Audrey shook her head. Always a rule follower, Kat never ducked out on a shift or questioned an order. Like images in a film, the nurses waiting at the mouth of the cave flickered through her mind. They'd looked straight ahead toward the horizon where help would soon appear. An older nurse who'd shattered her wrist, Ruby from Idaho Falls, who had begun hallucinating, screaming about flaming, decapitated heads as they tried to sleep, and others who were sick—sicker than the rest, stricken with malaria or dysentery or severe malnutrition, barely able to stand upright. They'd been chosen because they were most in need of rescue.

Audrey pictured Kat's eyes, the odd way they shone, her tendency to gaze off into the distance as noise exploded around her. How difficult she'd been to rouse from sleep. The weight she'd lost and gained. Her face pale, perhaps with pain. The way she used to press her hand against her stomach.

The mop Audrey had been holding clattered against the floor.

"Is she sick? Kat's sick, isn't she?"

She should've thought of it before. She had been so convinced the three of them would emerge unscathed, meant as they were—destined—for survival, for a lifetime of friendship, wherever their lives took them after the war ended.

"Well, it's true she's not in good health," the lieutenant said.

"When she gets home, she'll get medicine. She'll find help," Audrey said. She suspected the situation was dire if Kat wasn't allowed to stay. But she had no family in the States, no relative to nurse her back to health, no money to pay for help.

Lieutenant Johnson touched Audrey's arm, a deep wrinkle between her kind eyes. "It's not only that. Kathleen is pregnant."

"That can't be right." The idea was so ludicrous Audrey feared she might be delirious. "We had all those tests before we came over. They checked for pregnancy, didn't they?"

"She wasn't pregnant then. She is now."

"Why wouldn't she tell me? Or Penny? She simply left."

"She was ashamed, I suppose. Couldn't bear it."

Lieutenant Johnson offered no other details, no explanation. Her words hovered in the air and Audrey tried to absorb them, to make them fit with some version of reality. *Kathleen is pregnant.*

Kat had been the life of the party those nights in Manila. She'd stayed out later than Penny or Audrey, who would wander back to the barracks arm in arm laughing about a joke they'd heard, their voices cottony with a pleasant tiredness while Kat remained behind at the dwindling party.

"Pregnant," Audrey repeated.

Lieutenant Johnson nodded. "And I'm worried about her. Physically, that's the biggest concern. She might be in bad shape. Until she recovers, that poor girl could stand to have someone at her bedside."

"I wish she had family to pitch in." Audrey's voice broke on the word *family*.

"There's also Kathleen's mental state to consider. Her spirits are awfully low. If there's any way you can help her, any way at all—"

Penny muttered from her metal hospital bed and Audrey leaned closer to decipher what she was trying to say. "Didn't know."

"I didn't know either. Not until Lieutenant Johnson told me. I never would've guessed."

"You had to go after Kat," Penny said. "That changes every-thing."

Audrey's throat constricted at how quickly she had understood. Even in her weakened state, Penny was able to see reason. And she was right. Kat's pregnancy had changed everything.

"I was selfish too, of course," Audrey said. "In all honesty, I desperately wanted out. I practically jumped at the chance."

From her bed, Penny nodded. "The letter I sent—I didn't know what to think about you."

"I left you there to rot."

"You cut me out of your life. All these years I never heard a word from you." Penny's voice broke as she coughed.

Audrey studied her friend's gaunt face and tried to voice what she meant. She felt guilty for leaving Penny on Corregidor. And for never reaching out to her after the war too. It was all tied up together, her shame expanding until it hardened into a boulder that blocked the path between them.

Laurel tilted her head in Penny's direction. "I don't think she begrudges you the life you've had."

"But her letter—" Audrey trailed off.

Its threatening tone had masked years of hurt. Even if Penny didn't blame Audrey for leaving Corregidor, she might have been startled to come across her picture, the stark realization—perhaps humiliation—that her once close friend lived two states away and had never reached out. Just as a gardener tearing up a dead plant might uncover a hidden disease in the soil, Penny had unearthed an old bitterness. This same friend broke a promise long ago and left her to suffer alone.

From her bed, Penny sighed and closed her eyes.

"Did you find Kat?" Laurel asked. "And why haven't you come to see Penny before now? You've had all these years to explain." Her tone was kind, but curious.

"I only wanted a chance to explain myself." Audrey tried to keep her voice low so as not to disturb Penny. "I didn't want her telling my family. I thought if Penny understood—"

At this Penny grunted and jerked her head. Audrey wasn't sure what she meant.

"I think she wants you to come closer," Laurel said and Penny grunted again as though in confirmation.

Audrey limped to her bedside and Penny took her hand. She was nothing but bones wrapped in thin, papery skin and knotty veins.

"It was an impossible choice—leave one of you to go to the other," she told Penny. A soldier doesn't leave another behind, but she'd left Penny. "I'd promised Kat we would be each other's family. I never had a chance to tell you—"

"We promised," Penny said. Audrey thought she saw a weak smile.

Her fingers still pressed against Penny's, Audrey didn't bother explaining that she'd made a second promise to Kat.

"If I could have, if there'd been any way, I would've gotten you passage as well."

Penny squeezed her hand. She knew.

"I had to see if I could help Kat. Lieutenant Johnson would've told you. Except with her knee injury, she ended up leaving too. I didn't know—I couldn't have known—what would happen to you." She touched Penny's palm with the tips of her fingers. She'd poured over the news clippings. Fallen asleep to an imagined newsreel of Penny's years of captivity.

"Anyway, you were the strong one. Didn't we always tell you that?"

When Penny tried to speak, Audrey couldn't understand her. Penny coughed and tried again.

"Kat had nobody," she said. She looked at Audrey's face as though she wanted to memorize her features and squeezed her hand tighter. Then she took a deep breath. "But that's not right. She had you." Penny's grip on Audrey's hand loosened and her eyes fluttered closed. These few words seemed to have sapped the last of her strength.

"Thank you," Audrey whispered. She smoothed Penny's forehead and her friend opened her eyes and nodded. She didn't have to say anything else for Audrey to know she was forgiven. Almost seventy years ago, Penny had given her the jade brooch. Now she'd given her one final gift.

CHAPTER 36

A hospice nurse interrupted to check on Penny and ask if she needed to rest. From the bed, Penny shook her head.

The nurse adjusted her morphine drip and tapped at her watch. "No matter what, I'm kicking you all out in fifteen minutes."

"What about your medicine?" Laurel checked her own watch and twisted it around her wrist, a gesture so familiar it made Audrey glance between her and Penny as if they might somehow be related.

"Back at the inn," Audrey said. "I didn't think to bring it." Penny's eyes had closed, and Audrey wasn't sure if she was still awake.

Laurel pulled a pharmacy bag from her tote. "I didn't know you'd manage to get a refill on your own."

Audrey thanked her and hurried to swallow her pills. Even if Penny was no longer able to listen, she would tell Laurel. She would make her understand.

The day after Lieutenant Johnson's offer, Audrey hurried across the rocky shoreline, her eyes fixed on the rescue boat. The moon dangled bright, an almost harsh glow against the dark sky. In the distance, the sea shimmered.

"A submarine is coming for a handful of us," Lieutenant Johnson had said. "The *USS Spearfish*. You could follow Kathleen and be there to help her. As long as the weather cooperates, it'll happen tonight. This will be the last group out as far as I know. It's likely now or never."

"Kat doesn't need my help," Audrey said, although she knew it wasn't true. "Besides, I couldn't leave Penny." They had promised each other, she started to say. Her words sounded childish and naïve. "Anyway, I'm sure there are others who deserve to leave."

"I have a list I'm working on." She patted her pocket. "The only reason I brought it up is that you have a commendation. You get a boost up the list."

Audrey stared at Lieutenant Johnson. The train journey, the cold metal of the pistol, seemed so long ago. The unexpected and peculiar nature of that task had led to a commendation, which now meant she could leave. Although she saw the sense in it, she still felt lost, underwater, confused.

"It's your decision," Lieutenant Johnson said. "But I need to know within the hour."

When she finished mopping, Audrey went to find Penny, who would know what to do. Any resentment she'd felt toward Kat faded when she thought of her pregnant and sick, alone and scared. Audrey would do anything she could to help her. But she wasn't sure whether she had anything to offer.

Wherever she ended up, Kat would have access to medical care. But if she was as sick as Audrey feared, she might not be able to care for an infant. Yet she wouldn't dream of giving up the baby. Nobody would want their baby to grow up in a children's home, least of all Kat, who'd grown up that way herself.

Audrey could find—and pay for—a place for Kat and the baby to live. She would help with diapers and feeding and cooking. Once Kat was healthy, Audrey could return home to her family or sign up for another tour with the Army. Perhaps by then the war would finally be over.

Audrey raced through the underground halls. Her time there might be coming to an end. The early days seemed far gone, the dances in Manila a vague memory. Jimmy Dorsey and Glenn Miller on the Armed Forces Radio, the swish of chiffon skirts, wrist corsages fashioned out of lush tropical blooms. And the rosy-cheeked soldiers, freshly shaven and smelling of cologne so delicious she had once blushed to imagine licking it off a boy's neck.

Audrey tried to remember the name of the handsome officer Kat most often danced with, the one with a mustache and big, beefy hands. He'd been from Florida. Cliff something. Or Frank. Maybe Franklin. She could picture his arm around Kat's slender waist. A gold wedding ring glinting on his finger.

According to the assignment board, she'd missed Penny. She would be in emergency surgery for hours. Audrey slapped her hand against the wall, impatient, impossibly frustrated. Everything on Corregidor was pointless, the meals too small to make any dent in their hunger, so many of the soldiers—boys who should've been home betting on horse races or playing baseball—too far gone, too crushed and mangled, to save.

When she slapped the wall again, her watch broke and clattered to the mud-caked floor. Her fingers tingled in pain as she imagined them stroking an infant's downy cheek or resting cool against Kat's hot forehead.

She could help Kat. She could get out of this godforsaken place. She bent to the floor and picked up the pieces of her watch. The glass dial had cracked, but the strands of soft leather still braided together to form a tightly woven band. Her twin desires—one altruistic, the other selfish—seemed just as intertwined.

Hours later, from the rescue boat, light flashed against the rocky island—more bombs falling on Corregidor, the troops' pathetic last stand, surely doomed for defeat. God only knew what the flashes meant for those left behind or what might happen to Penny that day or the next. How long she might be stuck in an underground hell. If she would ever make it out alive. If she did, what condition she would be in.

At the thought of Penny rounded up by Japanese soldiers, Audrey leaned over the side of the boat, nauseated and dizzy. Bile burned her throat until the meager contents of her stomach emptied.

Lieutenant Johnson rubbed her back and, once she was finished, handed Audrey her helmet and pointed at the sky. As warplanes crossed overhead, the whaleboat's phosphorous wake made them an obvious target. Everyone scrambled to the bottom of the boat. Audrey couldn't be bothered to move. Frozen in place, she refused to look back at the rocky island or imagine what might be happening there. She vowed not to think of Penny roaming the tunnels looking for her, calling out her name, the disbelief that would strike her, Penny's face crumpling when she discovered the truth.

Her bag at her feet, Audrey stared straight ahead. If she'd had the chance to talk to Penny, her friend might have understood. She would've encouraged her to escape.

Without such a blessing, leaving at the first opportunity felt like the coward's way out. The worst, most shameful decision of her life. When she'd first set foot in Manila, she'd been selfish and spoiled. She'd meant to improve herself, to make good use of the life she'd been given. Now look at her. Audrey was leaving Penny behind with no one, nobody at all, to lean on. What kind of person would do such a thing? Instead of keeping her promise, she'd grasped at the first prospect of freedom.

More than anything, more than shelter or water or rice, Audrey wished for a way to quiet her thoughts, to ease the aching in her head. For a fleeting senseless second, she imagined she could take a tattered Army blanket and wrap it around her brain, smothering the frontal and temporal lobes until she no longer questioned her decision, until she had no thoughts at all.

As she looked out at the Pacific, she pretended its murky depths had snuffed out the fires raging shoreside and the plumes of smoke rising above Corregidor. The boat drew closer to the Spearfish and the waves tossed and churned with foam. Like some mad scientist's fantastical creation, the submarine rose from the bottom of the sea.

One by one they climbed out of the boat and Audrey, her mind already veering away from this shattered and broken place, slipped through the narrow hatch.

*

Toward the end of May, they arrived in New York. By then, according to reports, everyone on Corregidor had been taken prisoner. Audrey wandered the city streets bewildered at the restaurants serving hamburgers and piping hot coffee, the women wearing gloves and perfume, the blinking traffic lights.

She was on a fool's errand, frantic to find Kat yet unsure where to start. She decided to take the first train to Washington, D.C. For lack of anything better, she planned to investigate the PBY planes that had left Corregidor. The Army would have records of where they'd landed. In her condition Kat wouldn't have gone far.

Audrey waited in the lobby while an Army official looked up the records. Behind a glass window a secretary pecked at a typewriter. She stopped only to take a drag from her cigarette. The clock on the wall clicked ever so softly with every passing minute.

When the man returned, he carried a thin file folder.

"Only one of the planes made it to the States," he said. "After a refueling stop at Mindanao, the other plane crashed."

CHAPTER 37

The hospice nurse returned as promised and forced them to say goodbye to Penny. They might never see each other again. In all likelihood, this had been their last lucid conversation. Although Penny hadn't heard the remainder of Audrey's story, she now understood why Audrey had no choice but to betray her. And it was a betrayal, Audrey was still convinced of that. At least now Penny knew why.

Audrey leaned down and kissed Penny's cheek one last time. She didn't stir. As they turned to leave, Audrey recalled the officers' club in Manila when a young Penelope Carson—wearing her neatly pressed white uniform, twisting her man-sized watch around her wrist—chose to take a seat next to Audrey Merrick and Kathleen Brooks. Back then, despite not knowing what lay in store, Penny managed to put on a brave front.

"She's brave now too," she said to Laurel, who nodded as though she understood exactly.

Back at the inn, Laurel seemed anxious to drive back to Savannah, reminding her of the hearing the following morning. They'd spent the entire day with Penny and hadn't done anything to prepare.

"We can get supper and see how you're feeling," Laurel said. "But I don't think we should wait much longer to get on the road."

At the window, Audrey pushed the drapes aside. She wished she could see all the way to the hospice center. Beyond the live oaks, the Cape Fear rolled by, its current steady and inky-black. To the right, seafood restaurants dotted the riverfront, their patio umbrellas tilting in the slight breeze.

Laurel brought up grouper sandwiches and steamed broccoli for their dinner.

"I talked to Oliver and he said his school report is ready. He asked what you were doing here and I told him you came to see a friend."

"Probably wise to leave out the dying part."

Audrey wondered about the losses Laurel had suffered. She wanted to know more about what happened to her before they met, what her happiest and most difficult days had been. They'd become attached in a way she hadn't anticipated.

Without meaning to, Audrey began explaining how Whit died, the way the morning sun came through the plantation shutters in the kitchen and glowed in lines across her husband's face. How he chuckled, shaking his head at the silly pet photos which had been entered in a contest run by the newspaper. He showed her a white Maltese in a Superman shirt, a close-up of a turtle that appeared to be winking. She looked where he pointed and laughed, then pulled down a cookbook to search for a new pound cake recipe. The dishwasher rumbled beside her. She tilted the shutters to shield them from the sun.

At the rustling of the newspaper, she glanced back. Whit appeared lost or confused. She reached for him as the paper fell from his hand and his coffee cup clattered to the floor, the sand-colored liquid pooling on the wood. His eyes narrowed in confusion, but he stood rooted in place instead of moving away from the spill. He wasn't wearing socks and the heat from the coffee reddened his pale skin. Audrey called his name as loud as she could. Grabbing the sides of his face, she willed him to come back. His mouth drooped and his arm hung slack and useless.

"It was an intracranial hemorrhage," Audrey said. "A type of stroke. He suffered another on the way to the hospital, which was too much for him to overcome. He didn't survive."

Laurel climbed onto the bed beside her. She put her arm around Audrey's shoulder and said she was sorry, that it must have been so hard to see it happen.

Audrey wasn't sure which was worse—to be with a loved one as they were ripped from you or, as was the case with Tripp's plane crash, to be hundreds of miles away and, once the news broke, left to imagine one horror after another.

For weeks after her son's death, she couldn't sleep. Every time she closed her eyes, she saw a plane hurtling toward the earth, out of control, flames bursting from its bulkhead. She heard the most horrible screeches of pain. As a nurse, she'd seen what a plane crash could do to a body. In her sleep-deprived confusion, she would rush to the room down the hall that had been Tripp's since he was an infant. The screams in her head sounded like his first cries, his panicked wailing some sixty years earlier when he was wet or hungry or tired. In the dark, she found herself reaching for Tripp. She anticipated the way his tiny body would be damp with sweat in his cotton sleeper. She wanted to prop him against her shoulder, to rub circles on his back until his cries quieted and his whimpering slowed, until he grew calm and sleepy again. She reached for him, but found only air.

Once they finished eating, Laurel brought up a bag of ice for Audrey's swelling.

"Let's leave this elevated for an hour or so. Then we really need to head back to Savannah."

"I'd like to be out of this thing—"Audrey pointed to the brace—"before I have to see Deanna again, much less a judge who will decide if I'm fit to manage my own affairs."

Laurel looked at her watch. "It's seven o'clock and the hearing is tomorrow at eleven. Sixteen hours. I doubt that's enough time to lose the brace. We're supposed to meet Suzanne first thing tomorrow morning. She'll meet us at your house to get ready."

Suzanne was Audrey's personal lawyer, whom Laurel had contacted about the situation with Deanna.

"She'll need to convince the judge that I can take care of myself—with your help of course," Audrey said. She was stating the obvious, but it comforted her to have a plan.

"She claims by the time this is all over everyone in town will know how greedy and conniving Deanna is."

Laurel spoke with such satisfaction that Audrey realized how much the younger woman disliked her granddaughter. She shifted her weight on the bed and tried to work out the kink in her hip. "Of course, it's not that simple. Nothing ever is."

"Well, she jumped at the first opportunity to take advantage of you. As soon as you left town, she called her lawyer."

"I was wrong to leave like I did. It was careless of me. You could say reckless."

"But she acts like you're practically senile."

"My granddaughter rushes around without taking the time to investigate. I'll admit she has no interest in truly understanding me or what I'm capable of. That doesn't mean she wishes me harm."

Laurel checked the time and sighed. "I don't know—Suzanne said she'll argue that she's trying to take your house." Her tone seemed to have lost some of its confidence.

"Do we know that for sure? Look, it's not appropriate to throw Deanna to the wolves. You said it yourself—I was selfish. I wasn't thinking straight."

She could see Laurel trying to find the proper place for Deanna in her mind. For all her caregiver's patience, she left little room for nuance when it came to Deanna.

"We can figure all that out with Suzanne. She's worried there isn't much time to prepare, and your ankle doesn't help." Laurel checked her watch again and spun the clasp around to the top. "Anyway, we should probably get going. We've got a five-hour drive ahead of us."

"Longer if we get lost like I did."

Laurel shook her head. "Surely we won't get lost." She adjusted the pillow under Audrey's foot. "If you're dreading getting back in the car, I don't mind staying here for a little longer. But we'll need to keep an eye on the time. It's going to be a long night."

"It feels better to have my foot elevated like this," Audrey admitted.

"Once we're in the car, we'll keep it iced as much as possible. I don't hold out too much hope though, about being out of the brace, I mean." Laurel patted the bag of ice as if for good luck.

For a few minutes, Audrey rested on the bed and Laurel dozed in the chair by the window. When the ice slipped off her foot, Laurel jumped up to fix it.

"I can't remember the last time I hopped up from a chair like that," Audrey said. "Or, let's be honest, did any sort of hopping at all."

This made Laurel laugh, a nice moment in what had been an otherwise draining day.

Audrey leaned against the pillow. "The truth is, the bed feels nice and I'd like to stay a bit longer before we head back. But I don't need to sleep. Would you like to hear the rest?"

CHAPTER 38

Audrey realized it might have been for nothing—Penny left behind to suffer, Kat and her unborn child drowned or taken prisoner. Although the man at the war office offered to look up the passenger lists, he warned it might take a few days. Perhaps sensing her desperation, he promised he would let her know as soon as possible, regardless if the news was good or bad.

Running out of money and almost certainly out of options, Audrey checked out of The Mayflower and bought a train ticket home. She telegraphed ahead to let her family know she was coming. Her mother would have thrown a fit if Eugenia, their live-in maid and cook, had to add another place setting at the last minute.

That first hot shower she'd taken at the hotel—she might never forget the elation she felt, the sheer wonder. Back home in her childhood *en suite*, Audrey marveled at the variable water temperature, letting it wash over her, pooling on the hexagonal marble tiles, until her skin shriveled. Had Kat done the same thing? She grew cold thinking of Penny who might never experience the same simple pleasure.

In Washington, she'd scarfed down a takeaway sandwich and coffee from a street cart. Once she was back at home, dinner was served in the formal dining room, complete with fine china and heirloom silver, the flower vases and decanters made of Waterford crystal. After greeting her parents—a kiss on the cheek from her father, a firm handshake from her mother—Audrey sat stiffly, surprised she'd ever felt comfortable in the silk-paneled room. She might have been playing a role in a film, cast as the interloper in a sophisticated family gathering.

Apart from Eugenia, no one at the house asked what she had experienced in the war. It seemed not to matter. From the start, Audrey explained she might not be staying for long. Either she would receive word about a friend who needed help—what type of assistance she didn't elaborate as she wasn't sure herself—or she would return to the Army, a possibility Audrey's mother considered a distasteful joke.

After dinner, she took her father's Packard down the lane lined with ancient-looking rock walls and rolling green pastures to Whit's family's neighboring estate, a red brick columned mansion only slightly smaller than their own. In her absence, the Thorpes' house had been well-maintained. The white columns looked freshly painted and the slate roof was in good repair.

She found her childhood friend smoking on the back porch, which overlooked the stables. He'd aged since she'd last seen him. His jawline was a bit fuller and a hardness had settled around his eyes. In the past, he'd always been clean-shaven, but now thick stubble covered his chin.

"Where is everyone?" Audrey asked, fanning herself against the humidity.

"Audrey?" Whit jumped out of his chair to scoop her up in a hug. He smelled of expensive, woodsy cologne and cigarette smoke. "I can't believe you're back and you didn't tell me. Are you all right? You're awfully slim." He stepped back to appraise her and she fiddled with the belt on a shirtdress she'd found in her closet.

After he'd brought out drinks, they took seats in the porch rocking chairs. Whit crossed his legs. His slacks were neatly pressed, his narrow feet sheathed in cotton socks.

Audrey took a sip and coughed, no longer accustomed to the taste of bourbon. She wanted to tell him about Kat. In what seemed another betrayal, she wished James was sitting on the porch with her instead of her oldest childhood friend. She slipped off her pumps and rested her bare feet on the warm porch stones.

"Your last letter didn't mention coming home." He took a drag on his cigarette. "It's a nice surprise."

"They called my name. I got on a submarine. The *Spearfish*," she said, disappointed in herself for not sharing more. It had been so long since she'd seen him in person. She wasn't sure whether he was the same Whit she remembered, the boy she'd once let style her hair for a school dance, a friend she could tell most anything. Cicada music sawed from the thick undergrowth.

When Whit plucked Audrey's hands from her lap, she realized she'd been kneading her knuckles. "What's the matter with these fingers of yours?"

"Probably the first signs of arthritis."

"But you're so young."

She looked at the hands she used to protect with cream and gloves. "When you've cut off the bloody uniforms of hundreds of soldiers—"

He rubbed her sore knuckles with his smooth fingers. The ceiling fans whirred above them on the cedar-planked ceiling. His parents had gone to Nashville to visit his sister and her family so he was alone with the household staff. They caught up on the horses and the whereabouts of their childhood friends.

When she stood to leave, Whit crushed his cigarette in a brass ashtray.

"Why the rush?" he asked. "Stay as long as you'd like. We've got more." He held up his mostly empty glass and the crystal caught in the light of the lanterns swaying between the fans. She shook her head and reached up to give him a hug.

"There's something you're not telling me," Whit said as soon as she let go. His eyes searched her face.

Audrey opened her mouth to speak, to tell him about Penny and Kat, to explain why she was anxious to get a telegram from Washington. On that muggy summer evening, in that genteel place a world away from the cramped and miserable tunnels of Corregidor, she found she couldn't. Instead, she looked down at the porch floor and wedged her feet back into her pumps.

"You'll tell me when you're ready," Whit said so gently he might have been speaking to an adored child.

Over a week passed with no word from the war office. Audrey spent her time scouring the old newspapers stacked in a corner of her father's study. Although news from the Pacific was scarce, she read about the prisoners on Corregidor being moved to an internment camp at Santo Tomas.

At night from the comfort of her childhood brass bed, she imagined telling James everything that had happened since she'd last seen him—about Kat's pregnancy, Penny left behind. At least he was safe in Australia, or at least she had no reason to believe otherwise.

One weekday afternoon Audrey started the journal, finding a heavy pair of scissors in her father's desk drawer, the blank leather-bound book in a cabinet beneath his bookshelves. Each evening before changing for dinner, she hid the journal among her underthings, convinced not even Eugenia would look there.

In the newspapers, she also found a brief mention of the PBY planes. Six hours after leaving Corregidor, the planes stopped at Lake Lanao to refuel. As the man from the war office had said, the next morning, as it attempted to take off from Mindanao, PBY 1 crashed into a coral reef. The seaplane, its starboard wing completely submerged, was declared unsalvageable. The passengers were believed to have been taken to a nearby base, but since Japanese troops had recently landed at Cotabato, some thirty miles away, the article noted their fate was far from certain. For the next several days, the phrase *far from certain* rang through Audrey's mind until she grew sick of it.

At last, when she received the telegram, the news from the war office provided a welcome relief. Kathleen Brooks was listed as a passenger on the second plane, PBY 7, which had, after a stop in Darwin, successfully made the long trip home. They'd landed in

San Francisco, not New York, but Audrey could get there by train in a few days' time. She left a note for her parents on the foyer table explaining that she was leaving to visit a sick friend. Then she took money from the petty cash drawer in the parlor, the key to which had always been kept in her mother's nightstand.

CHAPTER 39

Laurel tried to picture Audrey returning to her childhood home with her pregnant friend in tow, how stunned everyone would have been. "What exactly were you planning to do?"

"I didn't know precisely. I hadn't thought it through. All I knew was that my friend needed me."

"Kind of like how I went looking for you. Of course, Kat was in much worse shape. You didn't really need my help at all."

"Oh, that's not true, Laurel. Think of it, I'd been stripped of my car, the bank froze my credit card, I'd injured my ankle—" Audrey tapped her bare wrist. "I'd almost forgotten about my watch."

"What do you mean? What happened to it?"

"Last I saw, it was in a seedy motel. Locked up for safe-keeping and yet it doesn't necessarily seem very safe."

"If you remember where, we can stop on our way back."

"It's too far out of our way and I might not be able to find it again."

When Laurel looked out the window, it had gotten dark. According to her own watch, it was almost eleven o'clock. "Never mind about stopping on the way back. It'll be the middle of the night. We won't have time. But if you remember the name, I'll call them next week."

"The way Deanna will see it, I've made a mess of things."

"You managed to get your medicine and money from your bank account. And you made it to Wilmington where you'd planned to go all along. You did pretty well for a ninety-year-old."

"It's surprising what I've discovered."

"What's that?" Laurel asked, thinking Audrey would agree to give up her driver's license. Or she might shift in the other direction, deciding she didn't need any in-home help after all.

"Sometimes the kind of assistance we need isn't what we anticipated."

Waiting for her to elaborate, Laurel stared at the room's blue and cream striped wallpaper.

"I'm surprised to realize," Audrey continued, "this is what I needed most of all. This," she said again, motioning between their two bodies like she was looping an invisible ribbon around them. "Someone, a real friend, to listen. To really know me."

Laurel couldn't think of what to say. Swallowing against the lump in her throat, she crossed the room and eased herself onto the foot of the bed, careful not to disturb Audrey's ankle. The matelassé coverlet was made of thick cotton, its stitches tiny and even, and she rubbed it between her finger and thumb.

Audrey leaned back against the pillow, her silver bob flattened against her head. Her pale pink scalp showed through until Laurel reached up and fluffed her hair back into place.

"We're not finished," Laurel said. "I want to hear the rest." She pointed to their luggage at the foot of the bed. "I'll drive through the night. Tomorrow morning, you can get ready at home and be fresh for the meeting with Suzanne. You can tell me the rest in the car."

But Audrey didn't hear, or she was so comfortable propped against the bed pillows that she didn't want to move. Laurel frowned, impatience stabbing at her stomach. The sooner they got back to Savannah, the better she would feel. Audrey had to attend the hearing and defend herself. They couldn't let Deanna win, not after everything.

"It took me weeks to travel across the country and find the rooming house where Kat was spending her leave," Audrey said.

"How was she when you found her?" With another glance at the luggage, Laurel turned her attention back to Audrey.

"Very bad shape. So swollen all over that she appeared misshapen, her skin unnaturally pale, the whites of her eyes shot through with red. She could hardly eat or sleep."

"But she must have been so glad to see you."

"She was astonished. Kat looked at me like I was an apparition. She hugged me as though she might never let go." Audrey's voice sounded tired and hoarse. "It took all the strength Kat had. I sat by her bed, brought her crushed ice from a deli down the street, told her everything would be all right once the baby was born."

"Did she ask about Penny?"

"Constantly. I had no answer. I could only grip her hand tighter and remind her how strong Penny was."

Sounding more tired by the minute, Audrey described how Kat was drawn and lethargic, completely unswayed by Audrey's attempts to discuss the future. No matter what Audrey said or how cheerful she tried to act, Kat wouldn't discuss baby names or make any sort of plan.

One afternoon at the rooming house, Kat pressed her jade brooch into Audrey's hands.

"Kat said she wanted to give it to me, even though I already had a matching one of my own." Audrey closed her eyes, then opened them again. "She wouldn't take no for an answer. For all these years, I've had both brooches hidden away."

"You got one out for that night at the museum."

"Even considering the Filipino connection, I still don't know what possessed me. I felt drawn to it somehow."

"That's how Penny recognized you."

"Imagine, after all these years."

Laurel fingered the brooch in her pocket, remembering Audrey's question about whether it was the broken one. She didn't know she had two to herself.

"When Kat went into labor," Audrey continued, "the doctors whisked her away, leaving me to pace up and down the hospital hallway."

"Everything turned out okay though, right?"

"She gave birth shortly before dawn the following day," Audrey said. Fading quickly, she stared off into the distance and Laurel figured that, instead of the inn's striped wallpaper, she saw the crowded city hospital, her friend shaking with exhaustion as she reached to hold the swaddled infant.

When Oliver was born, Laurel had laid him on her chest to feel his heart beating against hers. A moment she felt certain she would never forget—but since then it had rarely come to mind.

By the time Laurel glanced her way again, Audrey's head had slumped to one side and her mouth hung slightly open. Laurel removed her glasses, positioned a fresh bag of ice on her ankle, and decided to let her sleep for a few hours. It was already so late, what difference would it make? As long as they left by four o'clock in the morning, they should make it back in time—but it was hard to say what kind of shape Audrey would be in after such a long night. Staring at the frail older woman—the deep creases at the corners of her eyes, the sagging skin at her neck, her thin arm flung over her chest—she wondered why she'd ever doubted her.

Sometime later Laurel woke with a jolt, surprised to find herself stretched out on the bed beside Audrey. The ice had melted and left a damp spot on the coverlet. She raised her arms overhead to stretch, telling herself she had to get up. They were running out of time.

Outside, the sky was still velvety dark, the only light a faint pulsing at the river's edge. Laurel's watch said four-thirty in the morning, which meant they were already behind schedule. Wanting to leave Audrey in peace for as long as possible, she hurried downstairs with the luggage and checked out at the front desk.

When she couldn't wait any longer, she woke Audrey and escorted her downstairs to the car. She scooted the passenger seat as far back as it would go. Since Audrey wasn't very tall, she had plenty of room to stretch out her leg. Laurel propped her injured ankle up on a small cooler from the trunk.

"Very industrious," Audrey said, her voice groggy, as she fastened her seatbelt.

"We'll figure out about getting your car back later, okay?"

But she'd already fallen back asleep.

As she pulled onto the road, Laurel kept herself awake by thinking about what she'd heard. The more she knew, the more she wanted to be sure nobody took Audrey's independence away.

By the time Audrey woke up, the horizon glowed pink. After a quick bathroom break at a rest area in South Carolina, Laurel got her settled back in the car. They were making good time but cutting it close.

Laurel reminded Audrey where she left off. "I need to know if the baby was okay," she said and pulled back onto the highway. "Was it a boy or girl?"

Audrey leaned forward to tighten her ankle brace, taking her time. Eventually, she seemed to gather the strength to explain. "You don't know how it was back then, how the children's homes were. They meant well, of course."

"What are you talking about? I don't understand."

"They would've taken him away, Laurel."

When Audrey spoke again, her voice sounded strained, like she still hurt even after all this time. "The doctors said Kat barely had a chance giving birth in her condition. She was already so weak. And she lost a lot of blood. Then the placenta ruptured."

Laurel glanced at Audrey, then back at the highway. "Are you saying Kat died? She didn't make it?"

Audrey's hand shook while she fiddled with the ankle brace again. She took a deep, shuddering breath. "I had this silly notion that my journey to find her, the way I'd abandoned Penny to go after Kat, to take care of her, meant she would be saved. I was young, you understand. Even after everything we'd been through, I didn't fully understand how unfair life could be. That it often doesn't turn out the way we anticipate."

"I'm so sorry, Audrey. I didn't—I thought she'd make it. You couldn't have known how it would turn out. Not when you set out after her."

"A decision that meant leaving Penny behind."

Outside the car windows the muddy-looking fields and run-down farms gave way to acres of salt marsh, their bronze depths gilded by the early sunlight. As she stared at the road, Laurel wondered what she might have done in Audrey's shoes, about unexpected crossroads, the paths chosen and the ones foregone. Sometimes people gave, other times they took. They left, they stayed. They gave up too soon, they persevered past all reason.

"It was impossible," she said. "A decision nobody should have to make."

Silence settled over the car for a few seconds before Laurel spoke again. "So if Kat died, what happened to the baby?" She was starting to think she might understand. "You didn't let the government take him, did you?"

"Kat never asked me to take the baby. Even as much as she worried, she never voiced the possibility out loud."

"But she knew you'd come all that way for her."

"And she gave me her brooch. That meant something." Audrey touched her blouse on the spot where a brooch would lay. "I think to some extent she knew what was coming."

Laurel hesitated to share her suspicion aloud. But, like Kat, on some level she already knew.

Chapter 40

In silence, they passed fireworks stands, the equestrian center for Savannah's College of Art of Design, the manicured entrance to the resort on Hutchinson Island. As they crossed over the bridge into Savannah—industrial factories on their right, the tourist district to the left—the golden dome of City Hall shone in the morning sun. The next time Audrey headed north, it would likely be for Penny's funeral.

By now Laurel knew that Audrey had telegraphed Whit from the hospital and asked him to come to San Francisco as quickly as he could.

"Why would he drop everything? Was he pining away for you the whole time?" Laurel checked the clock on the dashboard and sped up. They had to hurry to prepare for the hearing. The car smelled of stale coffee, her cup from the inn long emptied.

Audrey had long suspected Whit would never love any woman. Not in that way. He'd paved his own path, a life his parents would never have endorsed, not in those misguided times. Whit loved her, of course, but like a brother. When she telegraphed him from California, she told herself they would do anything for each other.

*

Whit arrived in San Francisco in a matter of days. She never asked what excuse he'd given at home. At twenty-two he was both old enough to make his own decisions and young enough to still believe the possibilities were limitless. He arrived with a crocodile leather suitcase and an armload of questions, Audrey's telegram having included only the sparsest of details—the address of her hotel and that she desperately needed him to come quickly.

When he saw the bassinet in the corner of her hotel room, Whit's gaze darted to her abdomen. She could imagine his mind working, wondering if she'd been pregnant when he'd seen her in Lexington. Shaking her head as though to answer his question, Audrey touched Whit's forearm and led him over to where the baby slept, his tiny hands balled into fists, batting at the air whenever some unknown dream disturbed him.

At the sight of the small body stretched out on the cushion, Whit drew in his breath. He leaned closer for a better look, his hand on his heart. Audrey knew her childhood friend well enough to gauge his likely response. They might never have had a fairytale romance, not the way people thought, but Whitney Trevor Thorpe II was an admirable man.

"If you'll agree, we need to raise him," Audrey said. "Together."

He nudged the wicker bassinet so it rocked ever so slightly. They watched together as the baby settled, his fingers easing out of their fists, the crease of worry marring his forehead all but disappearing.

"I don't know how it will work," she said. "The legal paperwork, what we'll tell people—"

He held up his hand to stop her. "We'll figure out a way."

Before they left town, Audrey and Whit arranged a burial service for Kat. It seemed impossible that she would never hear her friend's laugh again, that Kat wouldn't see her infant son learn to walk or toss a ball or read a book. At the graveside, Audrey held him in her arms.

"I'll take good care of him," she whispered.

*

Days later Audrey and Whit boarded a train back to Kentucky. To anyone they passed they must have looked like a young family— Whit dressed in a charcoal gray suit and hat, Audrey in a red skirt and matching jacket, her hands stuffed back in the doeskin gloves she had once bemoaned as impractical. The baby swaddled in a flannel blanket, blinking as he breathed in the unfamiliar fumes from the engine. The porter, none the wiser, helped them aboard and got them settled in their sleeper car.

As they traveled across the country, Audrey had plenty of time to tell Whit, by then her fiancé, about Kat. Her beauty—the way her blue eyes glittered, how her high cheekbones looked sculpted from marble, the tidy economy of her birdlike hands. And more importantly, so essential Audrey's throat closed up whenever she approached the subject, the way Kat grasped life in her palm. The way she threw back her head to laugh at a funny joke. The ease with which on the first day they met she bestowed new nicknames upon herself and Penny, as though most anything was possible. How when Kat was thrust into the heart of war, she rushed toward bleeding young pilots with no hesitation and no thought of her own safety.

In much the same way, Whit cast aside his own plans, any aspirations he'd once harbored, to help Audrey. Whit's married siblings, Audrey's sister, they all had lives of their own. They moved so quickly, their days so full, that Audrey couldn't broach the subject of Kat's infant or bother them with such a request. The universe of options seemed circumscribed to encompass only herself and her childhood friend.

Together they told their families about their plan. They gave them no choice but to agree. Although they were not in love, and would never be, they would get married. They planned to raise the baby as their own, to give him a chance at a normal life. With their parents' money, if not their blessing, Audrey and Whit, together with the baby they now called their own, set out to start anew.

"But why Savannah?" Laurel asked. "So far from home."

"A fresh start. A place where we didn't have to explain anything." Whit's family had houses all over. They had their pick of places. It was an overwhelming luxury at a time when they felt desperate—and exceedingly nervous—to embark on their new life together.

As soon as Whit's father mentioned Savannah, Audrey envisioned the Georgia coastline, the gold-tinged salt marshes and centuries-old oaks. And there would be palm trees. A place with palm trees, James had once said. The way things had turned out, she would never have him, could never dream of falling asleep in his arms. She might at least lie in bed with the rustling of palms sounding in her ears.

"So you started a new life," Laurel said, her hands gripping the steering wheel.

"I had to put the past behind me. We owed it to the baby."

Apart from her research about the prisoners on Corregidor, Audrey pushed away any thoughts of the Pacific or what happened there. After the war ended, she didn't attend any of the parades or victory celebrations. She wrote a letter to Anthony Delfino's family, but after she mailed it, she cut all ties to anyone she'd known during that part of her life.

"I went to visit your housekeeper's grandmother. Remember Noreen? She described this beautiful family arriving at the mansion on Victory Drive," Laurel said, like she could picture the scene herself, the smiling, nervous couple emerging from the brand-new Lincoln. The trunks of clothes and heirloom place settings. The baby boy in his carriage decked with blue satin ribbons, the infant they called Tripp. Audrey's father had dealt with all the legalities and their families went along with it—anything to avoid a scandal.

For years Audrey kept busy with committees and galas. She surrounded herself with tasteful, well-made possessions. She doted on Tripp. Whenever she remembered all she'd given up, she focused on what remained. She never told anyone the truth. As time passed, she let everyone—especially her granddaughter—rely on the family name.

Now, if Deanna had her way, Audrey's house and garden would be stripped away, her independence signed over to a woman who, when she looked at her, saw only dollar signs.

In some small way, Audrey was likely to blame for Deanna's obsession with what people thought of her. As she and Whit raised Tripp, they second-guessed their parental abilities at every turn. But they could give him a place in society.

Once Audrey took Kat's baby as her own, she tried to cast aside any memories of James. She didn't know his current location, but guessed he was in no position to marry her. They'd never even had the opportunity to go steady. Occasionally she whispered his name out loud as she wandered around her mansion on Victory Drive. She would eventually forget the deep timbre of his voice, the taste of his mouth on hers. She wasn't sure which would be worse, to remember or to let the memory fade.

Walking down Broughton Street, Audrey asked herself what she would do if James appeared around the next corner. His face would light up at the sight of her.

At night as she tried to sleep, she heard his whisper in her ear, felt the brush of his fingertips across her collarbone. If he came home safely after the war, perhaps he'd found someone else and gotten married. With time, thinking about James grew too difficult. All of her longing, Audrey's raw and desperate yearning, had to be snuffed out, her youthful eagerness sacrificed at the altar of what she knew to be the right thing. Whenever his face or voice appeared in her mind, she pushed it aside.

The afternoon of Tripp's first birthday party, Audrey excused herself and went upstairs to retrieve her letter from James—the one she'd received from him in the jungle, the news long since out-dated—from its hiding place in the closet. She read it one last time, letting the page rest on her face as though the lines and strokes he'd formed might seep into her pores.

Then she took the lighter they'd used moments earlier for the candle on their son's cake and burned the letter in the bathtub. As the edges of the paper blackened and disintegrated, the words she'd once said to Kat sounded in Audrey's head. That their children would one day celebrate their birthdays together.

When she returned downstairs, the sleeves of her dress were soaking wet from where she'd rinsed out every last trace of ash from the elegant clawfoot tub. Whit handed their son to her and, with him in her arms, the wet fabric of her dress pressed against his tiny chest, Audrey told herself this life would need to be enough. For the baby's sake, it had to be.

Tripp, who smelled of buttercream icing from the cake smeared across his cheek, looked tired. He blinked against Audrey's shoulder, his eyelashes like the smallest of wings. Gently, she bounced him up and down as she looked out over the back yard. Within moments she envisioned how it might be transformed into a garden, what hours she might spend there engaged—so thoroughly her mind had no inclination to roam—in the work of transforming a common-place patch of dirt into something extraordinary. *It would have to be enough.*

"You've been in the paper so much," Laurel said. "You must have worried about someone finding you, someone who might know the truth. What if James had found you? Do you know if he ever looked?"

Audrey shook her head. "You forget, my dear, for most of my years, nothing appeared online like it is now. I was in the public eye, yes. How could I not be? I'd been brought up to believe that meant a happy life. We were in Savannah, a new place, an insular world unto itself. I had no reason to think anyone would come across me there."

"He would've looked in Lexington."

"That's right. At a family gathering my father once intimated that James had written. I didn't, I couldn't, ask for details. And James couldn't find me in Savannah. No one could. People from the war—Penny, James—they all knew me as Audrey Merrick, not Thorpe."

Laurel, her eyes still on the road, held up her finger like she'd thought of something. "Is Audrey your real name? Your first name, I mean?"

Audrey shook her head. "For generations every firstborn girl in the Merrick family has been named Helen after my great-many times over grandmother. We started going by our middle names to avoid confusion. Why do you ask?"

"I'd looked up—never mind. Did you ever want a brother or sister for Tripp?" An undercurrent of sadness crept into Laurel's tone and Audrey guessed she was thinking of Oliver and how she'd longed for another baby.

"I wanted to give him that, but it wasn't meant to be." Her voice trailed off as she pictured the expansive master bedroom with its antique mahogany furniture, the slip of her satin night-gown between the crisp sheets, the sound of Whit snoring from his bedroom down the hall. "And Tripp died so young," she reminded Laurel. She wanted her to understand all the sadness Audrey had accumulated over the years.

"I thought he was in his sixties."

"But to be taken like he was—" She shuddered at the memory of the plane crash.

"No time is a good time for something like that. Did you ever tell him the truth? Did he know?"

Audrey shook her head again. Once Tripp grew older, it was easier not to bring up the past. Over time, they let the Thorpe name and reputation carry them through Savannah society, float-ing from one glittery cocktail party to another, until it seemed as though they'd always been there and harbored no secrets. "Imagine if Deanna knew she wasn't even a real Thorpe. She puts so much stock in the name."

"Never mind her." Laurel brushed her hand through the air. "Look, you gave Tripp a good life. Not just the nice house and con-nections—what I mean is he spent his life with people who loved him."

It wasn't long before Laurel, whom Audrey had re-hired as her care-giver, pulled the car under the porte-cochere. Beneath its shade, they looked up at Audrey's white house. Although the Boston ferns needed watering, the columned front porch, bathed in morning sun, appeared welcoming, like nothing had changed.

Especially on so little sleep, the day ahead would be challenging. First, Audrey would meet with Suzanne, due to arrive any minute.

She stretched her foot in the brace, still unsure if she could remove it for the hearing.

"Well, here we are," Laurel said cheerfully, like they'd merely been away for a bite to eat. Audrey couldn't help but laugh. Laurel joined in and the sound, surprising after what they had been discussing, seemed almost magically healing.

"I'll help you inside and then there's something I need to do," Laurel said. "I'll check in as soon as I can."

Beside the car Audrey reached out her hand, remembering their arrival so many years ago, how it felt to scoop the infant Tripp from his carriage, the instinctive way her hand cradled the back of his downy head, the panicky hesitation that twisted her stomach in knots. A new life awaited, but it wasn't one she'd ever imagined. And yet now, all these years later, she knew she would make the same decision again.

Laurel grabbed her outstretched hand and held it. "You gave him a good life," she repeated as though she would brook no argument.

Chapter 41

Laurel checked in with Clay to make sure Oliver had gotten to school. After leaving messages with Jacqueline and Noreen, her next stop was to see Deanna.

At Your Service advertised itself as "a locally owned shop offering hand-selected accessories and gift-appropriate housewares." Sure that everything was too expensive, Laurel had never considered shopping there.

At this time of morning, the sign dangling on the glossy teal door said *closed*. But she noticed movement inside and she didn't have time to wait. The hearing would begin in a couple of hours. The unlocked door jingled as she pushed it open.

Inside the shop, the air smelled like spicy fruit. A mirrored table held white candles labeled *blackberry & saltwater*. She flipped one over and read the price tag. Fifty dollars.

"We're not quite open yet, but I'll be right with y'all." Deanna looked up from the counter. "Oh, it's you. Back in town finally? I'll admit I've been so relieved since you found her."

Laurel set the candle down and squeezed past a display of bright floral tablecloths and tortoise shell keychains shaped like pineapples. "When we called from the inn, it sounded like you started to cry."

Deanna nodded. "I've been extra emotional—look I had no idea where she'd gone or if she was even okay. Honestly, I figured—I hoped—she'd waltz back into town whenever she felt like it. She's like that, you know. Always doing her own thing."

"You could've helped me look for her."

"I didn't even know where to start. My mind's been going a million miles an hour. Calling the authorities seemed like our best bet."

"Speaking of the authorities, isn't there a hearing today?"

"I guess so. It's good you made it back." Deanna adjusted a stack of tasseled necklaces arranged around the neck of a mercury glass owl. "I'm meeting Spencer in a few minutes. He can go over your testimony."

"That's not why I'm here."

"Why did my grandmother go to Wilmington anyway? Who was this friend she was seeing?" Deanna peered around Laurel's shoulder as if she might spot Audrey. "Why didn't she come with you? No offense, but I'd like to lay eyes on her myself to make sure she's in one piece."

"She's at the house meeting with her own lawyer. She's ready for whatever might happen today," Laurel said, bluffing. *And she's not really your grandmother.*

Deanna sighed and arched her back in a stretch. Laurel glimpsed the tiny pudge of her stomach poking out from her patterned top. Deanna, who must have noticed her staring, patted her belly.

"I'm sure you've heard, the way gossip gets around. Almost forty years old and pregnant. Didn't see that one coming."

She nodded half-heartedly while she absorbed Deanna's news. Audrey's granddaughter sounded happy enough, but she sensed desperation behind her words. A vein twitched in Deanna's otherwise smooth forehead and the longer she tapped the granite countertop with her manicured nail, the more something inside Laurel loosened. Another time she might've been jealous of Deanna. Not anymore. Taking care of Audrey wasn't the same as mothering another child. But, as it turned out, the hole she once imagined in her heart wasn't so empty anymore.

Deanna stuffed her keys in her suede tote. "I've got to get to the courthouse. Samantha was supposed to open the shop, but she's not here. One more thing I have to deal with."

Laurel made no move to follow her out. "You really should leave Audrey alone. She can still take care of herself."

"Look, I can't go through this again, not with the baby coming. I can't have her scatterbrained and disoriented. She'll get hurt or forget to take her medicine or make a mistake with her money."

"Wouldn't you be better off not adding one more thing to your to-do list?"

"What do you mean?"

"If you're trying to take over managing her affairs—her bank accounts and things like that—isn't that more work for you?"

"Of course it is. But I'm obligated. I'm her granddaughter."

Laurel wondered how quickly Deanna would tire of her obligations and stick Audrey away in an assisted living facility.

"We'll see how today goes," Deanna continued. "But first we had to hire in-home help. Then she evaded the care provider to leave town—"

"Except you didn't have to hire any help in the first place. Not really."

"Are you saying I shouldn't have hired you?"

Laurel ran her fingers over a silver beaded coaster and tried to slow her breathing. She was so upset, so starved for sleep, that the room started to spin. "What are you going to name the baby?" she asked finally.

Deanna frowned like she wasn't making any sense, but answered anyway. "Fielder if it's a boy."

"Fielder?"

"Yes, Fielder. Lily Grace if it's a girl."

"It's up to you if it's a boy."

"Excuse me?"

"If the baby is a girl, you should name her Penelope."

Deanna wrinkled her nose. "Lily Penelope? That's a mouthful."

"Just Penelope. Or Kathleen. One or the other. They're both pretty names. They were friends—really close friends—of your grandmother's from a long time ago."

"Not to be rude, but how is my baby's name any of your business?"

271

Laurel leaned closer. "You need to tell your lawyer to drop everything. Nothing more about Audrey or her estate. Cancel today's hearing."

"We'll need to take care of her sooner or later. Why not get it over with?"

"Audrey can take care of herself, at least with a little help. If that changes, we can make adjustments. Convince her to stop driving—I think that's probably in the works. Put in an elevator to keep her off the stairs. Isn't that enough for you? I'm not sure why you need lawyers to be involved."

The vein in Deanna's forehead twitched again.

"What do I need?" She flung her arm in the air and her bracelets clanked against each other. "You have no idea."

Laurel shook her head. "Like I said, you need to call off your lawyer."

"I'm not sure why you've barged in here—"

"You care about what people think of you, right? And your family?"

Deanna plucked at the gold chain glinting at her collarbone. She looked like she could plop down on the floor and take a nap.

"If you go forward, you'll be surprised at the story that comes out. You won't like it." Surely Deanna had to realize she'd never heard of Penelope or Kathleen, these supposedly good friends of her grandmother's. Deep down, she probably suspected Laurel had discovered something.

"I have no idea what you're talking about," Deanna said. "What story?" She'd worked the clasp of her necklace around to the front. Now she gripped it so tightly it was a wonder the gold didn't snap.

"By now your grandmother and I have had plenty of time to talk. She said what she told me would take care of you." At this, Deanna's eyebrows shot higher on her forehead. "I realize now what she meant," Laurel continued. "All the stuff you think is important—your family's pedigree, the Thorpe name—you'd be surprised at the truth. Everyone would."

Without waiting for an answer, Laurel turned and walked out.

Outside, the sounds of the historic district offered a welcome liveliness, the clomp of horse-drawn carriages, the whizz of a group of cyclists. The air smelled of chocolate from the shop next door. She paused to take a deep breath and her stomach growled. She'd accomplished what she set out to, but the victory felt hollow. She couldn't shake the image of Deanna plucking frantically at her necklace and the tired-looking creases that lined her eyes.

Laurel had been so intent on giving people the benefit of the doubt. She'd defended Audrey every time Clay questioned her motives. Meanwhile, Deanna made such an easy villain that Laurel assumed the worst. The truth, of course, lay somewhere in the middle. Deanna might be misguided. She jumped to convenient assumptions and inflated both her own importance and the mounting pressures she pictured hanging over her head. But surely, when all was said and done, she didn't wish her grandmother harm. As relieved as she was to have salvaged Audrey's independence, at least for now, Laurel felt sorry for her granddaughter.

Once she confirmed with Audrey's lawyer that the hearing had been cancelled, Laurel spent the rest of the morning with Clay, who rescheduled his appointments. Of course, the saying claimed that absence made the heart grow fonder. She didn't know if it was completely true. She did know they were able to talk—really talk—like they hadn't in a long time. They arrived at the topic of IVF in a meandering way strewn with false starts and deep, jittery breaths. For so long Laurel assumed Clay had given up. Not only on another baby, which would have been bad enough, but on her too. When she said these words out loud, he squeezed his eyes shut like he was in pain.

"Not at all," he said. "From what the doctors said, it might not have worked. So what was the point?"

"I thought we wanted the same thing."

"We did. We do. I hated for you to be disappointed again. The way you got before—"

"I'm doing a lot better now."

"If you still want to, we could look at our options." He lifted his hand to his eyebrow, started to rub, then stopped. "I worry it's not a good idea. But if you want—"

Down the hall in Oliver's room, his Legos were strewn across the floor. Laurel motioned for Clay to follow her. She walked in, picked up a handful of blocks and snapped them together with satisfying clicks. Their family fit together too, in a way she didn't see, or at least didn't appreciate, before.

"What we have now is good enough for me," Laurel said. Besides, between Oliver and Audrey, she would have her hands full. She saw it now. For all the ways her days would depart from what she'd imagined, she'd somehow ended up in this abundant and sustaining place.

That afternoon, Clay said he would pick up Oliver at school if Laurel wanted to rest. Once she was alone in the house, she went down the hall and paused at the door to the guest room. She'd once viewed the potential nursery as a gaping, dark pit, a reminder of what their family lacked. Now she stepped into the room, the carpet soft under her bare feet. At the window, she drew back the toile curtains and let the warm sunlight ease the stiffness in her bones. She had to talk to Clay about the school, about how much better Oliver was doing. He would say Episcopal was too expensive. He already worked all the time. But they had to figure something out.

When Clay and Oliver got home, Clay disappeared into the home office with a stack of papers. As soon as Oliver saw Laurel, he flung himself at her, saying "Mama" over and over again in a way he hadn't since he was much younger.

Once she let go, Laurel asked how school went. "How did it go with your World War II project? I need all the details. Will you let me see it?"

"I want to show you and Miss Audrey together. I'll read it aloud to you, okay? Because I've been working on my reading a ton at school. But it has to be both of you at the same time so I only have to do it once."

Something between a laugh and a sob escaped Laurel's throat. "Sounds like a plan."

"Right now I've gotta show you the videos I made." Oliver tugged her toward the couch and Laurel sat beside him.

"Okay, let's see this video."

"Videos—plural," he corrected her cheerfully, tapping his laptop. When he handed it to her, the screen filled with images of his friends—Ford, Anderson, Josh, and other boys from school he'd talked about. Oliver had made videos, complete with special effects and music, of them on the football field, kicking a soccer ball, doing karate moves. All the activities he'd never been interested in himself.

"They're going to love this." She snuck a kiss on the top of his head.

"They do already." He pressed a button to make the screen go dark. "I showed them at lunch. Sullivan even gave me his brownie."

"I'm pretty impressed, buddy. You figured it out on your own."

"Figured what out?"

"How to make friends at your new school."

Oliver shrugged. "You just have to be yourself."

"That was good advice from Miss Audrey, being yourself," Laurel said. Audrey embodied a truth she wanted her son to carry with him—the lengths people would go for one another.

"You're the one who said it, Mom."

"Was I? Are you sure?" She cast her mind back to that day in Audrey's rosemary-scented kitchen, replaying the conversation until she realized he was right. She'd promised her son that being himself was good enough. His friends, the real ones, would eventually come around.

"Yeah, you told me and Miss Audrey a long time ago."

She traced the line of freckles on Oliver's wrist. "It does seem like a long time ago, doesn't it?" Back before Audrey disappeared. Before Laurel went looking for her—and they ended up finding each other.

CHAPTER 42

Monday evening, Laurel and Oliver stopped by to see Audrey. She answered the door, but soon settled in the rear parlor with her foot propped on the ottoman.

"I'll fix some food," Laurel said on her way to the kitchen.

Oliver rummaged in his backpack and pulled out some slightly crumpled papers. "After you eat, I've got something to show you," he said.

Laurel brought a tray of cheese and crackers into the parlor, then returned with Audrey's medicine and a cup of chamomile tea.

"Looks like Jacqueline cleaned the house and stocked the refrigerator while we were gone. I called to let her know you're okay."

"Looking back, I'm sorry I caused so much trouble."

"Who's in trouble?" Oliver asked. "And how many crackers can I have?"

"Nobody's in trouble. You may take three. Here, use a napkin." Laurel handed him a monogrammed linen cocktail napkin.

After they ate, Oliver stood in the center of the room and cleared his throat. He held the papers in his hands.

"Ready to hear my report?"

"Most certainly," Audrey said.

Laurel took a seat in the wingchair and clasped her hands on her lap.

As he began to read, his voice trembled. Laurel closed her eyes like she couldn't bear to watch. His hands shook, rattling the papers, and his voice trailed off.

"It's okay," Laurel started to say.

Oliver blinked rapidly, trying not to cry. "It's hard reading out loud."

"Would you like to try sitting down?" Audrey patted the seat next to her on the couch.

"I guess," he said. He settled down, his legs dangling off the edge of the couch cushion.

Audrey held her breath as he began again.

"The Air Battles of the South Pacific," he started. "That's the title."

With each word, Oliver's voice grew more confident. Audrey breathed more easily and snuck a glance at Laurel, who looked as though she might cry from pride. He stumbled on some of the locations and almost gave up on a difficult string of plane names—Liberator, Marauder, Airacobra. But he persisted to the end and thrust the paper in the air as a final flourish.

Laurel clapped and hugged him. Even in her ankle brace, Audrey managed to give him a standing ovation.

"You worked really hard, I could tell," she said. "Excellent attention to detail. And you have a lively imagination."

"My teacher said so too. The detail stuff." Oliver stuffed the papers back in his backpack. Spots of red had appeared on his cheeks.

Audrey settled back on the couch and propped her leg up again. His scholarship at Episcopal, in her estimation, ought to be supplemented with a stipend for unforeseen fees.

"Laurel, will you bring over my portfolio? I need to jot down a note so I don't forget an important call."

Oliver brushed his mother aside and ran to the desk. "What's a portfolio?"

"That blue leather case on top of the stack." Audrey pointed from the couch and he brought it over.

He pressed his fingernail against the soft leather. "This is pretty fancy."

"Someday we'll get you one for your schoolwork." Audrey showed him the lined paper inside and wrote *Call board chair re stipend*. She flipped it closed before Laurel could see and Oliver returned it to the desk for her. In this short time, she'd grown quite fond of him and his mother.

Laurel gathered up their plates and took them to the kitchen. When she returned, she pointed toward the staircase with its wall of framed pictures. "Now I get it. I felt like there was a gap. There aren't any wedding pictures of you and Whit. All those family por-traits and there's not one of your wedding. You'd think it would have been a big society event, covered in all the papers."

"You'd think so, wouldn't you, my dear?" Audrey said. "As it turns out, it was a hasty, low-key affair. No flowers, no champagne toast. An appointment at City Hall to go through the formalities." She could still summon to mind the clacking of the typewriters, her pumps slipping on the freshly mopped tile floor, Whit's steadying hand at her elbow.

"After Whit died, did you ever think of looking for James?"

"Not seriously." She shook her head. "It had been so long. Assuming he made it home safely, we'd each lived full lives since the war. Too much time had passed."

"But you must have wondered about him."

Oliver interrupted them, bringing Audrey what she assumed was another paper airplane. When he corrected her that it was a raven in honor of her house's new name, Audrey met Laurel's eyes and tried not to laugh.

"That's right," she said. "Raven Hall." Audrey fingered the care-ful folds and angles and complimented his creativity. "We'll have to be sure and tell Ford about the new name."

Oliver gave a thumbs up. "I bet he'll think it's awesome."

When he hurried out to the garden to play a little before the sun set, Audrey turned her attention back to Laurel. "It might be nice to know what happened to James. Now that so much about the past has been re-visited, I mean."

"Yeah, that's what I was thinking too." Laurel sorted the stack of bills until Oliver tired of playing and they gathered their things to leave.

"One more thing before we go," Laurel said. She brought over the Bible and flipped to the page bearing the family tree. "When I looked around before—sorry, but I was trying to find a clue about where you'd gone."

"Did you find the note I left you? You haven't mentioned it."

"It was for me? Deanna intimated it was for her. Never mind. It doesn't matter."

Audrey frowned, realizing she should've left word with them both. Deanna's feelings might have been hurt to discover Audrey had written to the new caregiver instead of her. And the note hadn't been specific. She'd only said she needed to take care of something and would be back by the end of the week. No wonder everyone had started to worry.

Laurel handed her the Bible and a pen. "Look, I don't care how you choose to do it, who you list as Tripp's mother. But don't you think it's time to fill this out?"

The following week, Laurel drove Audrey back to Wilmington to attend Penny's funeral. When he'd called with the news of her death, Penny's nephew said she wanted Audrey to have her jade brooch. During her time in captivity, the Japanese stole anything of value. Penny was clever though. She wrapped her thick hair into a bun and hid the brooch inside where no one could see it.

Since Audrey already had her own and she'd given Kat's to Laurel, she would save Penny's brooch. If Deanna's baby was a girl, she might like it one day.

Much to her surprise, Mr. Branson had asked Audrey to say a few words at the funeral, which she rehearsed during the car ride. Once she stood in front of the crowd, she felt unstable and Mr. Branson hurried over with a chair. Laurel handed her the notecards, but Audrey's eyes were too watery to make out the words she'd so carefully written. Someone in the front row coughed and she felt everyone's collective impatience for her to begin.

At first, she stumbled a bit. Eventually, as Audrey described the Penny she knew, her voice strengthened. The crowd quieted and the coughing gentleman leaned forward with his elbows on his knees.

The woman beside him dabbed at her eyes with a tissue. These people were Penny's family and friends, those who knew her best. After the service, Audrey would ask them to share how Penny spent her life, to describe how she filled her days. Although she never had her dance hall wedding reception with a fourteen-piece orchestra, perhaps Penny fell in love. Or played bridge with her friends or won prizes for her glazed pottery or got up early every morning to swim. After all, the time Audrey spent with Penny in the Philippines constituted only a small percentage of her life. The almost three years she spent as a prisoner must have affected Penny in unimaginable ways. Even as her suffering followed her like an unwelcome shadow, she lived an entire lifetime since then.

Considering how, at the very end, Penny managed to forgive her, perhaps it was time for Audrey to forgive herself.

CHAPTER 43

Once they returned to Savannah after Penny's funeral, Laurel's husband offered to find out what happened to James. It was too much to hope that he would still be alive. After all, he'd been older than Audrey. Even so, when Clay handed her a folded newspaper printout, frowning ever so slightly, she couldn't bear to read it. Only after he left and she forced down a cup of tea did she unfold the page.

All this time later, Audrey was pierced with what she could only describe as joy to discover that some years after the war he married and became a father and grandfather. As much as she would have liked James for herself, these were gifts he richly deserved. The life he always wanted.

He died only a little over three years ago, a day Audrey must have spent in Savannah like any other. Perhaps they were still somehow linked. She might have suffered that day from a headache or an unexplained throbbing in her chest that came and went as quickly as their time together.

Now James was buried in Portland, surrounded, Audrey imagined, by towering pines. According to his obituary, he was survived by a granddaughter, Clara Williamson.

At first Audrey brushed off the sense that her name sounded vaguely familiar. But something, old-fashioned curiosity she supposed, made her circle back, picking at the name as though at a loose thread. With only the faintest glimmer of an idea, she pulled out the packet of materials about the Filipino artifacts exhibit, the one distributed to the museum's board members when they first considered hosting it. Growing more anxious by the second, she flipped through the color pictures, the dense descriptions in print too small to read.

Since the exhibit originated at the Virginia Museum of Fine Arts, the packet included a list of contacts. Under "registrar" appeared the name Clara Williamson. Audrey studied it and tried to work this out. Normally, the registrar kept track of a museum's holdings and maintained ownership and borrowing records. Occasionally they might manage requests for rights or reproduction of certain images. Since it was almost unheard of for a registrar to be involved in planning an exhibition, she had never before seen one listed in the materials.

Curious, Audrey tried calling her, but she couldn't navigate the computerized directory to reach the proper extension. So she wrote Clara Williamson a letter, letting her know how much the exhibit meant to her and asking if she'd been involved with planning it. Clara must have thought the request odd, having no idea of Audrey's connection to her grandfather. All the same she answered with a letter of her own.

According to Audrey's watch, which was back on her arm where it belonged, she'd arrived early for today's outing. When she'd called Deanna to make plans to see Ford, she agreed in the begrudging way Audrey had grown accustomed to. In several months' time, she could only hope the new baby's arrival would soften Deanna, perhaps open her granddaughter's eyes a bit, reminding her of all that was pure and innocent. Despite her age, Audrey trusted she would not only meet her new great-grandchild, but survive long enough to make memories with her as she'd done with Ford.

With her cane in hand, she hobbled around the museum's lobby, stopping by the gift shop where an Edward Hopper print, one of his train paintings, hung on the wall.

When he was young, four or five years old, Tripp had a wooden toy train he pulled around the house on a string. One morning, so early Whit was still in bed, Tripp surprised Audrey by pulling something out of the cargo car. He kept it hidden, wrapped tightly in his tiny fingers, until his hand reached her mouth.

"Mama, look here." He uncurled his fingers to reveal a day-old cruller, his favorite treat, the powdered sugar all but gone. As he tore the pastry in half, her son grinned, his blue eyes sparkling the way Kat's used to. After he gave Audrey her share, which she pretended to savor, he popped the rest in his mouth and wiped his lips with the back of his hand. Then he tugged on the string again and urged her to follow him out to the garden where, if she recalled correctly, they filled the cargo cart with rocks for its next adventure.

As she waited for Ford on a bench near the staircase, she marveled at how the exhibition led to such an unexpected journey. If she hadn't worn the brooch, if Penny hadn't seen it in the newspaper photograph and reached out to her, then Audrey wouldn't have left town. Nothing would have changed. She wouldn't have had the opportunity to make amends to her oldest friend.

Without the exhibition, apart from Audrey's decision to wear the brooch that evening, it was hard to say when her granddaughter would have hired a caregiver. And yet it seemed inevitable that Audrey would have met Laurel Eaton eventually, that they would become much more than employer and employee. Now Laurel knew her story. Better still, Laurel knew her.

Thanks to the letter in Audrey's purse, she'd learned where the idea for the exhibit originated. Clara Williamson confessed to only a vague familiarity with the selection criteria, but after her maternal grandfather passed away, she had an idea. In her spare time, Clara began exploring the field of artifact history and preservation. Soon she was exchanging emails with far-flung experts. With the help of the newest on-staff curator, she prepared a proposal, which one Friday afternoon after normal business hours Clara slid under the director's office door.

According to her letter, approval for the travelling exhibition came swiftly, the idea having been deemed of wide appeal. Others took over, handling everything from acquisitions to catalog printing. In time, museums up and down the east coast, including Savannah, lined up to participate.

Audrey took Clara's letter from her purse and adjusted her glasses to read over Clara's explanation again. She meant the exhibit as a memorial tribute. The idea came to her when she was sifting through memories of her grandfather, whose full name she wrote in elegant, looping script. James Edward Strout. Clara bypassed the obvious, anything to do with medicine or cooking or sailing.

Then she remembered how, whenever James spoke about his time in the South Pacific, his cheeks turned pink. Her grandfather described the white columns marking the entrance to Fort Stotsenburg—his hands gesturing like he couldn't keep them still—so it was almost like Clara had been there herself.

More vividly than anything else, Clara said she could envision a hidden stone courtyard. A place of refuge, he said. Like another world entirely. When the sun rose in that tucked-away spot, the light suffusing the cobblestones with a rosy glow, he felt cradled in warmth and safety. In the re-telling, Clara said his fingers would spread wide like they were sunbeams themselves and he shook his head, the flush from his cheeks spreading to his neck. Not only safe, he corrected himself, trying to make her see. Full of possibility, like anything might happen.

Clara confessed she didn't understand exactly what he meant. But despite the war raging around the courtyard, she suspected her grandfather returned to it in his mind again and again.

Outside the museum's glass entrance, Deanna's car pulled up to the curb. Audrey tucked Clara's note away as Ford waved from the backseat, brandishing the bow he'd made for tomorrow's garden gala. Fashioned from bright pink ribbon to match her dress, he'd made her promise to tie it to her cane.

Despite recent events, the gala would proceed as planned. The oyster shell paths had been raked smooth, the iron bench freshly painted a glossy black. The catering company would serve whipped goat cheese tarts and chilled rosé wine. Claiming a conflicting engagement, Deanna sent her regrets and wouldn't be attending. Audrey suspected what was really behind her absence—her inability to fit into the designer sheaths she favored.

Audrey was already planning for next year's garden design, a profusion of yellow and orange blooms dotted with white lilies shaped like stars. And she wasn't too old to try something new. The time had come for a bloom she'd never tried to grow—common name frangipani, more properly known as plumeria. Having selected the right shade of coral from the catalog, she'd placed the order with the nursery just that morning. Already she looked forward to how its tropical scent would wind its way over the garden, as sweet as sugar, as enduring as memory.

For now, Audrey watched Ford wave goodbye to his mother and, skirting the sprawling live oaks by Telfair Square, jog down the sidewalk. Today she and her great-grandson would stroll through each display at their own pace. He would no doubt be slightly bored by the stem cup discovered in Leta-Leta cave and presumably by the copper plate inscribed in Kavi. When they arrived at the death mask, Ford might shiver and touch the tender skin beneath his eyes, imagining how delightfully scary he would look wearing it.

Ford pushed the glass door open and Audrey stood and leaned on her cane. Perhaps today she would teach him the word *legacy*, although he might not grasp the concept quite yet. As her great-grandson got older, there were many truths she hoped he would grow to understand. The human heart's capacity for devotion, for sacrifice and forgiveness. That as much luck as a stone can bring, goodness might as often be born from decisions, large and small, made every day. How the ties binding us to those we love are at once gossamer thin and iron strong.

ACKNOWLEDGMENTS

My heartfelt thanks to Jon Sealy, Carly Watters, Jane Smiley, Julie Cantrell, Silas House, Kimberly Brock, Susan Bernhard, Phillip Lewis, David Payne, Gina Heron, Melissa Hill, Melody and Doley Bell, Elese Adams, Susie and William Adams, my Bell and Ward families, Patricia Gibson, Kristin Caid, Pam Van Dyk, Agnes Stevens, Denise Smith Cline, Susan Hargrove, Andrea Short, Parul Kapur Hinzen, Pamela Reitman, Tinderbox Writers' Retreat, Looking Glass Rock Writers' Conference, the North Carolina Writers' Network, the Grassic Novel Prize, *Pisgah Review*, *The Petigru Review*, my son, Davis Adams, and my husband, Geoff Adams.

AUTHOR'S NOTE

After the fall of Bataan and Corregidor, the Japanese captured and imprisoned eleven Navy nurses and sixty-six Army nurses. During their three years as prisoners of war, these women continued serving as a nursing unit.

If you're interested in learning more about the nurses who served in the South Pacific, these books are a good place to start: *Pure Grit* by Mary Cronk Farrell; *No Time for Fear* by Diane Burke Fessler; *Helmets and Lipstick* by Ruth G. Haskell; *Angels of Mercy* by Betsy Kuhn; *We Band of Angels* by Elizabeth M. Norman; *I Served on Bataan* by Juanita Redmond; and *G.I. Nightingales: The Army Nurse Corps in World War II* by Barbara Brooks Tomblin.

Book Club Reader's Guide

1. As a story about friendship, *The Good Luck Stone* explores what it means to be truly known. In what ways do we curate what others discover about us? Is transparency important to cultivate meaningful relationships?

2. Do you believe in talismans—objects meant to protect from evil or harm? Have you ever owned one?

3. Once she learns Penny is still alive, Audrey feels desperate to tell her side of the story. What does she hope to accomplish when she sets out on her journey? Do her motivations change?

4. As the story progresses, we hear from both Audrey's and Laurel's points of view. Do you sympathize with one character more than the other? If so, why?

5. What are your thoughts about Deanna? Did your impression of her change by the end of the story?

6. As Laurel begins to hatch a plan to go after Audrey, are you cheering for her? Or do you think she's better off minding her own business?

7. Imagine being in the war and finding yourself in a similar position to Audrey's. Would you have made the same decision?

8. So many years later, does Audrey believe she made the right decision? To what extent is she satisfied with the life she has led?

9. Based upon what we see about their friendship, would Kat or Penny have made a similar sacrifice for Audrey if she'd needed help?

10. At the story's conclusion, are you optimistic about Laurel and her relationships with Clay and Oliver?

CPSIA information can be obtained
at www.ICGtesting.com
Printed in the USA
LVHW041605280720
661754LV00005B/865